Deceived by the Highlander

Daughters of the Isle
Book 2

Christina Phillips

© Copyright 2025 by Christina Phillips
Text by Christina Phillips
Cover by Kim Killion Designs

Dragonblade Publishing, Inc. is an imprint of Kathryn Le Veque Novels, Inc.
P.O. Box 23
Moreno Valley, CA 92556
ceo@dragonbladepublishing.com

Produced in the United States of America

First Edition September 2025
Trade Paperback Edition

Reproduction of any kind except where it pertains to short quotes in relation to advertising or promotion is strictly prohibited.

All Rights Reserved.

The characters and events portrayed in this book are fictitious. Any similarity to real persons, living or dead, is purely coincidental and not intended by the author.

ARE YOU SIGNED UP FOR DRAGONBLADE'S BLOG?

You'll get the latest news and information on exclusive giveaways, exclusive excerpts, coming releases, sales, free books, cover reveals and more.

Check out our complete list of authors, too!

No spam, no junk. That's a promise!

Sign Up Here

www.dragonbladepublishing.com

Dearest Reader;

Thank you for your support of a small press. At Dragonblade Publishing, we strive to bring you the highest quality Historical Romance from some of the best authors in the business. Without your support, there is no 'us', so we sincerely hope you adore these stories and find some new favorite authors along the way.

Happy Reading!

CEO, Dragonblade Publishing

Additional Dragonblade books by Author Christina Phillips

Daughters of the Isle
Beguiled by the Highlander (Book 1)
Deceived by the Highlander (Book 2)

Dedication

For Vicki, Charlotte, Olly, Danny & Kaveh
Never let go of your dreams!

Chapter One

Scotland. Spring 1566

"I<small>T'S TIME YE</small> took yerself a wife."

Alasdair Campbell swung about in the courtyard of Castle Campbell and eyed his half-brother Archibald, the Earl of Argyll, not sure if he was jesting or not. But the earl wasn't looking at him as he tended to his falcon before handing the magnificent creature to his man.

They'd spent the morning hunting in the forest, a rare privilege Alasdair had no intention of taking for granted. But it was gratifying to know his years of unquestioning loyalty to Archibald had been acknowledged, even if it had taken the death of the old earl before his bloodline had been formally recognized.

"A wife?" Alasdair repeated as the falconer took his raptor, and he pulled off his glove. In truth, he'd not given the matter much serious thought; his burning ambition to climb the ranks of Clan Campbell haunted every waking hour. There'd be time enough to look for a bride when the coveted barony he craved was his, and the gnawing sense of *not being enough* finally faded.

"A<small>RE YE COURTING</small> a lass?" The earl gave him an inscrutable look as they strode towards the mighty tower that dominated the courtyard and was the pride of the castle. A shadow streaked across the ground and Alasdair glanced up, where a golden eagle soared overhead, the sun glinting on its distinctive nape feathers, as anticipation burned through him at the earl's pointed question.

Did this sudden interest mean his half-brother had a prestigious alliance in mind?

It was a tantalizing notion. An outcome he'd hoped for since the day Archibald had formally welcomed him as his kin, four years ago, and the reason why he'd never become entangled with any woman, noble or otherwise, who had temporarily caught his eye. But it had always been a closely guarded wish, and he'd certainly never expected the earl to take an interest in such things until he'd really proved himself.

Until he'd secured that elusive barony.

It seemed he was wrong.

"I am not," he confirmed, and the earl came to a halt before they entered the tower.

"Good. I have a mission for ye. These political alliances are always easier when yer heart is not captured elsewhere."

Fierce satisfaction blazed through him. His suspicion was right. Archibald was rewarding his loyalty with a distinguished match. It scarcely even mattered who the earl had in mind.

God knew, he'd even marry a sassenach woman if it was of benefit to Clan Campbell and further proved his unwavering support to the earl.

"My heart is intact." And it would forever remain so. He had no intention of losing sight of what he'd wanted since he was nine years old and being pelted with filth and fists in the back streets of Oban. His lifelong friends, William and Hugh, had stood by his side, the three of them bruised and bloodied as the older lads surrounded them, but it was him they'd really been after.

There was no doubt broken bones or worse would've been his fate that day fifteen years ago, had the thirteen-year-old Archibald Campbell not appeared out of nowhere with a couple of friends. Within moments, the assailants had fled, not willing to stand up to lads bigger than themselves. Archibald had flexed his muscles, shot the three of them a smug grin, and swaggered off, and Alasdair's allegiance to the earl's son was forged in an unquenchable fire.

He'd made a silent pledge that one day he would be as untouchable as Archibald Campbell. That no one would deride him for his bastard origins or disdain his words.

One day, he'd be a force to be reckoned with. And nothing would stand in his way when it came to defending his half-brother or satisfying his own ambition.

"I'm told old Ranulph MacDonald of the Small Isles is on his deathbed. He has no living male descendants, and his granddaughter is to inherit Kilvenie Tower," the earl said, and Alasdair inclined his head, even though he had no idea who Ranulph MacDonald was. "Kilvenie holds a strategic position on Rum, and it's likely a prominent branch of the MacDonald clan will set their sights on acquiring the Tower through marriage with Ranulph's granddaughter. That's not an option we can afford. It'll grant far too much power to the MacDonalds of the Isles."

"Ye want Kilvenie to come under the jurisdiction of Clan Campbell."

"Aye. It'll strengthen our advantage on the Isles, and I've a notion if we don't act to prevent the possibility of such a union, the Crown will become involved. And none of us want that."

That was true enough. Although the Earl of Argyll, and by extension Clan Campbell, had sworn fealty to Queen Mary, the MacDonalds of the Western Isles had never forgiven the Crown for forcing them to relinquish their enviable position as Lordship of the Isles. Even though it had occurred generations ago, and Clans Campbell and MacDonald were now on amicable terms, old wounds still ran deep.

The earl's plan for a strategic marriage was far better than the alternative of allowing the MacDonalds to expand their influence across the Isles and disrupt the Campbells' hard-won balance of power.

"Is Ranulph MacDonald likely to agree to a Campbell match with his granddaughter?"

"I believe he'll favor the match. His wife was a Campbell, a cousin of my maternal grandmother, which we'll certainly exploit to our advantage. But that's not the issue. His granddaughter is Freyja MacDonald of Sgur Castle, on Eigg, and not beholden to Ranulph's command."

For the first time, interest in the mysterious bride-to-be flared through him. His good friend William had married Isolde MacDonald of Sgur Castle last winter, and on the occasions they'd met, he had found her most charming.

The prospect of wedding one of her sisters changed his opinion of the earl's political maneuver from a necessary duty into something far more enticing. Except for one glaring problem.

"If Ranulph MacDonald cannot command his granddaughter to marry, then how are we to ensure Lady Freyja complies?"

The earl's lips twitched in clear amusement. "Do ye doubt yer powers of persuasion, Alasdair?"

Alasdair stared at his half-brother as an unsavory notion slithered through his mind. "Ye want me to seduce her into submission?"

It was an age-old tactic. And although he didn't relish being ordered to play such an underhanded strategy, his first loyalty was always to Archibald, and he'd do anything to ensure his half-brother's interests were achieved.

The earl laughed and grasped his shoulder. "If that's what it takes, but don't look so stricken. Think of it as a last resort. Our strategy is to convince Ranulph that the only way he can be sure his legacy will remain intact is to ensure Kilvenie Tower goes through his late wife's noble Campbell line, upon marriage to Lady Freyja. 'Tis not even a lie, since I have a claim through his lady wife's kin. I want the Kilvenie land, and this way no blood is shed."

"Ye believe Lady Freyja will be agreeable to the alliance if her grandfather tells her this?" It sounded unlikely to him. Things would be far easier if Ranulph Campbell could merely command his granddaughter to wed.

"The MacDonalds of Sgur are canny and will see the sense in

aligning themselves with us. But one way or another, ye're to make Freyja MacDonald yer bride."

"How soon do ye want me to leave?"

"Tomorrow. As early as ye can book passage to the Isle. We don't want Ranulph to perish before he makes the necessary arrangements. That reminds me: yer manor is fine enough, but a MacDonald of Sgur bride deserves a more fitting household. I'm granting ye Dunochty Castle and its chattels. Don't make me regret it."

The earl grinned, but his meaning was plain enough. The castle was contingent upon procuring Lady Freyja and Kilvenie Tower. If he'd harbored any doubts about this marriage before—which he hadn't—the prospect of being laird of Dunochty Castle was incentive enough.

When he secured his bride, he'd be master of both the manor of his late stepfather, and a prestigious castle half a day's ride from Oban.

Two estates. A prerequisite for any baron.

Another step closer to achieving his goal.

"Ye won't regret it, my lord."

"I know I won't. Ye've never let me down, Alasdair. I know I don't need to tell ye to keep this business close to yer chest." The earl indicated they should enter the castle. "I've documents for ye, to present yer case to Ranulph once ye've eased any suspicions he might have about yer visit. And we'll drink to yer imminent success in bringing the Small Isles more securely within the jurisdiction of Clan Campbell."

ONCE ALASDAIR LEFT the imposing castle, he navigated the precarious path down the hill with only half his mind on the task as anticipation of his upcoming mission burned through him.

He was under no illusions about just how much importance

the earl placed on a successful outcome, and he had no intention of disappointing his half-brother. One way or another, Ranulph MacDonald would see the only possible way to secure peace among the Small Isles was to unite Campbell and MacDonald through the granting of Kilvenie Tower.

As he neared the bustling village that lay in the foothills, a rider approached, and he raised his hand in greeting. "Hugh. I haven't seen ye in a while. How goes it?"

Hugh gave a grim smile. "Well enough, if ye discount my brother's poor judgement." He sighed and shook his head. "Sorry. Ye don't want to hear about Douglas' latest exploits." Hugh glanced up at the castle, and a shadow passed over his face before he drew in a deep breath. "Although I've a feeling that's exactly what the earl wants to discuss."

Alasdair had faced a lot of shit over the years, but at least he'd never had to contend with a wastrel brother. Sometimes being the only child of his mother had its advantages.

"Good luck," he said with feeling. The earl was a fair man, but it wasn't wise to get on the wrong side of him. And although it was Douglas, and not Hugh, who had likely raised the earl's ire, there were times when the guilty one's kin were the ones to pay the price.

He hoped this wasn't one of those times.

"I'll be fine." Hugh's gaze sharpened on him. "Ye're looking mighty pleased with yerself."

He grunted in response. Despite how much he wanted to share his news, it was a sensitive matter and the earl's expectation to keep his counsel had been explicit.

It wouldn't be long, God willing, before he could tell his friends he was laird of Dunochty Castle. But first, he had to secure Freyja MacDonald as his bride.

Chapter Two

Isle of Eigg

"Nothing has been the same since Isolde left Sgur."

Freyja MacDonald glanced at her younger sister, Roisin, as they walked along the edge of the woodlands on the way to the local village with their terriers chasing after every scent, real and imaginary. The sky was a cloudless blue, birdsong filled the air, and a warm breeze rustled the grasses at her feet as she contemplated her sister's doleful remark.

As the elder sister, it was her place to reassure Roisin that just because Isolde was now wed to William Campbell and living in Argyll, it didn't mean everything had changed.

Except everything *had* changed. And pretty lies, even ones that might uplift the mood, did not come easily to her.

Still, she did her best.

"'Twas good to see her here last month. And don't forget, we all of us are visiting her and William in the autumn. That's something to look forward to, isn't it?"

Even their grandmother was taking the boat to the mainland before staying with Isolde at Creagdoun Castle for a fortnight. It would be an adventure for sure, but she couldn't help worrying about her patients. Who would care for them if she was away from the Isles for so long?

"Aye." Not that Roisin sounded especially thrilled about the notion of leaving their beloved Isle. Then she brightened. "Do ye suppose we might see Hugh Campbell there? He and William are cousins, after all."

It wasn't the first time her sister had mentioned Hugh Campbell since Isolde had wed William last winter, and Freyja never knew quite how to respond. It wasn't as though anything could ever come of Roisin's sadly misplaced affections. Hugh belonged to the Highlands, and Roisin, like herself, was bound to Eigg.

The way Isolde had been bound to their Isle. Until William had washed onto the beach on that fateful night and stolen her sister's heart.

She shook her head to clear her troubled thoughts. In the end, Isolde had been given no choice but to leave, and thankfully she loved her new life. But she and Roisin were destined to remain on Eigg, and that was all there was to it.

"It's possible," she conceded, in answer to her sister's question. "But ye shouldn't waste yer time dreaming of a Campbell. No good will come of it."

"Ye don't know that. He has a kindness about him, and I'm certain one day he'll return to the Isle."

Freya shot her sister a concerned glance. Roisin had never shown any interest in men in all of her eighteen years, until William's cousin had come to Eigg. Well, more than that. She scarcely spoke to anyone she hadn't known for most of her life, and it was a little disconcerting that she'd seemingly fallen for the silken charms of a Campbell within moments of meeting him.

A man who doubtless had forgotten all about her the moment he'd sailed back to the mainland.

For the last six months, she'd tried to persuade her sister to enjoy other interests aside from her passion for creating illuminated manuscripts of the fanciful myths of the Tuatha De Danann of Eire, and sharing the tales with the wee bairns on the Isle. Roisin spent hours every day in the solar with her inks and parchment, and while Freyja admired her skill, she couldn't help thinking the ancient stories from Eire were merely encouraging her sister's romantic notions about a man she'd likely never see again.

Unfortunately, although Roisin never complained whenever she accompanied her as she tended to her patients, the distraction hadn't worked.

For the life of her, she couldn't understand it. Roisin and Hugh had barely spent any time together. She was thankful *she'd* never be in such a disquieting predicament. There wasn't a man alive who'd be able to turn her head in such a way. The very thought of it was enough to send a shiver along her spine. There weren't enough hours in the day already. If she had a man who needed tending to, she wouldn't get anything done.

Once in the village, they made their way to a small cottage opposite the kirk. The door was open, and as they went inside, bidding the dogs to remain at the threshold, Laoise jumped to her feet and bobbed a small curtsey. Even though the young woman was no longer her patient, Freyja couldn't help assessing how well she looked.

At almost twenty-one, just a few months younger than herself, Laoise's eyes were bright, hair tidy, and despite having four bairns under the age of five, her energy was boundless.

That's what happened to a brow-beaten woman when her brute of a husband met an untimely death. And although she still wasn't proud of her reaction, even five months later, Freyja still held the opinion that his drunken stagger off a high cliff into the raging sea was nothing but a blessing. And scarcely in disguise, either.

"How is the cataloguing coming along?" she asked Laoise as Roisin took the four little girls outside, doubtless to share with them another fantastical story of the Sidhe from the legends she loved so well.

"Slowly, milady." A flash of anxiety crossed Laoise's face. "But I don't want to make any mistakes."

Freyja took the sheaf of papers from her and scrutinized Laoise's work. A year ago, she would never have guessed Laoise possessed the talent to sketch so well, never mind to learn to write the names of the medicinal herbs and flowers that Freyja shared with her.

But there was no doubt that now she was free of her bullying husband, and with no need to seek another now she earned her own wage helping Freyja, her quick mind had blossomed.

Freyja sat at the table and went through the latest sketches with their accompanying uses that Laoise had painstakingly copied from the notes she had left her. Although the other woman sometimes accompanied her when she visited her patients—on the occasions her mother could watch the bairns—she hadn't yet allowed Laoise to actually diagnose and blend remedies.

But she needed to. Otherwise, why was she teaching her about the less common medicinal uses that had been handed down from her foremothers for countless years?

"Well, that's all for today." She smiled as Laoise carefully packed her papers away and Roisin brought the bairns in. "Don't forget, I'll be in Canna for the next few days."

"Aye, milady."

They left Laoise and paused beside the kirk. It was plain Roisin was eager to return to the castle and her precious manuscripts, and Freyja smothered a sigh. If only Isolde were here. She'd know how to extract their sister from her baffling daydreams without hurting her feelings.

Even though she'd already asked Roisin to accompany her to the Isle of Canna, she tried again. "Are ye certain ye don't want to come with me? Tis a fine day for the crossing and ye know everyone will love to see ye."

"Ye'll be busy with yer patients, and I'll only get in yer way. Besides, I'm helping Amma with the embroidery she's doing as a surprise for Isolde when we visit her."

That was true enough, but the gradual decline of their grandmother's eyesight when it came to close work was simply something else to worry about.

"Very well. But remember, I'll be stopping off on the Isle of Rum on my way home to see Afi."

Concern wreathed Roisin's face at the mention of their long-widowed grandfather. "Give him my love. I hope he's feeling better than he was last week when we visited him."

"I will," Freyja promised, but the truth was, she was doubtful their beloved Afi would ever recover his strength after the fright he'd given them three weeks ago, when he'd inexplicably lost his balance and taken a bad fall.

She watched her sister leave the village, before calling Dubh to heel and making her way to the next cottage to check on an older woman who'd birthed a surprise babe the previous day. But she couldn't push her grandfather from her mind. Why was he so stubborn, refusing to leave his beloved Kilvenie, when there was plenty of room at the castle for him?

At least then they'd all be able to keep a watchful eye on him, instead of having to rely on messengers making the crossing from Rum to Eigg in case of bad news.

She sighed heavily. He'd even refused her offer to stay with him. Well, she'd see how he was in a few days, after she left Canna, and if he wasn't improving then he'd just have to put up with her, wouldn't he?

Isle of Rum

"Ye may be a relative of my beloved late wife's cousin, but ye needn't think that'll sway me when it comes to the happiness of my Freyja."

Alasdair inclined his head in understanding at Ranulph Mac-Donald's heated outburst, but inside he was reeling. Since he'd arrived on the Isle of Rum three days ago, and introduced himself to the laird, Ranulph had been most agreeable.

He'd been eager to hear news of the Earl of Argyll and welcomed Alasdair as an honored guest. The rapport between them had been so cordial, he'd not envisaged any problems when he'd raised the issue of uniting their bloodlines to ensure peace among the Isles.

But now suspicion lurked in Ranulph's eyes and despite his frail appearance, hostility radiated from him. How had he misread the signs so badly? He'd been so certain the old man would be happy for his granddaughter to be connected through marriage with the earl.

'Twas a setback, but they were far from finished. Ranulph transferred his glare from him to gaze out at the sea and Alasdair inhaled a calming breath. At least here on the beach they were alone. If he'd broached the subject at the tower, it was certain they would have been overheard by at least one servant, and any hope of keeping this between the two of them would've died.

He was used to finding an advantage in the unlikeliest of circumstances, and this one certainly worked in his favor. No one had witnessed this discussion and seen Ranulph's flare of distrust. All he had to do was reassure Ranulph that Lady Freyja's happiness was all he wished for, too, and surely the older man would see reason.

It was, after all, imperative that Ranulph was in favor of the marriage so he could persuade his granddaughter it was politically advantageous for her to agree to the match. And if that failed, then he'd have little choice but to set his sights on wooing Lady Freyja.

"My apologies," he said. "I didn't mean to offend. The earl wishes only for Clans Campbell and MacDonald to flourish in peace."

Ranulph snorted before sucking in a rasping breath. "I'm aware of what the earl wants. There's no need to ladle honey on yer words, lad."

Grudging respect inched through him as he eyed the man by his side. When he'd first met Ranulph, all he'd seen was an old man who had difficulty breathing and needed a sturdy stick to help him walk. But there was obviously nothing wrong with his faculties.

Maybe he should try a different tack.

"I'm not. 'Tis only the truth. Kilvenie is a coveted prize, and without a son to inherit, there are many who will risk much to claim the land for their own. But with direct connections to the earl, Lady Freyja's heritage will be secure."

"I'm not denying it's an alliance that's worth considering. I'm telling ye that my granddaughter is not a pawn to be bartered with."

The earl had warned him of this. He still found it strange. With her father dead, it stood to reason her paternal grandfather would step up to negotiate the best possible future for her.

And yet here they were.

"I respect yer stance." Even if he found it damned exasperating. "Lady Freyja is fortunate to have yer support."

Ranulph gave a raspy laugh. "Do ye know nothing of the MacDonalds of Sgur, Alasdair? A man does not wed into their line lightly, as my son was well aware. Freyja has my unwavering support, but 'tis the love of her foremothers that guides her. Best not to forget that, lad."

Unsure how best to respond to that comment, he gave a noncommittal grunt as they turned from the shore and headed back to Kilvenie Tower, where it perched on a hill, giving magnificent views across the Isle.

He knew Lady Freyja lived in Sgur Castle with her sister and grandmother. Was that the foremother Ranulph meant? It seemed an odd way of referring to her, considering she was still alive.

As they took the path up the rocky slope, with Ranulph's hounds leading the way, he offered the older man his arm. After a few moments where Ranulph steadfastly ignored his offer of help, he finally accepted, and an unexpected sting pierced Alasdair's chest.

It wasn't right for a man to lose his vigor like this. To be sure, he'd never seen Ranulph in his prime, but he'd overheard whispered conversations among both servants and villagers that confirmed his suspicions that until the last year or so, Ranulph had been a giant of a man.

It was strange for such a thing to affect him. He scarcely knew the man, and yet during the last three days, and against his better judgement, he'd become oddly attached to Ranulph's dry humor.

They entered the great hall, and servants offered mulled mead for Ranulph and ale for him. The older man sat before the fire, his hands wrapped around his cup, as his hounds lay at his feet. Ranulph glanced about, a frown creasing his weathered brow. "Where's Ban?"

"We'll find her," his steward said.

"She shouldn't be unsupervised. She could whelp at any moment."

"We'll find her," the steward repeated, undeterred by the sharp note in his laird's voice and Ranulph sighed before draining his mead and pushing himself to his feet.

He glanced at Alasdair. "I'll speak with ye later. There are matters I must attend to."

Alasdair gave a brusque nod and watched the older man amble across the hall, his hounds following in his wake. He knew full well Ranulph needed to rest after the exertions of the morning, but if he wanted to give the impression he was attending to matters of his estate, it was none of his concern.

Maybe he'd see if he could find the laird's favorite dog. It might cause Ranulph to look more kindly on his proposition.

Smothering a grin at the fanciful notion—no man was that fond of his dog, surely—he strolled back to the courtyard. Despite the steward's assurance, it didn't appear anyone was searching for the creature, and as he approached the stables he paused and swept his gaze across the stronghold.

There was no doubt Kilvenie Tower was in an enviable position, with views not only across the Isle but also across the sea. But the earl wasn't interested in its spectacular views. It was for the formidable foothold it held in the Western Isles.

A muffled howl penetrated his ruminations, and he swung about and stared at the stables. The door was ajar, and a quick glance around confirmed no one else appeared to have heard the sound. Goddamn. Had he really found Ranulph's missing hound?

He strode over and entered the stables. The aroma of horse and hay filled the air, but it was the metallic tang of blood that hit him. And then he saw a young woman kneeling in the corner, where the dog lay panting.

"'Tis all right, Ban, my love," the lass said in a soothing tone as she used a dagger to cut a length of material from a blanket she held. Fascinated, he gazed at her as she hastily folded the material before moving closer to the dog. "Don't ye worry now. Ye're doing a grand job. We'll have yer babies out before ye know it."

He'd never encountered anyone helping to birth puppies before. Dogs simply whelped without any need for assistance. At least, to his knowledge they did.

Without quite meaning to, he took another step closer, and she swung about, her red-gold hair glinting in the sunlight that filtered through the door, and her blue eyes widened in obvious surprise at seeing him.

The breath stalled in his throat as his gaze locked with her beautiful blue eyes. A smattering of freckles dusted the bridge of her nose and across her flushed cheeks, and he'd be damned if he'd ever seen anything more enchanting in his life.

Her dusky-rose lips parted, and his blood thundered in his head, obliterating the outside world and, God help him, any sense he'd once possessed. He had the mad fancy of dropping to his knees beside her, taking her into his arms, and claiming her delectable mouth.

Yet his feet remained immobile, and his tongue remained transfixed, as though, if he moved or spoke, the vision before him might vanish.

She hitched in a jagged breath, breaking the spell, but before he could gather his wits, she spoke.

"Don't just stand there gaping, man. Get over here and make yerself useful."

Chapter Three

Freyja tore her gaze from the stranger. It was far harder than it had any right to be, especially since sweet Ban was in such difficulties. She gripped the piece of blanket expectantly, and then almost forgot how to breathe when the man crouched beside her.

"How can I help?" His voice was hushed and the very sound of it sent illicit shivers skating through her blood before colliding between her thighs. How . . . *mortifying*.

Did he have to be so close to her? The evocative scent of leather and woodlands momentarily dazed her senses before she forced such foolishness aside. She'd not lose any of the puppies if she could help it, and she licked her dry lips and jerked her head at the bundle by her knees.

"The pup needs warmth. Pick him up and hold him close while I deliver this poor wee creature."

"Like this?" He held the puppy, wrapped in a piece of the birthing blanket she'd had with her, at arm's length, as though he'd never held a newborn puppy before. But she supposed she couldn't hold that against him. Not many men would have.

"Hold him against yer chest." She only just managed to stop herself from admiring his fine chest, which filled out his shirt most admirably. Hastily, she returned her attention to her task. The puppy was stuck, and now she could focus on helping Ban deliver without worrying about the first pup. "I got him breathing, but he needs bodily contact."

The stranger gave a grunt of what sounded suspiciously like

alarm, but she couldn't waste time soothing his manly pride right now. If she didn't get this pup out, Ban would die.

She wrapped the bit of blanket around her hands before gently grasping the puppy's shoulders and pulling it down with Ban's contraction. "Come on, lass," she whispered.

It took longer than she liked, but finally the pup slid out onto her hands, and she hastily cleared its nose and mouth. The poor wee thing was as lifeless as her brother had been, and after she cut the cord, she wrapped a length of the blanket around the tiny body and blew on her face.

Nothing happened. She shifted position and gently rubbed a dry corner of the blanket over the pup to get her vitals working.

Come on.

Time stood still as she worked on the pup, and kept an eye on Ban, who thankfully wasn't in distress as she licked up the afterbirth with relish. When the pup gave a wee shiver and hitched in a breath, relief rushed through her leaving her lightheaded.

"Thank ye, blessed Eir." She sent her customary prayer to the ancient Norse goddess of healing, and even though usually her patients were women and bairns, and these were puppies, at the end of the day they were all babes in her eyes. She held the pup against her breast and chanced giving the fair-headed man by her side a quick glance.

And then couldn't look away.

He cradled the puppy she'd handed to him against his chest, and there was an expression of fierce concentration on his face, as he eyed his charge with clear trepidation.

It was unaccountably endearing, and it took her more than a few moments to realize she was smiling at him in a completely ridiculous manner.

Who *was* he? She was familiar with most of the inhabitants of the Small Isles, and if she'd ever met this man before, she wouldn't have forgotten it. Or him.

Especially him.

Was he a MacDonald from the mainland, visiting her grandfather?

"Am I doing this wrong?" He caught her gaze, and his deep brown eyes, framed with thick black lashes that no man had any right to possess, were frankly bedazzling.

Good Lord, what foolishness was she thinking? Bedazzling? It was the kind of thing Roisin would imagine. And it was more than a little disconcerting.

"Not at all," she responded, but her voice sounded alarmingly husky, and she cleared her throat before she had the chance to further embarrass herself. "Indeed, I must thank ye, for I'm certain he wouldn't have survived without ye."

He smiled, dissolving the tension that had wreathed his features and she all but melted on the spot. The sensation was most inconvenient. And irregular.

And annoyingly irresistible.

"I'm glad to have been of assistance. I confess, I've never done anything like this before. Do ye often birth puppies?"

She laughed. "I do not. But when I saw poor Ban in distress, I had to help. Anyone would've done the same." Except she knew that wasn't true. Although here, on Rum, it was likely someone would've assisted Ban if they had found her. The hound was, after all, her grandfather's favorite. "D'ye mind holding this wee one? I must cut a length from my blanket for the next arrival."

Gingerly, he eased one hand away from the pup he held, and she carefully transferred the second pup to him. Her fingers brushed against his, and jagged lightning streaked across her skin at the contact, causing her heart to slam painfully within her chest.

How utterly *absurd*. Was she sickening with something? Hastily she pulled back, gripped her dagger, and cut through her blanket. As she glanced over her shoulder to check on Dubh, who sat patiently behind her, his bright gaze fixed on Ban in seeming empathy, her grandfather's steward, Miles, came into the stable.

"Thank God," he said with feeling, his gaze fixed on Ban.

"Aye, 'twas lucky I arrived when I did and saw her in difficulties. Poor lass was struggling."

"I've had the servants searching the whole damn Tower for her. Ranulph will be relieved all is well."

"How is he?" Anxiety threaded through her question as she tore her watchful gaze from Ban to Miles. The two men had grown up together, and she knew that, after herself and her sisters, there was no one who loved her Afi as well as Miles did.

"He'll be all the better for seeing ye, lass. Don't worry. He's resting. I'll let him know ye've arrived when he wakes."

Then Miles' glance slid to the stranger by her side, and a definite smirk twisted his mouth. "I see ye've met our Campbell guest."

A Campbell? It was foolish, and yet she couldn't help the flare of disappointment that he wasn't, after all, a MacDonald. But then she caught his glance, and the amusement gleaming in his dark eyes vanquished the thread of regret in an instant.

"A Campbell, are ye?" She ran a gentle hand over Ban's belly. "Well, I'll forgive ye, seeing how ye helped save two puppies' lives."

"Alasdair Campbell, at yer service." He gave a wee bow of his head, and it was utterly charming, not least since he still tenderly held the pups against his chest. "I'm honored to make yer acquaintance."

There was a definite question implied, and she couldn't help returning his smile. "My name is Freyja MacDonald, and Campbell or not, I'm also honored to make *yer* acquaintance."

His smile faltered, and for a heartbeat, shock sparked in his dark eyes. How odd. She'd never received that reaction from anyone before, but then, she so rarely needed to introduce herself to anyone, here on the Small Isles. But before she could wonder further, he grinned, and the sight fairly took her breath away.

"The pleasure is all mine, Freyja MacDonald."

She was quite certain his response wasn't altogether decent, and had he been anyone else, she would've had a sharp word or two for him. But somehow, coming from Alasdair, she found his remark enchanting.

It was a novel experience. And she had to admit, 'twas most intoxicating.

"Do ye need me to bring anything?" Miles cast his gaze between Ban and the puppies in Alasdair's arms. "A maid to assist?"

"I'm at Lady Freyja's disposal," Alasdair said, which caused warmth to bloom deep inside, although God alone knew why his honeyed words should affect her so. It was plain he was merely flirting, and just as obvious he was well practiced in the art.

But even that probability didn't cast a damper on her mood.

"I need some waterbags filled with warm water," she said to Miles. "We can't move Ban into the hall yet, and I don't want her pups getting chilled from drafts in here."

"I'll see to it," he promised before leaving the stables, and she returned her attention to Ban. Thankfully, the dog delivered her next pup without any problems, and Freyja gave a relieved sigh as Ban finally understood what she needed to do for her newborn.

"Let's hope the rest of her pups come out as easily," she remarked, as she cut up another strip of her blanket in readiness for when Miles returned with the waterbags. She shuffled around on her knees to check on the two pups Alasdair still held. "Are ye all right there?"

"Aye. Don't worry about me. I'm fine here."

That he was. Hastily, she averted her eyes before he realized she was all but drooling at the sight of him cuddling two wee animals. And since Ban was no longer in imminent danger, her curiosity got the better of her. "So, what are ye doing, visiting Ranulph MacDonald?"

"Sending regards from the Earl of Argyll."

"The earl?" She couldn't help the scoffing note in her voice, and Alasdair gave her a questioning look, as though he wasn't used to anyone referring to Archibald Campbell with disdain. Too bad. She was a MacDonald to her core, and proud of it. And MacDonalds didn't worship the ground the Earl of Argyll walked upon. "Why?"

"Why?" he repeated as though he wasn't certain he understood her question. "Because there's a blood connection between him and Ranulph MacDonald's late wife. At least, that's my understanding."

"Oh." Of course. She'd never met her paternal grandmother, and while she knew, of course, she had been a Campbell, it wasn't something she generally thought about. "Aye, that's right. But are ye aware my grandmother died twenty-five years ago? I don't know why the earl should think to send his regards after all this time."

"I'm merely the messenger, Lady Freyja."

She shook her head and returned his smile. "I'm not accusing ye of anything, Alasdair Campbell. I have a habit of thinking out loud. Don't take it to heart."

"I wasn't offended, if that's what ye think."

"Good. There's nothing worse than a man who finds offence in every wee remark that goes against his leanings."

He laughed. "My leanings? What are ye saying? I'm flummoxed by yer thought processes."

"Ye wouldn't be the first, and that's the sorry truth."

"I see nothing wrong in a woman speaking her mind."

"Is that a fact?" She raised her eyebrows. "Then ye're a very unusual man, Alasdair."

"'Tis better than keeping secrets and lies for fear of causing offense."

"Ye don't have to persuade *me* of such things. I'd far rather face an unfortunate truth than be victim of a pretty lie."

For a moment, a shadow darkened his expression, but it vanished in an instant, and she gave herself an inner shake. What was she thinking? It seemed meeting Alasdair had utterly addled her good sense.

"Then for the sake of not hiding anything from ye, I feel 'tis only right to tell ye up front I'm a half-brother to the earl. Is that an unfortunate truth?"

"Ye're already a Campbell, which is unfortunate enough. I'll not burden ye with further condemnation for being related to the earl. 'Tis hardly yer fault, is it?"

Before Alasdair could respond, a maid entered the stables with several waterbags. She took them from her, carefully placing them on the ground next to Ban, and wrapped strips of her ruined blanket around them. The maid left, and she glanced at Alasdair.

Good Lord, she needed to take those puppies from him. Never in her wildest dreams had she imagined a broad-shouldered warrior—and a Campbell at that—could look so irresistible while holding a pair of newborn pups so tenderly. The juxtaposition should have been jarring. Yet it felt strangely right, and once again she couldn't help smiling at him.

'Twas a relief Roisin wasn't here to see how foolishly she was reacting to Alasdair's easy charm. Her sister would never have let her live it down.

She wasn't certain she'd ever live it down herself.

Chapter Four

Freyja MacDonald smiled at him, and Alasdair couldn't tear his gaze from her. He was still reeling from the revelation that this vision was his intended bride.

He'd resigned himself to wedding Ranulph's granddaughter and had certainly been intrigued to know Freyja was Isolde's sister. But nothing had prepared him for the woman herself. Damn, she wasn't simply a beauty who ignited his lust. She made him laugh. And that was something he'd never expected his future wife would do. The prospect of marriage was no longer merely a strategy he had no option but to undertake. It was something to look forward to.

"Here." Freyja interrupted his thoughts, her hands reaching for him, and for a mad moment he thought she meant to take him in her arms. Until he realized she reached for the puppies.

"Huh." He glanced down at them, although all he could see were the tops of their heads, wrapped as they were in strips of blanket. An inexplicable tug of warmth heated his chest at the sight of the helpless wee creatures. "Are they out of danger now?"

"We've given them a good chance, and that's all we can do." She carefully extracted one of the pups from him, her fingers brushing against him, and lust roared through his blood at the contact. If it wasn't so damned inconvenient, it would be funny. Since when did the merest touch of a woman's hand cause him to half lose his mind?

The answer knelt beside him, as she placed the pup by the

heated waterbags next to its sibling, before she retrieved the second pup he held. And as she turned her attention to Ban, a deep sense of satisfaction settled through him.

It would be no hardship to woo her, if Ranulph continued to be stubborn. What was more, Freyja was refreshingly practical and would surely see the advantages in such an alliance.

'Tis better than secrets and lies. His lighthearted comment echoed in his mind, and unease flickered through him as he recalled her retort.

Except he wasn't lying to her, nor did he intend to. But even if his half-brother hadn't commanded him to keep this business close to his chest, he could hardly tell her of the earl's plan when they'd only just met. He was under no illusion she wouldn't hesitate to tell him to go to hell.

All he needed was a few days to win her favor. With luck, Ranulph would change his stance and have his back when he saw how committed he was in securing his granddaughter's happiness, but one thing was certain: He would not leave the Isle of Rum until Freyja had promised to be his bride.

IT WAS LATE in the afternoon when they left the stables and made their way to the stronghold. The dog had delivered six puppies in all, and the unexpected tug of warmth that had assailed him when he'd held two of them still lingered deep inside. 'Twas an odd thing, and yet he couldn't deny its existence. Almost as though he'd helped to deliver a prized foal.

"Well." Freyja gave him a sideways glance with a smile that was already feeling enjoyably familiar. "That was a productive day, although I'm sure ye've never had one like it before."

"Ye're not wrong. But I can't say it wasn't enjoyable, thanks to the company."

"'Tis kind of ye. I'll be sure to pass on yer compliment to Ban when I next check on her."

"I'm sure she'll be thankful for it." He caught Freyja's glance and grinned when she rolled her eyes at him. "What?"

"'Tis very odd for a strange man to accept my comments without trying to . . ." she paused for a moment, as though contemplating her words, "correct them."

"I can't be that strange anymore. We just spent hours together in a stable."

"I happen to think ye're very strange indeed."

"If ye're attempting to insult me, ye'll need to try harder. I've been called far worse than that in my time."

Her lips twitched as though she was trying not to laugh. "Ye can take it as a compliment if ye wish."

He gave an exaggerated sigh. "If ye insist."

The jet-black terrier that had been in the stable with them raced up to the doors of the stronghold before swinging about and darting back to Freyja's heels, its tongue hanging out as it gazed up at her in evident adoration.

She came to a standstill and crouched down, tickling the dog's throat. "Aye, ye're a very good lad indeed, Dubh. We'll go on the beach to stretch yer legs shortly."

Amused, he glanced at her as they once again continued walking. "Apt name."

"I don't see what else he could be called, do ye?" She sighed and shook her head. "My sisters both tried to persuade me to pick something fancier, but between ye and me, I'd feel foolish calling him anything else. Besides, I'm certain he likes it."

He was certain the dog didn't give a damn what he was called, but he had to agree no name could suit it better. "I like it."

"Well, that's a relief, for I doubt he'd take kindly to me changing his name after more than ten years."

He smothered another grin as he held the door open, and together they entered the great hall, where Ranulph was once again sitting by the fireside.

"Afi," Freyja said as she went to his side and wrapped her

arms about him. "How are ye? Roisin sends her love."

Alasdair stood at the other end of the hearth as Ranulph responded to his granddaughter. It was plain the old man adored her, and he dropped his gaze to his boots, feeling suddenly like an intruder.

He wasn't used to witnessing such displays of affection between family members. God knew, he'd never experienced it in his own divided family. His mother had scarcely acknowledged his existence, and his stepfather had considered a roof over his head more than enough compensation for the temerity of having been born.

"Miles tells me ye tended to Banphrionsa," Ranulph said. "Is she well? What of the puppies?"

He gave a wry smile at Ban's full name. *Princess*. Aye, the hound was certainly treated like royalty.

"She did a grand job and is the proud dam of six. But ye must thank yer guest for that, Afi. If Alasdair Campbell hadn't arrived when he did, I fear I would've lost two of the puppies."

Ranulph eyed him. It was impossible to guess his thoughts. "Must I, indeed. If my granddaughter says it is true, then I believe her. How fortunate for ye, Alasdair."

Somehow, he felt compelled to defend himself, since it was obvious Ranulph thought the worst of him.

"I heard the dog howl and entered the stables but had no idea Lady Freyja was already attending to her."

"Why would ye know that before ye saw me?" Freyja shot a questioning glance between him and her grandfather. "Why is that fortunate, Afi? I feel I'm missing something."

"'Tis fortunate he helped and didn't hinder ye in any way."

"Ye're talking in riddles." There was a hint of exasperation in her voice, but he heard the edge of concern, too, and inexplicably a flicker of guilt ate through him. "I'll prepare ye a soothing tea to calm yer mind."

Ranulph gave an unexpected laugh and held onto her hand. But he spoke to Alasdair.

"I wager ye've learned already that my granddaughter is a canny lass." Then he turned to Freyja, who looked understandably bemused by her grandfather's remarks. Alasdair hoped the old man wasn't going to spill the real reason why he'd traveled to Rum just yet. He was certain Freyja wouldn't appreciate it. "My mind is fine, Frey. I don't need one of yer calming teas. But I wouldn't say no to a cup of yer special willow bark. No one makes it like ye do."

After another doubtful glance in his direction, as though she somehow thought he was to blame for her grandfather's request, she nodded. "Very well. I'll be back directly."

He watched her walk across the hall and disappear through the door at the far end before returning his attention to Ranulph, who was regarding him with narrowed eyes.

"I take it ye didn't discuss the earl's idea with my granddaughter, did ye?"

"I did not."

"At least ye possess some sense, then." For some reason, Ranulph appeared to find that fact amusing. "Ye couldn't have picked a better way to have her look kindly upon ye, than by helping her with Ban."

Although he believed it, he was also irked by Ranulph's insinuation. "I didn't know she was Lady Freyja until yer steward came into the stables. I was helping out regardless."

It wasn't a lie, but it wasn't the truth, either. He'd been captivated by her, long before he discovered who she was, and that was why he'd crouched in the straw and tended to two newborn pups. Would he have done the same if she'd been a stable lad?

It was possible, but he suspected he may have gone outside and hailed a maid to assist, instead. Not that he intended on telling her grandfather that. He had the feeling Ranulph would find fault in it.

And he knew, without a doubt, that Freyja would.

"Keep yer counsel, lad, and so will I. We'll see where fate leads my Frey."

Alasdair inclined his head. Aye, he'd keep his counsel for now. But he wasn't leaving the outcome of his future in the fickle hands of fate. When the time was right, he'd do everything in his power to win Freyja MacDonald and Kilvenie Tower.

And by doing so, earn the right to be laird of Dunochty Castle.

Chapter Five

THE FOLLOWING MORNING, Freyja examined each puppy as Afi fussed over his beloved Ban. Who, thank the blessed Eir, was doing very well. Her grandfather had caught her before breakfast and had insisted on seeing his dog before doing anything else, so here they were.

Not that she minded. She'd intended to visit her charges in any case before she left the Isle for Eigg. Although, if she was truthful, she'd been hoping Alasdair might've accompanied her. But she hadn't seen him since last night, and they'd had no opportunity to talk without others surrounding them from the moment they'd entered the hall yesterday afternoon.

She shook her head, exasperated by how she couldn't seem to get the charming Campbell from her mind. Curse the man, he'd even invaded her dreams.

And what breath-stealing dreams they'd been.

Heat flooded through her, burning her cheeks, and she crouched lower over the puppies so neither her grandfather nor Miles would notice. But she couldn't stop her besotted smile at the memory of Alasdair's dream kisses.

God help her. She was going soft in the head.

"Why did ye whelp in here, lass?" Afi, sitting on a low stool Miles had brought with them, gave a heavy sigh as he scratched Ban's throat. "We had a grand corner set up in my chamber for her," he added to Freyja, who dragged her wayward thoughts together and nodded in sympathy before handing him a puppy.

"We can't move her yet," she reminded him. "But the stable lad is under strict instructions to keep a close eye on her and ensure they're all kept warm, and ye know Miles won't let anything happen to her or the pups."

"They'll all be fine," Miles said as he kept a watchful eye on her grandfather as he inspected each puppy in turn. "There's no need to stay," he added to her, nodding his head at Dubh. "Go take the lad for his run on the beach. We'll see ye back at the stronghold before ye leave."

She shot him a grateful smile, kissed Afi on the cheek, and left the stables. It was another fine day, and as she made her way down the rocky path that led to the beach, with Dubh enthusiastically chasing elusive rodents, she breathed in deep. The scent of sand and salt drifted in the fresh breeze, and she was glad of the extra shawl she'd borrowed from her late grandmother's possessions that Afi had refused to dispose of.

The beach was deserted, and only a few red deer grazed at the fringe of the woodlands. After a quick glance over her shoulder to ensure she truly was alone, she picked up her skirts and raced along the shoreline, Dubh barking ecstatically at her heels.

Laughing, she came to a halt and scooped him into her arms for a quick hug. He licked her nose, and she shook her head. "Aye, I love ye too, ye little rascal."

She put him back on the beach, but instead of chasing gulls, he faced the way they'd come and barked in greeting. Heat flashed through her. Who had witnessed her undignified dash along the sand? To be sure, 'twas nothing to be ashamed about, but she did have a reputation to uphold. And not just because she was a MacDonald of Sgur Castle.

Her healing skills were everything to her, and she was well aware there were some among the Western Isles who'd take great delight in disparaging her for such a seeming lack of decorum.

Not here on Rum, though.

I hope.

Since it was a fool's wish to hope whoever else was now on the beach hadn't noticed her unseemly behavior, she straightened her shoulders and swung about.

And not two horses' length from her stood Alasdair.

"Where the devil did ye appear from?" She hadn't meant to sound quite so accusatory, but good Lord, it was as though he'd materialized from the sand itself.

He glanced to the edge of the beach, where the sand merged with grassland, strewn with massive, irregular boulders, that in the distance converged into woodland, before he offered her the same smile that had haunted her dreams overnight. "I didn't mean to startle ye."

"I'm not startled," she corrected him, which wasn't quite the truth but better than admitting every time she saw him it seemed her heart was determined to hammer in her chest like a creature possessed. "But ye could've said something, instead of skulking behind me like that."

"To be fair, I wasn't skulking." He appeared to find her charge against him entertaining. Why didn't that irk her? Instead, she found herself returning his smile. "I'd just come from the woodlands and thought for sure ye'd seen me. I was about to hail ye when yer wee dog greeted me."

"Dubh is a grand guard dog, and that's a fact."

A frown flashed across his brow. It was disconcerting how fascinating she found it. "He's a good dog for warning ye of a stranger's approach, but he's no guard dog, Lady Freyja. 'Tis none of my business, I'm aware, but do ye sail between the isles alone?"

He was right. It wasn't any of his business, and yet she didn't mind his question. It wasn't as though it was a secret, after all. "I do not. My grandmother would never allow such a thing, even though I'm perfectly able to navigate the waters between the Small Isles. One of our most trusted warriors, Clyde, accompanies me."

"Yet ye walk the beaches alone."

This time his remark did take her aback. "Of course. Why shouldn't I? The beaches of Rum are as familiar to me as those on Eigg. And I'm as safe here as I am there."

He sighed. "Ye're likely right. I grew up in Oban, and no lady would walk alone with only her dog for company. I've been to Skye before, but this is the first time I've visited one of the Small Isles."

"Aye, well ye can't compare the Isles with Oban, or any of yer towns on the mainland. I'm thankful I don't need to heed the restrictions imposed beyond our Isles. Eigg is where my heart lies, and Rum is very dear to me, too."

And it was just as well, since she was bound to Eigg by the sacred Deep Knowing that had been handed down for countless generations of her foremothers.

The bloodline of the Isle must prevail beyond quietus.

The meaning was as clear as the sun in the sky. If the daughters of Sgur abandoned the Isle, their bloodline would die.

But what of Isolde? She had left Eigg against the edict of their Pict queen ancestor and was blissfully happy with her decision. It was a puzzle, and one Freyja had not yet managed to solve.

"What if ye wed a man not of the Isles? Ye might find life in the Highlands to yer liking after all."

"I don't think so." She cast him an amused sideways glance as they continued to stroll along the beach. In the sunlight, his blond hair glinted with elusive shimmers of auburn, and it was an effort to drag her mesmerized gaze from him before he noticed and questioned her on it. She drew in a deep breath of salt-laden air, but the mad urge to reach up and run her fingers through his windswept hair lodged in her mind.

It was most distracting.

"Ye don't think what? That ye'll wed a man not of the Isles, or ye won't enjoy living in the Highlands?"

There was a teasing note in his voice that was frankly irresistible. Which was intriguing since usually she wasn't thrilled when a man insisted on questioning her views. But Alasdair wasn't arrogantly overriding her with his own opinions. Despite his smile, he sounded genuinely curious.

"Both. Whoever I wed will make his home with me at Sgur."

"Is that so?"

She laughed. "Aye, it is so. Why do ye sound so skeptical? 'Tis the way it's been for the last nine hundred years."

"Nine hundred years? Isn't it time for a change, then?"

"Why change something for no reason? That's simply foolish."

"Wait. Are ye telling me that no MacDonald woman has left Sgur in almost a thousand years?"

"'Tis the legacy we inherited from our foremothers. We travel, of course." She waved her hand to encompass the sea and the beach. "But our hearts are forever entwined with our beloved Eigg."

"Huh."

She couldn't quite fathom what he meant to convey with his *huh*, but she could take a guess, since it was something that was often on her own mind of late.

"Ye may be aware that my sister, Isolde, recently wed William Campbell of Creagdoun. And before ye say anything, I'll tell ye straight: I'm still flummoxed by it. I can only suppose it's because just one daughter of Sgur is needed to continue our legacy, and that's why Isolde is happy in her new life."

He gazed at her as though he had no idea what she was talking about. She couldn't really blame him. There was no reason why he'd know of the legacy of Sgur that had been passed down from mother to daughter since their infamous Pict queen ancestor. And no one outside the female line of her family knew of the Deep Knowing.

She hoped he didn't ask what she meant. She really should have kept her mouth shut, but he was so cursed easy to talk to.

"I've known William since I was a wee lad," he said, unexpectedly, and she blinked at him as relief swept through her that she didn't need to deflect any awkward questions about her matrilineal heritage. "And I've met yer sister, Lady Isolde, several times."

"Oh." She came to a halt and stared at him, unsure why his remark so surprised her. Indeed, now she thought about it, it made sense he knew William, who was, himself, related to the Earl of Argyll through his father. Alasdair may have been born out of wedlock, but noble blood flowed through his veins, and clearly he had been a favored son of the late earl. It made sense he had grown up with William who was, after all, the son of a baron.

"I don't know anything of yer legacy," he said, "but I do know William will do anything to ensure Lady Isolde's happiness."

She sighed, and of one accord they resumed their walk along the shore. "I know. He's a good man, for all he's a Campbell, and my sister loves him."

"He's not the only good Campbell, ye know."

"I'll take yer word for it." She cast him a teasing glance and he lightly bumped her shoulder with his arm. Illicit thrills raced through her at the fleeting touch, and she scarcely had the wit to berate herself for such an absurd reaction.

Without a doubt, it hadn't been an accidental touch. She wasn't sure how she should feel about such a liberty. Especially when Alasdair held her gaze for far longer than necessary.

She sucked in a long breath, but it didn't help ease her racing heart. Anyone would think she'd just climbed to the summit of An Sgurr on Eigg, rather than enjoy a leisurely stroll along the beach. But then, they wouldn't be taking into account the presence of Alasdair Campbell.

A liberty or not, she couldn't deny she'd enjoyed the brush of his arm against her. A revelation burst through her mind. Was this how William had made Isolde feel from the moment she'd met him? Flustered by where her imagination appeared to be leading her, she fished madly through her mind to change the subject.

"How long are ye intending to remain on Rum?"

"Until yer grandfather is tired of me and sets me on my way."

She shook her head. "Are ye ever serious? Don't ye have a grand castle waiting for ye in yer precious Highlands?"

"I have a trusted steward."

"A trusted steward is invaluable." Especially one as loyal as Miles. He was the reason why she and her sisters could rest easy that Afi always had the best care when they weren't on Rum themselves.

And then something occurred to her, and a shiver skated over her arms at how she hadn't thought of it before. "What of yer lady wife? Won't she be missing ye?"

"I'm not wed, Lady Freyja." Was that a hint of laughter in his voice, as though he suspected the possibility he possessed a wife had unsettled her? She hoped he suspected no such thing. How mortifying. "Do ye have an understanding with a man from the Isles?"

"That's a very personal question, Alasdair Campbell."

"I shouldn't wish to intrude if yer interest lies elsewhere."

"If my interest lay elsewhere, I shouldn't allow ye to intrude." Belatedly, she realized her comment might make Alasdair conclude she'd just invited him to continue, rather than letting him know she was more than capable of telling a man to back off if he was annoying her.

But continue what? She wasn't so starstruck by his charm as to imagine his flirting was anything serious. Even if she wanted it to be.

Which she didn't. Especially with a Highlander who had made no secret that he found the tradition of Sgur women remaining on Eigg after marriage to be somewhat odd.

They had reached the end of the beach, where a rocky peak towered over the bay and spilled into the sea. She'd often scrambled over the rugged coastline with Dubh, but she didn't have time today. She needed to get back home and see to her patients.

They came to a halt, and Alasdair turned to face her. "Since I'm not intruding, might I escort ye back to Kilvenie Tower?" He held out his arm and she eyed it with some suspicion. "Unless ye wish for a stroll through the woodlands?"

She laughed at that. "I've no intention of walking through the woodlands with ye. But I'll accept yer offer to accompany me back to the stronghold."

With that, she hooked her arm through his, and the tips of her fingers brushed against his wrist. His skin was warm, and she had to forcibly curb the urge to stroke the fine hair on his forearm. What on earth did this Highlander possess that made everything about him so fascinating?

She knew plenty of men from the Isles. She'd treated a fair number of men, too, and not one of them had ever come close to making her catch her breath. Never mind all but forgetting how to breathe in the first place.

It was as though he'd cast a spell upon her. Except she didn't believe in such fanciful fae tales, and she couldn't believe she'd even thought such a preposterous thing in the first place.

What the devil was Alasdair Campbell doing to her?

Chapter Six

Alasdair glanced at Freyja as she walked by his side, her arm linking his as though it was the most natural thing in the world. In truth, he'd doubted she'd accept his offer, but if there was one thing he'd learned about her in the short time since they'd met, it was that she never did what he expected.

Her hair was pulled back into a loose plait, tied with a blue ribbon that matched her eyes, but several long curls had escaped and danced around her face in the sea breeze. His gaze roved over her profile, snagging on the enchanting blush that highlighted her aristocratic cheekbones, and satisfaction streaked through him.

There was no denying the sparks between them. All he needed was a few more days, and he was certain Freyja would look favorably on an alliance between them. And once she accepted his proposal, Ranulph wouldn't raise any obstacle. All he wanted was his granddaughter's happiness, and if Alasdair made Freyja happy, his mission for the earl was accomplished.

"What plans do ye have for the rest of the day?" He was already envisioning a leisurely stroll to the local village, and he'd discovered a secluded cove the other day that would be perfect for an afternoon picnic. Not that he'd ever done such a thing before, but he'd heard it was a good strategy for romancing a lady.

"I'm leaving for Eigg shortly. This was only a quick visit on my way home from Canna."

His visions of spending the day with Freyja shattered around him. How was he meant to gain her favor if she left the Isle? But it was more than that. He'd been looking forward to her company.

"Yer grandfather will miss ye." And he wouldn't be the only one.

"I'll miss him too. But he's so much better than he was a few weeks ago. Ye wouldn't believe how hard we tried to get him to come and live with us at Sgur."

"Kilvenie must be in his blood." Growing up in his stepfather's manor, he'd never had a great attachment to the place, but he knew others had a fierce bond with the land of their forefathers.

Hell, look at Freyja. She'd told him plainly she had no intention of leaving Sgur Castle. What plans had she made for Kilvenie Tower, when Ranulph granted her the stronghold?

When William had introduced his wife to him, he'd had no idea Lady Isolde was the first woman of her lineage who'd left the Isle of Eigg in almost a thousand years. But she'd left Sgur for love.

He could only hope Freyja would, too. But that would never happen if she returned to Eigg before he had the chance to capture her heart.

"To be sure," she said, and it took him a heartbeat to understand what she meant. "Afi's forefathers have been custodians of the stronghold for more than three hundred years. I know he's grieved he has no grandson to continue his heritage, but it cannot be helped."

He wasn't sure how common the knowledge was that Ranulph intended to leave the stronghold to Freyja. It was likely best if he kept the fact that he knew to himself. "I'm certain he'll make the right choice when the time comes."

"Hmm." She cast him a sideways glance, and for a moment he thought she was about to say more. Confide in him, maybe. But instead she sighed and leaned closer to him as they continued along the beach. It was a torture he'd never imagined could exist and there was nothing he could do about it. Not when he needed to win her trust. "I hope it's many years before we need to face that choice."

He inclined his head in agreement, but all his wretched mind could think about was stealing a kiss. Would she slap his face or sink into his arms? The very fact he didn't have a clue how she'd react only made the prospect more enticing than ever.

"I'm sure ye're right." But even as he spoke, disquiet edged through him. The only reason the earl had sent him to Rum was because Ranulph was thought to be on his deathbed. While the older man was certainly frail, Alasdair hadn't seen any sign he was on the point of dying.

The truth was, the longer he stayed at Kilvenie, the less he wished for that outcome. And yet his future hinged on it.

But how long did the earl expect him to stay here? And more to the point, how long would Ranulph allow him to?

ALASDAIR WAITED IN the courtyard while Freyja said her farewells to her grandfather. Clyde, the warrior she'd spoken of earlier, eyed him from the door to the stronghold, his face an impassive mask. He was a great hulk of a man, and it was clear no one would attack Freyja with such an intimidating guard.

It was a relief, although he wasn't sure why. She had said herself, she was safe on the Isles, but that had more to do with her status as a MacDonald of Sgur rather than the inhabitants being more law-abiding than those from the mainland. Still, at least she had a man to navigate the boat between the Isles, and that was something.

Finally, she emerged with her dog, as always, at her heels, and he strode over to her. "I'll accompany ye to the boat."

She fell into step beside him, and after shooting him a dark glare, Clyde marched ahead of them.

"When ye leave Rum, do feel free to visit us on yer way back to the mainland." She smiled at him, and he once again had the overwhelming need to kiss those irresistible lips. Except this time, unlike when they'd been on the beach, they weren't alone, and he was certain Clyde would relish breaking his nose for taking such a liberty.

To hell with it. He threaded his fingers through hers, and she gave a soft gasp but didn't pull away. Who knew the gentle caress of a palm against his could be so arousing?

But then, this was Freyja, and it seemed anything she did had the power to fire his blood.

"I'll be sure to take ye up on yer kind offer," he promised. One way or another, he was determined to make her his bride, whatever happened here on Rum with Ranulph. Because if he was sure of one thing, it was that the earl would claim Kilvenie by whatever means he could. And Alasdair intended to support him, even if it entailed wedding Freyja while Ranulph was still alive.

They reached the sheltered cove, where her boat had been pulled up onto the sand beside a rocky outcrop. The sea was calm and Eigg, with its dramatic ridge that towered over the Isle, looked deceptively close.

As Clyde dragged the boat to the water, as though it weighed no more than a satchel of feathers, Alasdair grasped Freyja's free hand and swung her around to face him.

"I mean it," he said. "Watch out for me, Lady Freyja."

She gave a silent laugh, but her fingers tightened around his. "I shan't be standing on the beach waiting for ye, Alasdair, if that's what ye're meaning. But make yer way to Sgur Castle, and I'll see ye soon enough."

"Ye may count on it." Before he could think better of it, he brushed her lips in a fleeting kiss, and her elusive scent of roses and rain tormented him. Lust roared through him, and it was hell to pull back, but somehow he managed it. For an eternal moment her blue gaze ensnared him, as the erratic thud of his heart blotted out the sound of the gulls' crying overhead. He dragged in a harsh breath, forcing himself back to reality while he still could. "And now the promise is sealed with a kiss."

FREYJA COULD STILL feel Alasdair's lips on hers as she made her way across the bracken moorlands to where Sgur Castle, in all its majestic splendor, rose on its mighty hill in the shadow of An Sgurr.

Exasperated, she shook her head but couldn't dislodge the smile that had affixed itself to her face ever since his unexpected kiss.

The very nerve of the man to do such a thing. She really should be most irked with him, but instead she was having a hard time not wishing for a repeat performance as soon as possible.

He'd remained on the beach watching her departure while Clyde had rowed to Eigg, and although it had been completely unnecessary on his part, she'd found it utterly charming. Especially when he'd raised his hand in a final farewell, before he'd vanished beyond the sea mist.

As she entered the castle, Roisin came across the hall to greet her. "How is Afi?"

"He's looking well, but he still tires so easily."

Roisin crouched to give Dubh a hug. "'Tis good news, then. I couldn't bear it if anything happened to him."

"Oh, and Ban had her pups. Six of them. So Afi is well pleased."

Roisin straightened and gave her a curious glance. "Did something happen while ye were away, Frey?"

Sometimes, Roisin could be annoyingly perceptive. "I was kept busy."

But all she could think about was Alasdair. And that kiss.

"Aye, of course." Roisin gave her another probing glance as they made their way to their grandmother's chamber where she dealt with matters of the estate. "But there's a glow about ye I've never seen before."

"A glow?" Freyja scoffed, but only just stopped herself from pressing her hand against her cheek, to check if her skin was burning or not. Except she knew Roisin was referring to something completely different than whether the walk up to the castle had turned her face red. "I'm not one of yer fae folk. I don't glow."

"I'm reminded of how Isolde looked, when she met William."

Freyja came to a halt and planted her hands on her hips as she faced her sister. To be sure, Isolde had most certainly favored William from the moment she'd met him, but the truth was, Roisin had seen from the start how utterly their sister had fallen for the stranger from the sea, and she hadn't seen anything of the kind. Feeling a little aggrieved, she said, "I never saw such a thing."

"I know. But I also know ye're avoiding my question."

She shook her head, but it was impossible to remain irked with Roisin, so she hooked her arm through her sister's as they continued on their way. Besides, she had the unaccountable urge to tell her about Alasdair, even though she knew Roisin would immediately weave fae tales about how he was her soulmate, or something equally outlandish.

"Very well. Afi had a visitor, Alasdair Campbell, sent to Rum by the Earl of Argyll. His half-brother, would ye believe. A charmer such as ye would never imagine."

"Ye're not impressed by charmers."

"Who said I was impressed?" And who was she trying to fool? "Aye, all right then. His charm was most delightful, and I enjoyed his company. Satisfied?"

Roisin looked enthralled. "Will he visit ye here before he returns to the mainland?"

"I invited him to do so," she said with as much dignity as she could, considering she was battling the urge to smile at the memory of Alasdair standing in the cove as she returned to Eigg.

They had reached Amma's chamber, but instead of knocking on the door, Roisin halted before it. "But why did the earl send him to visit Afi? It's a bit odd, isn't it?"

It was, but she'd been so enchanted by Alasdair that she hadn't considered it too deeply. But it wasn't hard to see the truth. Even if she'd rather not.

"I expect the earl heard of Afi's fall and wanted confirmation on how his health was. Ye know how the Campbells covet MacDonald land. Maybe he thought to gather information on how well Kilvenie is defended."

"Ye mean the earl might try and take Kilvenie by force?" Roisin sounded distraught. "But the stronghold will be yers when Afi passes. Surely the earl won't want to cause bad blood between the clans by usurping yer claim?"

It seemed unlikely. Regardless of how her grandfather intended to grant her the stronghold, Clan MacDonald would not take kindly if the Earl of Argyll waged a battle for the prestigious land. It would undo all the goodwill between the two clans, and why would he want that?

THE FOLLOWING MORNING, Freyja was working in the castle's medicinal gardens with Laoise, as they tended to the precious stock of poppies Freyja had grown from seeds. Although the plants weren't best suited to the isle's weather, their remedial benefits far outweighed the extra care it took to cultivate them.

Dubh sat beyond the vast wall that surrounded the potentially deadly plants, and although she trusted him not to eat anything he shouldn't, he did love to investigate interesting smells and vermin. She couldn't risk him accidentally poisoning himself, but he always gave her a doleful look whenever she shut the gate on him.

"We'll take these back to the apothecary," she said, pointing at the pods in a basket at their feet. "And ye shall prepare the tincture."

"By myself, milady?" Laoise sounded startled.

"Aye. 'Tis time. Ye have the skill to tend patients on yer own, so 'tis only right ye start to prepare the remedies too. And of course, it'll mean ye get an increase in wages."

Laoise looked thrilled. "Thank ye, milady."

Freyja smiled at her. It was the right decision to make. Apart from all the practical concerns, it meant she could visit Afi again in a few days, for longer this time, without worrying that she was abandoning those who relied on her.

It certainly had nothing to do with the possibility of seeing Alasdair again. That was simply a side benefit.

She was still smiling at how she kept trying to justify her thoughts when it came to Alasdair when Roisin entered the gardens.

"Colban MacDonald has arrived," her sister announced.

Freyja glanced up from her work. She couldn't see why Roisin thought Colban's visit warranted such a dramatic declaration. It was scarcely noteworthy, since he often stopped off at Eigg on his way from Islay to Skye. "Aye?"

Roisin gave a loud sigh. "He's asked where ye are three times already, so I thought it best to come and get ye myself before he took it into his head to look for ye."

Irritation flickered through her. She'd known Colban of Tarnford Castle on Islay, who was a couple of years older than her, for most of her life, and truth be told, hadn't taken much notice of him or his frequent visits to the Isle. But last winter, while Isolde was busy falling for William, both of her sisters had commented on Colban's attention to her. And not in a good way. Even Roisin, who saw romance wherever she looked, had said he was merely trying to flatter her with insincere compliments instead of simply admiring her healing skills.

When she'd thought about it, she'd reached the same conclusion. It had left her feeling greatly out of sorts with him, and she'd managed to avoid him completely the last two times he'd stopped on the Isle.

It seemed her luck had run out.

She peeled off her gloves with more force than necessary and then caught Laoise's anxious glance. She took a deep breath and offered her a smile. "I'll leave this in yer capable hands, Laoise. I won't be long."

With that, she joined Roisin, but before they even reached the kitchens, Colban swung open the door. Had he actually followed her sister out here? She returned his smile of greeting with a frosty glare.

Which he appeared not to see.

"Lady Freyja, what a pleasure. It's been a good while since we last spoke."

"I hope ye're keeping well, Colban." Somehow, she managed to summon up a tight smile. She was, after all, a daughter of Sgur, and her grandmother's favorite piece of advice was to keep perspective in all matters to be a fair judge of truth. "Are ye on yer way to Skye?"

"No, we're heading to Oban. I have business with my cousin Peter on the mainland."

As they entered the kitchens, she shot him a sharp glance. "Why did ye come to Eigg? 'Tis hardly on yer way." Indeed, it more than doubled the journey.

"True, but I was hoping to see ye." They left the kitchens, and as they approached the great hall, he lowered his voice, presumably so Roisin, who walked ahead of them, wouldn't overhear. "Word reached us that yer grandfather is ailing. I hope that's not the truth of the matter. Ranulph is a fine man."

The tense muscles in her shoulders eased and she offered him a genuine smile. She'd allowed her sisters' suspicions to get the better of her these last six months, when she'd been right all along. Colban and his forefathers were old friends of the Sgur MacDonalds, and that was why he'd added hours to his journey to Oban by detouring to Eigg.

"I'm thankful to report my grandfather is far from ailing." To be sure, the fall he'd taken the other week had been alarming, but seeing him during the last couple of days had greatly eased her mind.

"That's good news." Instead of pausing in the hall, he continued to the doors, as though he wished for them to take a walk in the courtyard. And while she'd have rather returned to the gardens to continue with her work, she felt bad saying such a thing to him when he was being so solicitous of Afi, and so she swallowed her inclination to excuse herself and accompanied him outside. "Would ye come with me to Kilvenie, Lady Freyja? I'd like to pay my respects to Ranulph."

"My grandfather will be pleased to see ye. But I shan't accompany ye. I was with him just yesterday."

"Ah." Was she imagining it, or did annoyance flash over his face at her response? "Are ye certain I can't persuade ye, Lady Freyja? 'Tis a glorious day for a short trip to Rum."

"Aye, it is, but I'm cataloguing stocks."

"Surely the steward can oversee such a task."

"I'm sure he could, if I trained him in such matters." She didn't bother to try and hide the irritation in her voice. Who was Colban to try and tell her what tasks she should or shouldn't pass onto the castle's steward? Especially when part of cataloguing the stocks involved preparing tinctures that could be hazardous in the wrong hands. "But neither of us have time for that."

"Ye take on too much. I've said this to ye before."

He had, and in the past she'd ignored it as Colban just being Colban. But today his remark, with its hint of disdain, rubbed her the wrong way.

"If I took on too much, the work wouldn't get done. And it does."

He eyed her. It was obvious he wasn't sure if she was being flippant or not. "That's not what I mean."

She knew that wasn't what he'd meant. He had an abiding notion that getting her hands dirty in the gardens was somehow beneath her, and she should delegate such tasks, and spend her time in the solar with her needle.

Not that she had anything against embroidery. When she was in the mood, she found it soothing, but it wasn't any of Colban's business where she decided to spend her time.

Alasdair wouldn't have misunderstood her retort. But then, she couldn't imagine he'd ever say such a thing to her in the first place.

Since she'd only known him for barely a day, it made no sense for her to think such a thing, but that fact didn't change her mind. An illicit thrill sparked through her as she recalled the laughter in his voice and warm gleam in his eyes as they'd walked along the beach, and inevitably, their parting kiss lingered in her mind like an ethereal promise.

It was a wrench to force herself back to the present, where Colban stood beside her with a faintly affronted air. But it wasn't her fault if he took exception to her words, when he was the one implying she was in the wrong.

"Then ye should say what ye mean, Colban, so there's no misunderstanding between us."

"I mean no disrespect, my lady. We've been friends a long time and I hope ye always take my words the way they're meant. Ye mean a great deal to me, and I shouldn't wish to offend ye."

Freyja folded her arms and focused on Dubh. Colban had never said anything about how much she meant to him before, and the truth was, his comment made her uncomfortable. As though he wanted more than friendship.

Blessed Eir. She hoped she'd misunderstood. She had no interest in having anything more with him.

"I'm not offended," she told him, without looking at him. "And we appreciate yer concern." Inspiration struck on how she could steer this conversation away from awkward territory. "Indeed, if ye're planning to visit my grandfather, ye'll likely meet his guest, Alasdair Campbell."

This time there was no mistaking the annoyance that darkened his brow. "I don't know of this Alasdair Campbell."

"He's half-brother to the Earl of Argyll. And apparently a good friend of William's."

Belatedly, she recalled how Colban had taken exception to William's presence at Sgur in the winter. It had likely been a bad idea to mention his name.

"What the devil is the earl's half-brother doing at Kilvenie?"

It was a small relief Colban hadn't decided to make disparaging remarks about William, but the aggression in his voice was plain. And she understood why. As she'd said to her sister, there was logically only one reason why the earl had sent Alasdair to Rum, and she doubted it was from the kindness of his heart to ensure her grandfather's wellbeing.

Just because she was charmed by Alasdair didn't mean she was blind to the politics behind his visit. Yet for some reason she was irked that Colban appeared to have jumped to the very same conclusion.

"The earl is related to my late grandmother," she reminded him. "There's a blood connection."

Not that she'd ever felt the need to highlight that connection before. Maybe, if she'd ever had the chance to know her paternal grandmother, she would have learned of her Campbell relations. But, as things stood, she scarcely even acknowledged the Campbell blood that ran through her veins.

"Aye." Colban sounded grudging. "There is a blood connection."

She waited for him to continue, but it seemed that was all he had to say on the matter which, unaccountably, caused a shiver of unease along her spine. The blood connection, after all, was between herself and her sisters, not Afi, as her comment had implied. Yet there was a dark trace of veiled calculation in the way Colban eyed her. What wasn't he sharing with her?

Tension sparked in the air between them, as though a thousand spiders crawled along her arms, and finally she couldn't stand it any longer. "Well, 'twas good to see ye, Colban, but I must be getting on. Ye've a long day ahead of yerself too, if ye plan on sailing to Rum before heading back to Oban."

He smiled, but it didn't reach his eyes. "I'll visit Ranulph another time."

She didn't care what he planned on doing so long as this encounter ended. "Give yer cousin Peter my regards."

Colban inclined his head, took her hand—even though she hadn't offered it to him—and pressed his lips upon her knuckles.

"I will." His gaze locked with hers before he turned on his heel. As she watched him march down the hill, Roisin came to her side.

"What did he want with ye that was so urgent?"

She shook her head, even though she had a sinking sensation in the pit of her stomach that she did, indeed, suspect what Colban might want with her. "He wanted me to visit Afi with him."

Roisin was silent for a moment, before she linked her arm through hers. "I fear he may be courting ye in earnest, Frey." There was an anxious note in her sister's voice, that did nothing to ease the disquiet in her own breast. "Ye need to tell him straight, before he thinks he has a hope of winning yer hand."

She knew Roisin was right. But what if they'd misjudged him, and he had no thoughts of courting her? It would be highly embarrassing to confront him, only to have him laugh incredulously at her presumption.

Yet even that excruciating encounter would be preferable to having Colban ask for her hand.

Chapter Seven

Alasdair stood in the sheltered cove where he'd said farewell to Freyja two days ago, his gaze fixed on the Isle of Eigg. It was strange how he missed her lively presence, considering the short time he'd known her. But the fact remained, Kilvenie was inexplicably empty without her.

The afternoon sea breeze was fresh with a hint of salt, and he exhaled a long breath. There had been no further discussions with Ranulph concerning an alliance between his granddaughter and Alasdair, and he was reluctant to broach the subject considering how his previous attempt had been received.

But he could hardly remain on the isle indefinitely. The earl had been misinformed as to Ranulph's health, and although the older man was frail, he could easily live another five or ten years.

It was time to change tactics.

Freyja had invited him to visit her when he left Rum, and he had every intention of doing so. And after he arrived on Eigg, he'd do everything within his power to win her affection.

She was an intriguing woman he couldn't get out of his mind. A woman it would be no hardship to woo.

But the truth was, even without the earl's blessing, Freyja fascinated him in a way no other lass had before. How fortunate that the one woman who'd captured his interest was also the one his half-brother wanted him to wed.

Belatedly, he realized he was grinning like a witless fool at his thoughts. Thank God no one was around to see him. Now he'd made the decision to leave Rum, it was time to bid Ranulph farewell, and he swung on his heel and made his way back to the tower.

As soon as he entered the hall, the tension slithered around him like a fog. Standing beside the hearth was the steward, Miles, deep in conversation with the stronghold's physician and chaplain, and Alasdair's senses sharpened.

Despite the urge to march up to Miles to discover what had occurred, it wasn't his place, but neither could he bring himself to leave the hall. Finally, Miles glanced over his shoulder, his face an impassive mask, and gave Alasdair a brusque nod.

He took it as a sign to approach. And although he was a guest, and didn't even know Ranulph well, he couldn't stop himself from asking. "What is it?"

"Ranulph had a—" Miles hesitated, a dark frown distorting his brow as he glanced at the other two men. "Turn."

"A turn?"

"Aye. Ye saw him yerself earlier. He was perfectly well. And then he dropped like a felled tree."

Alarm streaked through him. "Is he injured?"

Once again, Miles glanced at the other men, and this time the chaplain responded.

"'Tis in God's hands, my son."

Alasdair stared at him as the words pounded through his mind. "He won't recover?"

Miles gave a low growl in the back of his throat, while he glared daggers at the chaplain. "He may. With Freyja's skill, he recovered well from the fall when others thought he was on his deathbed."

"His injured leg was something I could treat." There was an affronted note in the physician's retort before he cast a sideways glance at Alasdair, as if reluctant to continue, and it wasn't hard to guess his thoughts. As far as he was concerned, Alasdair was an outsider.

He turned back to Miles. "I'll fetch Lady Freyja, if ye think it will help Ranulph."

"Aye." Miles released a harsh breath. "He'll want to see her. But first, he wants to see ye."

"Me?" He hadn't expected that.

"He was most insistent." There was a grim note in Miles' voice. "I'll take ye to him."

Alasdair followed the steward across the hall and up the stairs. When Miles paused before a door, he couldn't remain silent any longer. "Is there nothing the physician can do?"

"Ye heard him." Miles gripped the door ring, but instead of opening the door, he cast a shadowed glance his way. "Not that I'd take his word on much. I put more stock in Freyja's opinion than I do his."

They walked across the small antechamber, and an elderly serving woman opened the door to Ranulph's bedchamber. The fire blazed in the hearth, thick rugs covered the floor, and the old man sat propped up in his bed, his gaze fixed on Ban and her puppies, who had been transferred from the stables yesterday afternoon.

Shock stabbed through his chest. In the short time since he'd last seen Ranulph, it seemed the man had aged twenty or more years. His face was sunken, and he slumped against his pillows as though all the strength had seeped from his body.

"I've brought Alasdair," Miles said, and Ranulph slowly turned his head to focus on them.

"Leave us," he said to his steward before nodding at the serving woman, and Miles glowered at the order, although he didn't appear surprised by it.

Alasdair waited until Miles and the servant had left the chamber before he approached the bed. "I'm grieved ye had a setback."

God knew he meant it. Even if the only reason the earl had sent him here was because he'd believed Ranulph was dying, he wouldn't wish this fate on anyone. Besides, there was a difference between meeting a stranger at death's door, and a man who he'd grown to respect during the last week.

"I almost believe ye." Ranulph's lips stretched into a grin, but the sight only caused a sharp pain to lance through Alasdair's chest. "Don't try telling me this isn't the outcome yer earl was hoping for when he sent ye here."

Guilt flickered through him. "Ranulph—"

The older man made a dismissive gesture with his hand. "Don't trouble yerself, lad. I know the political situation." He drew in a raspy breath. "I know why the earl wants to dig his claws in Kilvenie."

There was no point denying it. But there was one thing he needed Ranulph to understand. "I meant what I said before. With the backing of the earl, Lady Freyja's heritage will remain secure."

"As long as she weds ye."

"Are ye still against such a match?"

"I don't believe I ever said I was against it. I said I wouldn't use my granddaughter as a pawn in yer earl's game."

He didn't like the idea of Freyja being a pawn, either. Even though that was exactly what she was in the earl's eyes.

But the bald truth was he didn't have to like it to know it made strategic sense. And since Ranulph had brought the subject up, maybe it meant he now believed the advantages to the match outweighed his previous annoyance at the proposed alliance.

"Ranulph, I want ye to know, when it comes to Lady Freyja, I'm not playing a game."

"I want yer word, Alasdair, that ye won't trick her into marriage."

Unease slithered through his chest. Did his determination to win her affection amount to trickery?

"I've no intention of hurting her, Ranulph. But I cannot promise to walk away if she honors me with a pledge to be my bride."

Ranulph grunted. "Ye know full well what I mean."

Aye, he did. A forced marriage through seduction. It was what the earl expected him to do, should all other negotiations fail. And yet the old man's veiled accusation cut deep, even if he understood why Ranulph harbored suspicions about his integrity. After all, the earl himself was relying on that very same integrity to get what he wanted by any means possible.

While Alasdair hadn't relished the notion when his half-brother had raised the subject, the truth was he'd sailed to Rum with the intention of winning Freyja's hand at any cost. But having Ranulph fling the accusation at him made him face a stark reality.

There was a difference between wooing her and winning her with pretty words and sincere promises of ensuring her future happiness and leaving her no choice but to wed him because he'd ruined her reputation. He knew which future he wanted.

"I do." He sounded irked and Ranulph gave him an inscrutable look, which he ignored. And even though it went against Archibald's edict, there was no point lying to himself anymore. And he wouldn't lie to Ranulph. "I'd not disrespect Lady Freyja in such a manner. Ye have my word."

Silence reigned between them until finally, Ranulph spoke. "Very well." Briefly he closed his eyes as if their exchange had exhausted him, before once again holding Alasdair's gaze. "I'll hold ye to yer word as a Campbell and half-brother to the Earl of Argyll."

IT WAS LATE in the evening, but sunlight still bathed the isle when Freyja left the village and made her way back to the castle. After Colban's visit, she and Laoise had gone to the castle's apothecary where Laoise carefully cut the pods they'd gathered in the gardens and collected the milky fluid that they would later use in powerful tinctures.

Freyja couldn't fault her meticulous attention to detail, which was essential when dealing with dangerous remedies. The advantage of having access to the precious poppy, and the knowledge on how to use its potent properties, was invaluable, but in the wrong hands could be deadly.

Thank Eir she'd taken a chance on training Laoise. Maybe she should see if there were any other women on the Small Isles who she might teach. It hadn't occurred to her before. The mysteries of the poppy had been handed down from her foremothers, as sacred as the Deep Knowing, and yet there wasn't any edict to keep the medicinal knowledge a secret.

Well, that was a thought for another day. For now, she was grateful she could visit Afi again tomorrow, and that Laoise was more than competent on her own.

As she strolled across the bracken moorland, Dubh barked in greeting, pulling her wandering thoughts back to the present. In the distance, obviously on his way to the castle, was Alasdair, and pleasure rushed through her like a warm wave.

He'd come to visit her. Just as he'd promised. And far sooner than she'd hoped for.

She returned his wave and picked up her pace as he made his way in her direction. Good Lord, how had she forgotten what a breathtaking sight he was? His blond hair, with those intriguing auburn glints, was tousled by the wind, and he'd rolled up his sleeves, giving her an unhindered sight of his marvelous forearms.

She sucked in a jagged breath and tried to quell her amorous reverie. It would be too mortifying if he saw how easily he affected her, without even touching her, no less.

"Lady Freyja." He gave a charming half bow.

"Alasdair. 'Tis good to see ye looking so fine."

Wait. Had she said that out loud? What in the name of Eir was it about him that made her behave like a lovestruck maid of thirteen? It was all very well speaking her mind, but not when her mind was seemingly determined to bypass any good sense she usually possessed.

Thankfully, Dubh distracted Alasdair's attention before he could respond to her unwary comment, by placing his paw on his boot.

"Good lad." Alasdair scratched Dubh's head, which only made her smile like a fool as she recalled how adorable he had looked holding Ban's newborn pups. What a relief he was focusing on her dog instead of her.

"'Tis quite late to be visiting," she remarked, but he didn't look up at her as he continued to scratch Dubh, who abandoned all pretense of dignity as he rolled onto his back in unabashed ecstasy. "I'm certain my grandmother, Lady Helga, will be pleased to offer ye hospitality for the night."

"That would be most kind of her."

He continued to focus on Dubh, and the way he'd avoided looking at her since she'd reached his side finally penetrated her befogged mind.

Was she imagining it? To be sure, on Rum he'd always greeted Dubh, who had taken an uncommon liking to the Highlander, but there was something off about this encounter. If only she could put her finger on it.

"Is something amiss, Alasdair?" And then the blindingly obvious smashed into her with the force of a hammer and she clasped his arm before she could think better of it. "Oh, God. Is it Afi? Has he—?" The words caught in her throat, unsayable, but Alasdair instantly threaded his fingers through hers and pulled her close.

"Freyja, no. He lives." Then he dragged in a ragged breath. "I don't know how to say this. He was in fine spirits this morning. I cannot explain what happened, but I've come to take ye back to Rum, so ye might see him."

She gazed into his dark brown eyes that were so full of sorrow and understanding. She barely knew him, and yet how comforting it was, with their fingers entwined, as though in some incomprehensible way his touch gave her a sliver of strength.

"Did Miles send ye?" Her voice was barely above a whisper.

"I offered to fetch ye." Then he wrapped his arm around her shoulders, and she sank against him, his unyielding body an anchor against the ache unfurling through her chest. "I didn't know what else I could do to help."

"Thank ye." Her voice was choked, and a shudder racked through her. It was possible this was but another false alarm, like the fall Afi had suffered a few weeks ago when his physician had predicted a gloom-filled outcome. Yet deep in her heart, she knew she was fooling herself.

The concerned expression on Alasdair's face, and the unease in his voice, told her all she needed to know.

"'Tis the least I could do. And who knows, when we return to Rum, he may have regained his strength."

As they trudged across the moorland to the castle, she released a ragged sigh. "In truth, 'twas a miracle he recovered so well from his fall. I did all I could, but alas, I always feared it was a temporary respite."

"Don't give up hope."

As they entered the courtyard, she caught his gaze and couldn't help but give him a small smile. How compassionate he was for a man he scarcely knew. And although it was possible he said such things merely to remain in her good graces, she heard genuine concern in his voice. No one could pretend such solicitude.

"Freyja. We were on our way to the village to find ye."

Roisin's voice dragged her from the mesmeric depths of Alasdair's eyes, and she turned to her sister, who was approaching them with Grear, their young serving girl. Roisin gave Alasdair a curious glance but didn't say anything else, and Freyja quickly disentangled herself from him before introducing them.

"It's my honor to make yer acquaintance, Lady Roisin," Alasdair said.

"Roisin," Freyja said, knowing her sister was too shy to respond and not wishing Alasdair to think she was being rude by her silence, "Alasdair has worrying news of Afi."

Roisin's awkward smile vanished. "He had another fall?" She sounded distraught and clasped Grear's hand for comfort.

It was startling to realize she didn't know if their grandfather had taken another fall. She hadn't thought to press Alasdair for details which now she considered it, was completely incomprehensible.

"I'm going to Rum to see for myself."

"I'll come too."

Freyja nodded. "Of course. We must let Amma know." She glanced at Alasdair. "Maybe, if we make haste, we can return to Rum before sundown."

Chapter Eight

ALASDAIR RESISTED THE urge to drop his gaze from Lady Helga's piercing stare. Freyja and her sister had taken him to their grandmother's private chamber, where two warriors loomed at strategic positions, and the matriarch sat behind her desk as the late evening light flooded through the window behind her, giving her an unnerving, otherworldly glow.

"Amma, may I present Alasdair Campbell. He's the one I mentioned to ye, who was visiting Afi on behalf of the earl. But it seems Afi has grown worse since I returned home, and Alasdair was kind enough to come to Eigg to let us know."

Alasdair bowed, and Lady Helga inclined her head in acknowledgement. He had the unsettling notion that she knew exactly why he'd sailed to Rum and made Ranulph's acquaintance and was judging him for it.

Finally, she spoke. "Welcome to Sgur Castle, Alasdair Campbell. Although I regret 'tis not under happier circumstances."

"Thank ye, my lady. This is my regret, also."

"We must leave at once." Freyja glanced at him, the worry for her grandfather clear on her face, and he had the mad urge to take her hand and offer what comfort he could. It was an effort not to follow through, but somehow he kept his hands to himself. He was certain Lady Helga wouldn't take kindly to such impropriety.

"Ye are not sailing at night."

Freyja returned her attention to her grandmother. "But it's

still light. We should arrive at Rum before it's dark. I cannot wait until the morning, Amma. Suppose—suppose that is too late?"

He heard the catch in her voice but before he could do or say something that would seal his fate with Lady Helga—and not in a good way—the old lady addressed him.

"What say ye, Alasdair Campbell? Would Ranulph want his granddaughters to risk their safety by sailing to Rum tonight?"

He knew Ranulph wanted to see Freyja. He was also certain the older man would never want to risk her safety.

Lady Helga's keen gaze bored into him, and he had the oddest conviction she was testing him. For what, he couldn't imagine. All he could tell her was the truth as he saw it.

"I cannot speak for Ranulph, my lady," he said, and he could've sworn he saw a glimmer of approval in Lady Helga's eyes at his response.

"No, ye can't." Lady Helga took a deep breath before rising from her chair and walking around her desk before taking both Freyja's and Lady Roisin's hands. "I know ye are both eager to see yer grandfather. But the wind is picking up and the light is fading. We shall all three of us leave here at first light."

"But Amma," Freyja sounded outraged. "Surely ye—"

Lady Helga didn't say a word, but her gaze clashed with Freyja's, who sucked in a sharp breath and pressed her lips together. After a silence that caused the hair on the back of Alasdair's neck to rise, Lady Helga inclined her head and released her granddaughters' hands.

"Freyja, ensure a chamber is prepared for our guest tonight. Roisin, we'll need an extra place set for supper."

As he went to follow Freyja from the chamber, Lady Helga stopped him in his tracks.

"Alasdair, a word if ye please."

Freyja shot him a glance. It was obvious she wasn't happy with her grandmother's decision to wait until the morning before they left for Rum, but truth be told, he agreed with the older lady. Even though it wasn't far from Eigg to Rum, twilight wasn't the best of times to sail, and it was never a good idea to underestimate the fickle nature of the sea.

When the door shut behind Freyja, he returned his attention to Lady Helga.

"So the earl is yer half-brother." It wasn't a question, but it was clear Lady Helga expected an answer.

"He is, my lady."

"And he thinks highly of ye, no doubt."

Highly enough to recognize their blood connection. But he wasn't about to tell Lady Helga that. As much as he tried to deny it, deep down it still stung that his own father had ignored his existence.

"I believe so."

She contemplated him for a moment. "He must, if he entrusts ye on such an undertaking."

Unease slithered through him. Had Ranulph sent a message to her, telling her of the earl's proposal concerning Freyja?

It was possible. She was, after all, as much Lady Helga's granddaughter as she was Ranulph's. Yet until this moment it hadn't occurred to him that Ranulph would do such a thing.

He hoped to God Lady Helga had no intention of informing Freyja. While he still intended to wed her, he wanted the chance to woo her without the earl's expectation hanging over her head like a storm-filled cloud.

Besides, he had the feeling the time for telling her about the earl's motives in sending him to visit Ranulph had passed. If he ignored Archibald's edict and confessed now, she'd likely never believe another word he said to her.

Since a response was expected, he bowed his head. "Aye, my lady."

Let her make whatever she wished of that. If Ranulph had confided in her that was out of his hands, but he certainly had no intention of sharing the real reason why the earl had sent him to Rum.

Lady Helga shook her head, as though her thoughts troubled

her. "Ranulph is my kin through my late daughter's husband, and I'm most fond of him. I should be grieved to discover if he's been misled in any way."

It was likely wiser to hold his tongue, but her unsubtle implication that the earl was trying to hoodwink the laird of Kilvenie rubbed him the wrong way.

"With greatest respect, my lady, I doubt any man could mislead Ranulph. It's true I scarcely know him, and aye, he's lost his vigor, but his mind is sharp. I did not travel to Rum with any plans to deceive him, if that's yer concern."

"It is my concern," she said, which momentarily threw him. He hadn't expected her to confirm it so candidly. Although he wasn't sure why. Freyja didn't hold back her thoughts either, and now it was plain to see where she got that trait from. "Kilvenie is a jewel that I'm sure the earl covets. Perhaps he thinks to wrest it from a dying man's grasp."

"The earl is an honorable man." No one, not even Lady Helga, would disparage his half-brother in his hearing.

"I'm glad to hear it. I met his grandfather many years ago. Ambition flows in the veins of every Campbell. But then, ye could say the same about the MacDonalds."

"Ambition is not a bad thing."

"I agree. But sometimes it can blind us to what is truly important."

He knew it was best to simply agree with her and end this conversation before he said something to offend her. Yet despite that good advice, he was intrigued by her enigmatic remark. "Forgive me, my lady, but ye've lost me. I'm not certain what ye're referring to."

Finally, she smiled, but it was a sad smile as though she recalled things from long ago. "Ye're young, Alasdair. There's no reason why ye would understand. But one day, perhaps ye will." She glanced at one of her warriors, who he recognized as Clyde, the one who had accompanied Freyja to Rum, and the man came to his side with his usual grim expression on his face. "Clyde will escort ye to yer chamber after supper. We shall leave for Rum at first light."

ALASDAIR FOLLOWED CLYDE back to the great hall, where the long tables that had been against the walls when he entered the castle were now in the center of the room. A fire burned in the hearth, dispersing the chill that always seemed to cling to castle walls, even castles that possessed many fine tapestries, like Sgur.

He eyed the one closest to him, of a grand hunting scene. It was a little faded through time but impressive, nonetheless. Dunochty possessed fine furnishings, and the earl had promised all the castle's chattels would remain. But, if need be, he'd take a few good pieces from his late stepfather's manor to make the castle welcoming for Freyja until they acquired their own appointments.

Anticipation pumped through him at the prospect of taking his bride to their new home. Strange. He'd never thought of the manor as his home, despite having lived in it all his life, yet here he was, thinking such of a castle he'd only once stepped foot inside.

Except the castle would be his, with no childhood memories lingering in every dark corner to blight his existence. Dunochty, the gleaming steppingstone that would take him closer to the barony he coveted, and where he could start a new life with his bride.

But first, he had to win her.

He caught sight of Freyja as she strode across the hall to him with her sister by her side. The flames from the fire glinted on her red-gold hair, and when she smiled at him, lust speared through his groin.

God. Stealthily, he shifted his weight from one foot to the other, but it didn't help ease his discomfort. There was only one way to quench that flame, but the likelihood of Freyja sharing his bed tonight was as remote as the possibility of him becoming the Earl of Argyll himself.

"Are ye all right?" There was an anxious note in her voice as she caught his gaze. "What did Amma want with ye?"

"Merely to ensure I had no nefarious intentions." He smiled, so she knew he was jesting, but instead of smiling back she shook her head and let out an impatient sigh.

"I'm sorry for that." She sounded irked and cast a glance at her sister, who offered a doleful smile in return. "'Tis not yer fault ye were there when Afi . . ." she frowned and tilted her head at him. He'd not seen her do that before and he found it utterly bewitching. "What *did* happen, Alasdair? Did he have another fall?"

Her question wrenched him from his lustful thoughts but despite his best intentions, desire lingered in his blood like a tethered fever.

"I wasn't with him. I don't know what happened, Lady Freyja, but he looked . . ." he hesitated, unwilling to tell her how her grandfather had looked the last time he'd seen him. But she held his gaze, and he knew she wouldn't appreciate it if he tried to coat his words in honey to protect her sensibilities. With reluctance, he added, "As though his strength had seeped from him."

"I should never have left him."

"Ye weren't to know," he said. "He's in good hands. His physician is attending to him."

"Aye, with his damn leeches, no doubt." Freyja cast her sister a frustrated glance before looking back at him, and he recalled Miles' caustic comment that he trusted Freyja's opinion more than he trusted the physician's.

But bleeding was common practice. What else was there to do?

Freyja took him to the high table and indicated he should sit next to her as she took her place beside Lady Helga. Her sister sat on the other side of their grandmother, and servants carried platters ladened with food to the tables, along with jugs of ale and wine.

He hadn't realized how famished he was until the cold meat pies, bannocks, and a variety of fruits were spread before him. As he speared his knife into a generous slice of venison pie, he cast a sideways glance at Freyja, who was listlessly buttering a bannock.

She was concerned about Ranulph. Hell, so was he, but talking about her grandfather would only cause her worry to rise, and there was nothing they could do about it while they remained on Eigg.

He wanted to see her smile again, to distract her with lighthearted banter, even if it lasted for only a few moments. He swallowed his mouthful of pie and nodded to the tapestry-covered wall to their left.

"Sgur Castle is fine indeed. I can see why ye're reluctant to leave, even if ye do happen to fall for a man not of the Isles."

Her sudden smile was like a ray of sunlight, and he could scarcely believe such a bizarre notion had crossed his mind. How strong was Sgur's ale? But he already knew the answer.

It wasn't the ale that caused him to imagine such a nonsensical vision like a green youth. It was Freyja herself.

"The castle is my home. But that's not the reason why I'll never leave Eigg."

He recalled their conversation on the beach of Rum. "The legacy of yer foremothers. I confess I'm still intrigued by this. I've never encountered such a thing before."

"Ye've never encountered women who hold onto their legacy with such determination, ye mean? For I'm certain ye know plenty of men who would fight to the death to preserve the legacy of their forefathers."

He had to concede she was right. "'Tis not the same thing, though."

She jabbed her half-eaten bannock in his direction. "Give me one good reason why it's not the same."

It was galling that he couldn't come up with an instant rebuttal. "Because it's not."

"What of Queen Mary? Does she not fight for her legacy?"

How in the name of God had they managed to bring the Queen into the conversation? He had no idea, but one thing was certain: Talking with Freyja was anything but tedious. "The Queen tends to do as she pleases."

And how. Last year she'd all but disowned the Earl of Argyll when he'd voiced disapproval of her intention to wed the Earl of Lennox's son, Lord Darnley. But now Darnley was out of favor, and the Earl of Argyll was once again the Queen's favorite and likely to be present at her impending confinement.

"Aye, well, I am not a great royalist, but I admire her for standing up against all those who oppose her choices." Freyja paused, before adding, "Even if her choices are hard to fathom."

He was a royalist to the marrow of his bones, and was of the opinion the Queen had lost her senses when it came to some of her choices. "I confess I'm not clear on what point ye're attempting to make."

"My point," Freyja jabbed her bannock at him again and he struggled not to laugh when a piece dropped off the end and landed on the table, "is she fights for the right to continue the legacy of her forebears. 'Tis not her fault they were all foolish men, which has given her an unfortunate disadvantage."

"The only disadvantage is she was not the son her father hoped for."

"Again, not her fault. Now, if the crown went through the female line, things would be very different."

"Very," he said with feeling. "That's not the natural order of things, my lady."

"Ye poor misguided soul." She shook her head in apparent sorrow, although her gaze was warm. "'Twas the natural order of the Pict royal houses, ye know."

Finally, he understood where her intriguing beliefs came from. "The legacy ye told me about when we were on Rum. Were yer foremothers Picts?"

"Indeed. We are descended from the fierce Pict queen who once ruled this isle with her women warriors."

"Nine hundred years ago?" He couldn't help the skepticism in his voice, despite how her tale fascinated him. "Do ye really believe her warriors were women?"

"The history was handed down from her daughter to her granddaughter. Now I grant ye, perhaps I don't believe there were lights on the sea, but we are bound to the great queen, nonetheless."

"Lights on the sea?" Pie forgotten, he gazed at her, entranced. "Was this queen a sorceress?"

She scoffed. "There are no such things as sorceresses, Alasdair. But 'tis said she was a powerful druid who rejected the new religion when the monks came to Eigg. After she and her warriors slaughtered the intruders in their monastery, they went to the beach of the singing sands and saw the lights dancing on the sea. But 'twas likely just the reflection of the moon on the waves."

"They slaughtered the monks?"

"Of course." She sounded so matter-of-fact, as though it was no great shock that a group of women would do such a thing. But then, it likely hadn't happened. These were merely legends that had been handed down for almost a thousand years. No wonder the story was so fantastical. "And I'll tell ye plainly," she added, "I've never understood why such a formidable warrior as that queen would lead her faithful warriors into the sea. I cannot fathom it."

"Did they catch those mysterious lights on the sea?" He couldn't see how, but he was invested in this tale now.

She flashed him a mocking smile. "Don't be daft. They all drowned."

He grinned at the unexpected end to her story. "All of them? Are ye sure?"

"Well, no, clearly at least her daughter survived, so she could pass her mother's knowledge down to her own daughter. Sea lights aside, our Pict queen ancestor was very real and her blood flows in our veins to this day."

"'Tis a fascinating history. But I don't see why ye must remain on Eigg because of it. Yer Pict queen warrior will never be forgotten as long as her story is told."

Her smile wavered as though he'd overstepped, which was the last thing he'd wanted. But before he could make amends, she sighed.

"I know. But that isn't the reason. We're bound to this land by the word of our foremothers. And the truth is, even if we weren't, I shouldn't wish to leave. I'm happy here at Sgur."

Regret twisted through him at the wistful note in her voice. He didn't want to be the cause of her unhappiness, but the only way to ensure his own invulnerable future was if they wed.

Chapter Nine

It was still dark the following morning when Freyja and Roisin left their bed. Yesterday evening, Freyja had sent a message to Laoise, informing her of what had happened, so the young woman knew she would be tending patients on her own until Freyja's return.

As Grear combed Roisin's hair, Freyja went through the supplies in her medical satchel, even though she'd checked it last night before going to bed, to make sure she had everything she might need to make Afi more comfortable.

How she wished she could be confident that she could cure him of what ailed him, but some things were simply beyond her ken. Kneeling on the rug before the hearth, she heaved a great sigh. If only Afi had agreed to stay at Sgur when he'd first suffered his fall. Would it have made any difference if she'd been able to see him every day?

Maybe not. Alasdair had said her grandfather had simply faded, for no discernable reason.

But that didn't mean he was at death's door.

Her thoughts lingered on Alasdair and a shaft of warmth pierced through the gloom that wrapped around her heart. He was so thoughtful, to come and tell her of Afi's decline himself. And he seemed so genuinely concerned for her grandfather's health, even though he barely knew him.

If only he were a MacDonald from the Isles.

The foolish wish slid through her mind, and she mocked

herself for it, even though the notion was so tantalizingly alluring. And although she'd never admit it out loud, he was the first man she'd met who had ever made her think that, just maybe, there *was* a man worth compromising her beloved freedom for.

But it would never happen. Alasdair, as she had known from the moment she'd met him, possessed an enchanting way with words. She wasn't so naïve as to imagine he meant anything more than simple flirting with his enthralling interest in her conviction to remain on Eigg, even if she fell for a Highlander.

It certainly didn't mean he wanted anything more than a fleeting dalliance with her. And even if he did, it could lead nowhere.

She wasn't sure which outcome caused her heart to ache the most. The only thing she was certain of was that Alasdair Campbell had addled her brains more surely than the finest French wine.

"Shall I do yer hair, milady?" Grear asked, pulling her from her meandering contemplation, as Roisin pulled on her boots.

"Oh, 'tis all right, Grear, thank ye, but I'll do." She ran her hand along her messy plait. To be sure, it needed a good comb, especially after her restless night, but she was filled with an apprehensive energy and wasn't sure she could sit still for long enough while Grear re-braided it. "We'd best get going," she added to her sister who nodded, worry etching her face.

Their grandmother was already in the hall with Alasdair when they arrived, and his smile of greeting sent a now familiar warmth spiraling through her blood. As Amma spoke with the warriors who would be accompanying them, she went over to him.

"I trust ye slept well?"

"Well enough. How are ye, Freyja?"

His voice was low, for her ears only, and it was most absurd how much she enjoyed hearing him say her name so informally.

"I'll feel better once I've seen Afi. It's not knowing that is the worst."

He bowed his head in acknowledgement. "Maybe yer willow tea he likes so much will help him."

She had something far stronger than willow tea in mind to aid her beloved Afi if he needed it. But it wasn't something she was comfortable sharing with Alasdair. Because, for all his charm, he was a Campbell, and there was no telling if he'd be shocked by her understanding of the hidden benefits of the poppy.

"Come." Her grandmother's commanding voice cut through her thoughts, and they left the castle and trudged across the moorland, as the sun rose beyond the horizon, casting ribbons of pink and purple over the gently lapping sea.

They didn't take the rowing boat today. There were too many of them, including Amma's serving women and half a dozen warriors. Instead, they went to the sheltered canal where her grandmother kept her ship. It took several trips in the small rowing boat before they were all aboard, but finally they were on their way and the rugged coastline of Rum grew ever closer.

Freyja stood at the prow, gripping the gunwale, Dubh at her feet and her precious satchel secure over her shoulder. Sea spray spattered her cheeks, and the early morning sun warmed her skin, but all she could see was Afi's smile as he bid her farewell just days ago.

Blessed Eir, please don't let me be too late.

Alasdair came to her side and grasped the gunwale. Distracted, she gazed at his strong, tanned fingers, so close to her own it would take little effort to shift her hand until they touched.

She exhaled a shaky breath; thankful it went unheard beneath the creaking of the ship and the splashing of the waves. It was all very well for Alasdair to know she enjoyed his company. But it was something else altogether if he guessed just how much his presence affected her.

Soon he'd be gone from the Small Isles, back to his castle in the Highlands. Not that he'd ever spoken of his castle, but he was the favored half-brother of the earl, so doubtless he possessed one. Or two. It was not an unusual circumstance for acknowledged bastards of the nobility to be elevated and enjoy all the privileges of their legitimate half-siblings. It was likely Alasdair was even welcomed at court, considering the cordial relationship the Earl of Argyll had with the queen.

There wasn't the slightest chance he'd consider remaining on Eigg with her.

As if I even want him to stay.

But it was a hollow rebuttal. She might be able to fool Alasdair that she hadn't fallen for his undoubted charms, but alas, she couldn't fool herself.

DESPITE HIS BEST efforts, Alasdair couldn't help but steal a sideways glance at Freyja. She gazed into the distance, her cheeks flushed a becoming rose by the brisk breeze, and it took more willpower than he cared to admit to stop himself from entwining his fingers through hers.

If he hadn't kissed her, if the memory of how her lips tasted hadn't haunted him ever since, would he still find it so hard to resist her?

He had the feeling he would.

Resolutely, he tightened his grip on the gunwale as though that might somehow help shore up his resolve to keep his hands to himself. Freyja was a noblewoman, and despite his connection to the earl, he was merely a commoner. Lady Helga would be well within her rights to have him slung overboard if she saw him take such liberties with her granddaughter.

God, what was wrong with him? He had never found it so hard to keep his mind on a task before. The only reason he was here was because of the earl and his need to claim Kilvenie through Alasdair's marriage to Freyja.

It was a straightforward mission. But he hadn't envisaged becoming attached to Ranulph. And it certainly hadn't occurred to him that Freyja herself would have him questioning the ethics of his assignment.

He sucked in a deep breath, the fresh salty air filling his lungs as he tried to clear his mind of his troubling thoughts.

One step at a time.

If Ranulph had kept his counsel, no one else knew the real reason why he'd gone to Rum. When the inevitable occurred, he'd be there for Freyja, and when he asked for her hand, she'd overcome her reluctance to leave her isle in favor of a life with a Highlander. Leaving their homes to be with their husbands was, after all, what women did.

His brow furrowed, and he wasn't certain it was only because of the wind buffeting his face.

"Alasdair."

He thrust his uncomfortable notions aside and turned to smile at her. "Aye?"

"I'm glad ye're here."

Before he could stop himself, he laced his fingers through hers where she still grasped the gunwale. Her hand was cold, but her responding smile was warm, and his momentary doubts on her willingness to leave Sgur Castle when the time came vanished.

"So am I, Freyja."

THE STEWARD, MILES, met them as they entered Kilvenie's courtyard, a grim expression on his face. Alasdair stood back as the family gathered around him where, doubtless, he updated them on Ranulph's condition. From Freyja's reaction to what Miles was saying, at least the old man hadn't died yet, which was something to be thankful for.

When Lady Helga led her entourage into the hall, Freyja came back to him. "It seems after ye left yesterday my grandfather had another setback." She drew in a ragged breath and once again he took her hand, a silent gesture to remind her that he was there for her.

"I'm grieved to hear that. I had hoped for better news."

She gave him a sad smile. "My grandmother, sister and I are going to see him now, but Miles said Afi requested that if ye accompanied us, ye should join us."

"Of course." With reluctance he released her hand, but as they followed her family across the hall, unease stirred. Was Ranulph going to denounce him in front of Freyja?

When they entered the old man's bedchamber, the odor of sickness and blood hit him, as the physician hovered over Ranulph like a specter of death. Freyja shuddered beside him, and concern tightened in his chest as he glanced at her, but she didn't look on the verge of breaking down in tears. She looked enraged.

"Ranulph." Lady Helga went to his side and placed her hand on his shoulder as Freyja and her sister took their places beside her. At an unobtrusive gesture from Miles, the servants silently left.

Alasdair remained by the door, feeling like an intruder. Apart from the physician, only the family remained—including the two terriers who were busy investigating the tolerant Ban's puppies. Not even Miles had stayed in the chamber. Yet he could hardly back out of the door, since Ranulph had specifically asked for him.

After a swift glance in the old man's direction, Alasdair's faint hope that he might have improved since the last time he'd seen him vanished. Pain twisted Ranulph's face, his hands shook where they lay on top of the bedcovers, and the color had leeched from his skin, leaving him looking little more than a corpse.

He'd never say it aloud, but it would be a blessing for Ranulph when he passed.

After Freyja greeted her grandfather, she stood back and pulled her large satchel from her shoulder and placed it carefully on the floor.

"Let's make ye more comfortable," she said before turning to the physician. "Lamont, a word if ye please."

She inclined her head, indicating they should move away from the bed and Alasdair watched, fascinated, as the physician pressed his lips together in undeniable displeasure at her request but obeyed, nonetheless.

They stood a short distance from him, and he tore his gaze from Freyja and focused on his boots, so it didn't appear he was eavesdropping. Yet despite how they kept their voices low, he heard every word.

"I should be obliged if ye'd kindly cease the bloodletting." Even though she framed it as a request, it sounded far more like an order, and Alasdair couldn't help casting an incredulous glance her way.

In his experience, no one, least of all a woman, questioned a physician's method of treatment. But then, this was Freyja, and she was unlike any other woman he'd ever met. Her gaze was fixed on the physician, who stiffened in clear affront at her words.

"That's most unwise, my lady. The treatment is working as it should."

"Indeed. And it's time to try an alternative."

"Yer grandfather is my patient, and I'll not allow anyone to use the devil's work on him."

Devil's work? Who the hell did the physician think he was, to speak so disrespectfully to Freyja? He'd taken a step towards them before he even realized, ready to defend her integrity against this educated oaf, when she jabbed her finger in the physician's chest. Staggered by her action, he halted, even as admiration for her nerve spiked through him.

"Ye're living in the past, and that's a fact. Have ye not heard the poppy is no longer reviled in yer rarefied circles?"

"Lady Freyja." Condescension dripped from each word. "Yer obsolete remedies may ease the peasant women ye are graciously inclined to assist in their hour of need, but ye must leave real medicine to those who know what they are doing."

Pompous turd. Irritation surged through him, and he took another stride closer to them. It didn't matter that Lamont was likely correct, he had no right to devalue Freyja's skills in such a manner.

"I know what I'm doing." There was a sharp note of frustration in Freyja's voice now and her cheeks flushed a deep red. "Just as my foremothers knew for generations, while yer profession turned its back on ancient wisdom. But I'm not going to stand here arguing with ye. We shall see what my grandfather wishes to do."

"Yer grandfather is in no fit state to make such a decision."

He'd heard enough of Lamont's barely disguised contempt, and he went to her side, ignoring the poisonous glare the physician arrowed his way. "Lady Freyja, might I pay my respects to yer grandfather?"

She looked at him, and while he'd expected to see anger shining in her eyes, it was the hurt lurking there that stabbed him through the chest. She put on a brave face, but Lamont's contemptuous dismissal of her skills had wounded her all the same, and a surge of unexpected protectiveness burned through him.

By God, if he wasn't a guest of the MacDonalds, he'd damn well call Lamont out. But now wasn't the time, and he battened down the urge to grab the physician by the neck of his pretentious long dark robe and sling him from the chamber onto his arse.

It was a satisfying fantasy. A pity it was unlikely to ever occur.

"Afi asked ye to join us, so I'm certain he wishes to see ye." Freyja's reply to his question pulled him back to the present and he smiled at her, pointedly ignoring Lamont as they made their way to the bed.

Lady Helga turned towards him at their approach, her face a regal mask hiding her feelings, as Lady Roisin surreptitiously wiped tears from her cheeks with her fingers. And again, he felt like an outsider. Because he was. He always had been. Even in his own family. Yet how he wished he wasn't.

He drew in a deep breath, banishing the insidious thought.

He'd never harbored any desire to be a MacDonald, and that was the only way he'd not be an outsider here in the heartland of the seafaring clan.

Just as Freyja MacDonald would be an outsider in Argyll, seat of the powerful Clan Campbell.

Even as the thought slithered through his mind, he rejected it. Once he returned to Argyll, he'd be laird of Dunochty Castle and as his wife, Freyja would not only be accepted, but she'd also be welcomed.

He would never allow his bride to feel anything less than cherished.

Chapter Ten

Freyja gently took Afi's hand and forced a smile on her face as she gazed into her grandfather's pain-filled eyes. She pushed Lamont's scathing words to the back of her mind. Now wasn't the time to wallow in her wounded feelings, not when she still needed Afi's permission to cease the physician's treatment.

"Lamont needs yer consent to allow me to treat ye." She kept her voice soothing, even though it was an effort to keep the tears from falling at his frailty. But Afi needed her strength now, and falling apart wouldn't help him.

Alasdair stood silently by her side, but his presence was strangely comforting, and she cast him a quick glance. His expression was troubled as he gazed at her grandfather, and it caused a small pain to pierce her heart.

Aye, she was glad he was here. But she hated that he'd witnessed how dismissive Lamont—and all his ilk, to be truthful—was of her hard-earned skills.

"I've already given him my consent, lass." Afi's voice was hoarse but there was no hint of confusion in his words. Thank Eir his mind, at least, was unaffected by this cruel malady. "Miles will back ye, if needed."

She nodded and steeled herself to once again face Lamont. It wasn't that the man unnerved her but there was no denying his disparaging attitude rattled her.

The physician stood behind her, and it was obvious he'd heard Afi. "If that is yer wish." His voice conveyed his affront.

"But I cannot accept any responsibility for the outcome."

Afi exhaled a pained breath. "We know the outcome well enough. Thank ye, Lamont."

She feared he was right, but if there was one thing she always tried to give her patients, it was hope.

"I'll have no more of that talk." She smiled at him and despite his pain, he offered her a small grimace in return. Since removing the leeches was beneath Lamont, she took the jar the physician gave her and put her satchel at the end of the bed so she could find what she needed.

"Let me help." Alasdair took the jar from her, and she flashed him a grateful glance before finding the pouch of salt in her satchel. Carefully, she sprinkled a little under the head of the first leech, so it released its grip on her grandfather's flesh.

As she systematically removed them all and dropped them into the jar, she pressed her lips together at the sight of the wounds they left behind. It wasn't that she was against their use. Eir knew, she used them often enough herself when her patients needed bloodletting. But there was a time and place, and no one would convince her it was a wise course of treatment when the patient was already so weak.

As she tended to the small punctures, Alasdair sealed the jar and offered it to Lamont, who took it with barely disguised disdain.

"Lady Helga," he said. "Ye are my witness to these events, are ye not?"

"I am." She inclined her head. "Ye have discharged yer duty, and we are grateful."

He sniffed before swinging on his heel and leaving the chamber. Freyja released a long breath before giving Afi another encouraging smile.

"I'll soon have ye feeling more comfortable," she promised. But if only she could cure what ailed him. But when the heart grew weary, what was there to do?

She picked up her satchel and took it to the nearby table.

There were many uses for the poppy, but all she could offer Afi today was the chance to take away his pain. As she prepared the tincture, her grandfather motioned for Alasdair to come closer to him.

"Ye see how brightly my Freyja shines?"

Freyja bit her lip. It wasn't uncommon for those hovering between this life and the next for their mind to wander and speak in riddles. But how she wished Alasdair didn't have to witness it. She wanted him to remember her Afi as he used to be.

Or at least, as he had been last week.

"Aye." Alasdair sounded somber as though her grandfather's words made sense to him.

"Her light must never be dimmed. Ye must promise me that."

She cast Afi an anxious glance, but his gaze was fixed on Alasdair who, to his credit, didn't look alarmed by the strange conversation.

"Ye have my word," he said.

Freyja measured a precise dose of the tincture into a cup, and the scent of the spices she'd added to disguise its bitter taste filled the air. She went over to the bed and with trembling hands her grandfather took the cup from her. It was an effort, but she managed to keep her voice light as she said, "This will help."

He drank the medicine, and she took the cup from him as his head lolled back onto his pillows. Within moments, the deeply carved furrows of pain on his face faded as the powerful poppy took effect.

"'Tis better." He opened his eyes, and his gaze caught hers. "Ye could teach those physicians in that fancy college down in London a thing or two, and that's a fact."

"Why would I want to live surrounded by arrogant sassenachs? I'm happy here, helping the people of the isles."

It wasn't a lie. She had no desire to move to England, of all places. But there was no denying that the college founded by physicians for the furtherance of medical knowledge fascinated her.

"I know ye are, lass." A shadow passed over his face as though his thoughts pained him. "I need to speak with Lady Helga."

"Then I shall leave ye for now. Try not to tire yerself out."

He smiled, but it was a faint shadow of his normal smile, and a dull ache gripped her heart. "Ask Miles to join us."

"I will."

She went back to the table to collect her satchel, and Alasdair grasped the strap.

"Let me help." His voice was quiet, and as she gazed into his dark brown eyes her instant rebuttal faded.

She never let anyone else carry her medical satchel. Its contents were too precious, too potentially dangerous to entrust with just anyone.

But Alasdair wasn't just anyone. He was . . .

Well, whatever he was, she could trust him to carry her satchel for her.

"Thank ye."

She tried not to stare as he slung the strap over his broad shoulder, and it was only when she heard her sister call for her dog that she managed to sever her besotted gaze before he noticed.

"Come, Dubh." She followed Roisin into the antechamber, and Alasdair shut the door behind them.

Miles strode over. "How is he?"

"More comfortable than he was."

Miles gave a curt nod of understanding.

"He wants to see ye," she added, and without a word, Miles entered the bedchamber.

"Do ye think there is any hope, Frey?" Roisin whispered.

Much as she wished there was, and no matter how she always ensured her patients had a thread of hope to cling onto, there was no point pretending to her sister.

Her throat ached, but she pushed out the words. "I fear not."

"But he improved so much after ye administered yer elixir."

Alasdair sounded shocked by her prognosis and before she could think better of it, she took his hand. His fingers tightened around hers, and even though she knew it was foolish nonsense, his gesture seemed to infuse warmth into her.

"I relieved his pain, Alasdair. But I cannot mend what ails him." And then the frustration that always seethed below the surface when her knowledge failed her bubbled to the surface. "'Tis hard to treat when ye cannot see what lies beneath the flesh."

"Ye helped him as best ye could," he said. "No one can see beneath the flesh, Freyja. Don't disregard yer skills in such a manner."

A spark of pleasure ignited deep inside at his compliment. It wasn't often a man voiced admiration for her work.

"There's always more to learn. My knowledge comes from my foremothers and of course working with my patients. But I've heard there is an astonishing book that truly can let us see beneath the flesh. Can ye imagine that, Alasdair? It would be like exploring a new world."

"I confess, I can't imagine anything of the kind."

She sighed as they reached the door to the antechamber and stepped into the corridor. "Although I'd never wish to leave the Isles, I cannot help but wonder about that grand royal college in London. As I've said to my sisters many times, I'd love to install a spy there who could pass all the new learning onto me."

"I've the impression yer grandfather believes there's nothing they could teach ye, and if Lamont is the type of physician they produce, I'm of the same mind."

"Lamont is stuck in the past and is suspicious of all new ideas—even if those ideas aren't new at all." One only had to see his reaction to her understanding of the poppy's applications. Just because he had never been taught of its wonders, he refused to see its benefits even when he witnessed them with his own eyes.

If she was a man, he wouldn't be so dismissive of her knowledge.

Deflated by that unassailable truth, even though it wasn't a new revelation by any means, she descended the stairs in silence. As they entered the hall, she forced a light note into her voice as she turned to Roisin.

"Let's blow away these cobwebs and walk along the beach. Miles will find us if he needs to."

Roisin glanced at Alasdair before answering her. "I'm fine. Ye go with Alasdair. I shall find Grear."

Concern for her sister tightened her chest even if the prospect of spending some time alone with Alasdair was more than tempting. "It was just a suggestion. I can stay here with ye, Roisin."

"No. Ye need to clear yer head. Don't worry about me, Frey." With that, her sister headed in the direction of the kitchens, where doubtless Grear would be found.

When she looked back at Alasdair, who was regarding her with a brooding expression on his face, it occurred to her she hadn't even asked him if he wanted to walk on the beach with her.

She'd just assumed. As though there was an unspoken understanding between them.

But there wasn't. Just because she couldn't forget the kiss they'd shared a few days ago didn't mean it had affected Alasdair in the same way. She wasn't so foolish as to imagine it had been *his* first kiss, too. The man had likely kissed a dozen or more women. Aye, and enjoyed doing a lot more than simply kissing them as well.

She refused to dwell on it. Even if she couldn't quite help herself.

"Do ye want to accompany me to the beach?" Thankfully, she sounded serene, and not as though she'd just spent countless moments dissecting something that was of no earthly consequence one way or the other.

"I should enjoy that." As they entered the courtyard, he offered her his arm. "Tell me if I'm being too familiar."

"Don't worry. I will." She linked her arm through his and had to forcibly stop herself from tracing her fingertips over his wrist. If anyone had told her a week ago how she'd find a man as utterly irresistible as Alasdair, she would've laughed in their face.

Well, maybe it was for the best. Until now, she'd never quite been able to understand why women would do baffling things for the man they loved. And while she certainly didn't love Alasdair, because that notion was simply absurd, at least now she had an inkling of how easily one's wit could vanish when a man's charms dazzled one. A healer should be able to empathize with her patients, and now she could add *unfathomable attraction leading to diminished good sense* to her store of knowledge.

"I wish there was something I could do to ease yer worry."

His kindly words snapped her from her reverie, and remorse streaked through her. It was unforgiveable that she'd been daydreaming about Alasdair when Afi was so ill.

"Ye are helping simply by being here." She smiled up at him, and even though in a tiny corner of her mind she remained incredulous at how easily Alasdair had addled her brains, it was a trifling concern.

It didn't matter how it had happened. Only that it had. And she wouldn't change it for anything, even though she was destined for heartache when he finally left the Small Isles for his home in the Highlands.

Chapter Eleven

Instinctively, Alasdair pulled Freyja closer so there was no distance between them as they left the courtyard of Kilvenie Tower. She held onto his arm as though it was the most natural thing in the world, and God help him, but he liked it.

He was also greatly relieved Ranulph hadn't divulged to her the real reason why the earl had sent him to Rum. If she knew that, she'd never believe he was helping her because he wanted to, and not because the earl had ordered Alasdair to secure her hand in marriage by any means possible.

He stifled a sigh as they headed across the moorland to the beach where a few days ago he'd watched her throw propriety to the wind and race along the sand like a young lass. Was it truly less than a week since they'd first met? Sometimes, he found it hard to imagine he'd known her for such a short time.

She glanced at him, and he realized she was waiting for his response. With an effort, he buried the uneasy thread of guilt that he was deceiving her by not sharing the earl's strategic reason for sending him here, and instead focused on her mesmerizing blue eyes.

It wasn't hard to forget everything else but Freyja when she gazed at him with such trust.

"Then I shall stay."

As they reached the beach, her expression turned curious. "I'm glad to hear it, but I should hate yer extended stay on Rum be the reason why yer fine castle is neglected in the meantime."

Had he told her of Dunochty? He was certain he hadn't. It wasn't even his, yet, to claim. But since he couldn't explain that without revealing her part in the castle's acquisition, he could scarcely ask her. Besides, a noblewoman such as Freyja, with ancient royal blood in her veins no less, was sure to look more favorably upon a laird who owned a castle, rather than a commoner who had merely inherited his stepfather's crumbling manor.

"There's no need for concern. I'm here because I want to be with ye, Freyja. And that's the truth."

"If only the circumstances were happier. I hate to think yer memories of our beautiful isles will be cloaked by sadness."

"Aye, there will always be a lingering sadness when I think of Ranulph. But that doesn't mean I don't also have happy memories of Rum. 'Tis where I met ye, after all."

She shook her head. "Ye are a terrible flirt, and that's a fact."

She wasn't the first woman to tell him that. Even William and Hugh had mocked him over the years on how he always told women what they wanted to hear. He'd always shrugged and laughed, for what did it matter if a few well-chosen words caused a woman to smile with favor rather than frown with affront?

But for the first time the word rubbed him the wrong way. He didn't want Freyja thinking he didn't mean what he said to her. That he was only saying what he believed she wanted to hear. It was an uncomfortable revelation, and he didn't know what to do with it. So he shoved it to the back of his mind.

Her fingers caressed his forearm, a touch so light he should barely feel it, yet lightning sparked across his skin, igniting his blood like liquid fire.

Need roared through him, all but blinding him to reason, and it took every ounce of willpower he possessed to stop himself from wrapping his arms around her and possessing her irresistible lips once again.

Ah, God. How he longed to possess her in every sense of the word.

"I worry for Miles, though." Sorrow threaded through every word, and he wished there was something he could say to ease her heartache. He and Afi grew up together. They are as close as brothers."

The way he, William, and Hugh had grown up together. Unrelated by blood but brothers in every way that mattered. He gave Freyja a sideways glance as she gazed out at the sea and Ranulph's command echoed in his mind.

"Her light must never be dimmed. Ye must promise me that."

As far as Alasdair was concerned, the meaning was plain. Ranulph expected that whatever happened, he would keep his word and not trick Freyja into marriage.

When Ranulph's time came and he'd been laid to rest, Alasdair would be there to comfort her and show her how good their life together could be. God knew, none of that was a lie. From the moment he'd met her, he'd been thankful the earl had sent him to woo her, and not another of his loyal men.

And once she was his bride, there was no reason for her to know that he'd only gone to Rum to fulfil the earl's order to bring Kilvenie under Campbell jurisdiction.

WHEN FREYJA AND Alasdair returned to the Tower, Miles met her in the hall. After an inscrutable glance at Alasdair, Miles focused on her. "Yer grandfather is asking for ye."

"Of course." She kept her worry from her voice, but she hoped Afi didn't need another dose of the poppy. She'd given him the strongest tincture she had dared to, and it was too soon to administer another one yet.

She returned Alasdair's smile before leaving him in the hall with Miles and making her way to her grandfather's chamber. He was propped up against his pillows in bed, and thankfully it appeared the poppy was still keeping his pain under control. Amma sat on a chair beside him, concern etched into her features, as her grandfather greeted her.

"Frey." He held out his hand and she went over to the bed. His fingers clasped hers and although it was a frail touch, at least he was no longer trembling. "Come, sit beside me." He patted the edge of his bed with their linked hands, and she did as he bid.

"Ye're looking better." She kept her voice light. "How are ye feeling?"

"Don't fret about me. 'Tis ye I wish to speak of. Yer Amma tells me Colban MacDonald has been bothering ye."

Startled, she glanced at Amma. "I merely told yer Afi that Colban is sweet on ye. 'Tis nothing to be troubled about. I also assured him ye're not interested in him that way."

Although she hadn't discussed Colban with her grandmother, she wasn't surprised by Amma's remarks. It seemed she was the only one who had been blind to Colban's intentions until recently.

"Amma is right," she assured her grandfather, even though she wasn't sure why he would be so against such a match. Colban, after all, came from a prestigious line of MacDonalds from the Isle of Islay. "We're simply friends, that is all."

"Ye're too trusting, lass. Men such as Colban do not consider women their friends."

After her last encounter with Colban, she was inclined to agree, but she didn't want to discuss it with Afi since he was becoming agitated. "Ye're likely right," she said, hoping that would ease his distress. "Please don't trouble yer mind about it, Afi."

"But I must." There was an urgent note in his voice that sent a shiver of alarm along her spine. She knew how some patients, as their end drew near, became fixated on a seemingly small issue. But in their mind, it was everything. She hated to think her darling Afi was so worried about her. "I've done ye wrong, not ensuring yer future is secure."

"But it is secure." She glanced at Amma who shook her head. It was clear she hadn't expected Afi to react so strongly when she'd told him about Colban. "Ye know it is. And if ye're concerned I might wed Colban, there's no need. Ye know my views on marriage."

Although the question of her marriage had never been a subject they'd seriously discussed before, Afi was well aware she didn't harbor romantic notions of finding her soulmate the way Roisin did.

She had her healing arts, and she doubted there was a man alive who'd be willing to take second place when it came to her medicine and the wellbeing of her patients. Certainly, she couldn't see Colban allowing her such freedom.

Afi turned to her grandmother. "Helga, Freyja needs a strong alliance. I always thought I would have more time."

"Hush, Ranulph." Her grandmother patted his shoulder. "'Tis all right. I'll not let any harm befall Freyja or Roisin."

He sank back onto his pillows, clearly exhausted. "Aye." His voice was hoarse, and his eyelids flickered. "I know ye won't. Curse this malady." His eyes closed and his grip on Freyja's hand slackened.

Amma stood, and Freyja followed her to the door. "We were merely speaking of everyday things," her grandmother said, her voice low. "I would not have mentioned Colban if I'd known it would upset him so. But it seems the feud he had with Colban's grandfather so many years ago has suddenly surfaced in his mind and he's transferred his ire to Colban."

"'Tis not yer fault, Amma. Ye weren't to know."

Amma sighed. "Perhaps not. But in one thing yer Afi and I are in agreement: Colban isn't the man for ye."

LATER THAT AFTERNOON, Freyja was in her grandfather's apothecary, cataloguing the dusty vials and jars that filled the shelves. It wasn't that the job needed doing—after all, she'd completed a thorough overhaul of Afi's stores last winter—but she found the process of handling the dark glass and glazed earthenware soothing.

Even if there was nothing that could cure what ailed him.

She bowed her head and gripped the edge of the stone shelf as the familiar frustration burned through her, dulling, for a moment, even her grief. There was so much she didn't know when it came to maladies that could afflict the body. So much that was unknowable.

But how she longed to untangle those mysteries.

There was a knock on the door, and she drew in a deep breath and straightened her shoulders. It would never do to allow the servants to believe she'd lost hope.

"Enter."

The door opened, and Alasdair stood there, and her heart leaped in her chest, smashing against her ribs, even though such a thing was utterly impossible. But it was scarcely worth chiding herself for the fanciful notion, since fanciful notions had become her constant companions since meeting the charming Campbell.

Instead, she gave into her inclination and smiled at him. How could she not? He was like a vision emerging from the shadows of the corridor behind him, and the bewitching hints of auburn in his blond hair glinted in the light from the lantern he held.

"Am I disturbing ye?" There was a hushed note in his voice as he cast a wary glance around the apothecary.

"Aye, but I won't hold that against ye."

His dark gaze caught hers and her stomach pitched. Unfathomable, and entirely delightful. If only they could kiss once again, but with the cloud of Afi's ill health hovering around her, even thinking such a thing seemed despicably frivolous.

"Miles found me," he said, and instantly all thoughts of wrapping her arms around Alasdair's neck and feeling his hard body against hers fled her mind. "There's no need for alarm," he added hastily, and she released a relieved breath, not even minding that he'd witnessed the fear that had whipped through her at his words.

"Afi wishes to see me?" She hoped he wasn't still upset about Colban.

"He wishes to see both of us." There was a troubled expression on his face as though the news wasn't welcome. Not that she blamed him. It was strange how Afi had taken such a strong liking to Alasdair after such a short acquaintance that he wanted him present during these last difficult times.

Not that she objected. Far from it. But her opinion on this matter was purely personal with no medical benefit and she certainly wouldn't voice it.

"Then we'd better not keep him waiting." She picked up her satchel and went over to Alasdair, and Dubh pawed his boot in greeting. Alasdair crouched and gave her dog a quick scratch behind his ears before straightening, and she wasn't sure she managed to hide her besotted smile before he once again caught her gaze.

"I feel as though I'm intruding in private family matters." He kept his voice low as he took the satchel from her before they made their way along the corridor to the hall, where light flooded through the windows, and he doused the lantern. "But Miles was adamant Ranulph wants me there, too."

"He thinks highly of ye." Not that Afi had said as much to her, but it was obvious to anyone with a grain of sense. "And let me assure ye, he's not one to give his approval lightly."

Instead of easing the frown that carved his brow, which had been her intention, it appeared her words caused his expression to darken further. How odd.

Her grandmother stood by the great hearth with Roisin by her side and beckoned them over with a regal wave. Miles was nowhere to be seen.

"Amma, how is Afi?" To be sure, Miles had assured Alasdair there was no cause for alarm, but it had been hours since she'd last seen him, whereas as far as she was aware her grandmother had been with him all afternoon.

"He's very . . ." Amma hesitated, which wasn't like her at all, and dread seeped through Freyja's heart. But before she could say anything, her grandmother continued. "Animated. But his mind is sharp, and I have no reason to doubt he is in full possession of his senses." Amma took her hand and concern wreathed her face. "But I fear this is his last spark, Freyja."

She feared the same. "I should go to him."

Her grandmother led the way and after they'd climbed the stairs and were walking along the passage to her grandfather's chamber, Alasdair's knuckles brushed hers, before lingering in a comforting caress. Before she could think better of it, she interlocked her fingers with his and his thumb stroked a path of fire across her palm.

She kept her gaze locked on her grandmother and Roisin and with her free hand went to grasp the strap of her satchel, to focus her scattered thoughts. Except Alasdair carried her satchel, and so she gripped her skirt, instead, but it did nothing to help clear her mind of the image of the man who walked so confidently beside her.

Blessed Eir, she was in trouble, and that was a fact. But for now, she'd simply enjoy his company and hope she didn't fall any harder for him before he left the Isle.

When they entered Afi's bedchamber, he was propped up on his pillows, Miles standing by his side with a grim expression on his face. Hastily, she untangled her fingers from Alasdair's. It was absurd, but for some reason it felt disloyal to enjoy his touch when her beloved Afi was so close to passing through the veil.

She hastened to his side. "Do ye need something for the pain?"

He grasped her hand in a surprisingly firm grip. "Ye've done all ye can for me, my beloved bairn. I know my time is short, but there are things I must do before I leave ye."

Her throat ached with the knowledge there was nothing she could do to deny the inevitable, but somehow she managed to find a smile. "Ye must conserve yer strength. Miles can do whatever needs to be done."

"I'm not speaking of the daily upkeep of the estate. I worry about ye, lass."

Unease shivered through her, even though she knew it was likely her grandfather was merely speaking in riddles. And yet, as Amma had noted, there was no sign that his senses were addled.

"There's no need to worry about me. I can take care of myself, as ye well know."

"I need to see ye settled before I go."

How she wished he would stop talking about his impending death, but Afi had always been a straight talker and there was no reason to expect him to change his ways now.

"I'm settled, Afi. Truly, ye mustn't concern yerself about such things."

"Ye know what I mean." His intense gaze locked with hers, and heat blazed through her. She hoped he wasn't going to raise the subject of Colban again. Not when Alasdair Campbell would hear every word.

She dropped her voice to a whisper and leaned in close, so no one, not even her sister, could overhear. "We don't need to discuss this now."

"Aye, we do." Although Afi's voice rasped with the ravages of his ill health, she was certain half the inhabitants of the tower would've heard him. "I don't have the luxury of waiting, lass" He sucked in a jagged breath. "Ye must wed, Freyja. 'Tis the only way I'll know ye're protected when I'm cold in my grave. 'Tis the only thing that will give me comfort as I draw my last breath."

Her grandmother came to her side and Freyja glanced at her, hoping Amma might share some of her wisdom and calm Afi's distress. But Amma didn't say a word, and although her face didn't share what she was thinking, the gleam of sorrow in her eyes shook Freyja to her core.

Amma agreed with Afi.

It hadn't occurred to her that they would continue to discuss her future prospects after she had left Afi earlier. Had they also decided who they believed she should wed? At least she could be sure it wasn't Colban.

It was hard to shake off the sense of betrayal that two of the people she loved most in the world had gone behind her back to consider her future, But Afi was still her patient, and she'd not distress him further by her hasty rejection.

She gave his fingers a gentle squeeze and sat on the edge of the bed. The specter of death had shaken him, but she had to make him see there was no need for him to feel he had failed simply because he hadn't ensured she was betrothed. Maybe if she could make him smile, he'd see the truth through the fog of his unwarranted worry.

"Afi, ye mustn't think such things. I'm well protected, and ye know it. There's not a MacDonald alive that I couldn't best, if I put my mind to it, and no man wants that from his wife, now do they?"

But he didn't smile. Nor did his gaze waver, and unease slithered along Freyja's spine. What had she missed? Why did Afi look so fierce?

"'Tis not a MacDonald who can protect ye, Frey." He drew in a rattling breath and his fingers spasmed in her gentle grasp. "I know who ye need, and ye must promise me on the bloodline of yer foremothers that ye'll honor my final wish."

Alarm streaked through her at how he'd invoked the sacred lineage of her foremothers. An unbreakable bond, but surely her grandfather wouldn't enforce something so irrevocable when he knew how desperately she was against it? "Afi, please—"

"To protect yer safety, ensure the survival of Kilvenie, and ease my heart, ye must wed Alasdair Campbell as soon as possible."

Chapter Twelve

A LASDAIR CAMPBELL?

The name whirled around Freyja's mind as she stared at her grandfather in stunned disbelief. To be sure he appeared in full command of his senses, but how deceptive that had proved to be.

He wanted her to wed Alasdair Campbell.

As the roar in her head eased, she realized the bedchamber throbbed with a silence so profound that it hurt her ears. And a horrifying awareness slithered through her.

Blessed Eir. Alasdair stood not a stone's throw behind her, and he'd heard every word.

Her cheeks heated and fire burned her veins as mortification blazed through her. Her tongue felt stuck to the roof of her mouth, but since it was painfully apparent no one else planned on breaking this ear-splitting silence, she needed to say something. Anything.

"Afi." Lord, was that really her voice? She sounded like a wizened crone. "Ye cannot expect Alasdair Campbell to wed me. Ye—" Her thoughts splintered at what she'd just said. Why hadn't she simply told Afi there was no way *she* could marry Alasdair? Flustered, she scrambled to cover her inexplicable mistake. "It cannot happen, Afi."

The last thing she wanted was to look at Alasdair, but she couldn't help herself. He stood a short distance from the bed, as though he was frozen to the spot, and she'd never in her life seen such shock on a man's face. His gaze was fixed on her grandfather as though he'd just grown two heads and truly, she couldn't blame him.

It was simply a wonder Alasdair hadn't bolted from the chamber already.

"Give me yer word, Freyja."

"Ranulph." Her grandmother's voice was low but infused with regal authority. Finally, Amma would make her grandfather see reason, but why had she taken so long about it? "Ye must let Freyja and Alasdair Campbell digest this news. 'Tis not something they can decide in the blink of an eye."

It wasn't the response she'd hoped for, but at least it offered a respite from Afi's alarming fixation. She rose from the bed as Amma turned to her. "Go into the courtyard with Alasdair. Ye have a great deal to discuss. I'll wait for ye in the great hall."

A great deal to discuss? She was quite sure that when they reached the courtyard, Alasdair would make his excuses and escape this madness as soon as he could.

How she hoped he didn't, though. As tangled as the situation was, she dearly wanted him by her side when the inevitable time came and Afi drew his final breath.

As she turned to Alasdair, Roisin took her hand, but her sister didn't appear startled by their grandfather's pronouncement. She seemed strangely tranquil.

Unnerved by that thought, although to be sure there were times she didn't understand Roisin at all, she released her hand and braced herself to meet Alasdair's gaze. Instead of horror at the predicament her grandfather had put him in, he looked strangely wary. Almost as if he expected her to blame him for this mess.

What nonsense was she imagining? She took a steadying breath which only resulted in making her lightheaded and offered him a strained smile. "Will ye accompany me for some fresh air, Alasdair?"

"Aye." He responded so fast it sent a sharp pain through her breast. It couldn't be more obvious he wanted to leave Kilvenie without delay.

In silence, they descended the stairs and crossed the hall. Once they were in the courtyard, she tugged her shawl tightly about herself, as though that might give her the courage to face him again.

"Freyja." His voice was low, troubled, and she squeezed her eyes shut for a moment, attempting to gather herself, but it didn't work. Her thoughts remained fragmented, trapped in that excruciating encounter with her grandfather, but she had to ensure Alasdair knew she would never hold him to such a bizarre request.

She turned towards him but couldn't quite gather the nerve to meet his eyes, so she stared at his chest. The fine white linen molded his magnificent muscles perfectly and her gaze strayed to his impressive biceps before dropping to his plaid.

Sweet Eir. The power of speech had deserted her.

"Freyja," he said again, before sliding his finger beneath her chin and tilting her face so she had no option but to look at him. Why did the touch of *one finger* cause her heart to hammer so? If she didn't manage to drag more air into her lungs instantly, she feared she might faint.

A fine spectacle that would make.

She sucked in a ragged breath and Alasdair's thumb grazed her jaw in a tender caress. He was being kind, and while it was better than him marching off without a backward glance, the prospect that he now felt sorry for her made her feel ill.

Because there was no choice, she could bear him leaving the Isles, but she couldn't bear the idea that if he ever thought of her in the future, it would be with a sense of pity.

"Alasdair, I cannot apologize enough that ye were put in such a mortifying position." Well, she guessed he was mortified. She certainly was. "I'd no idea he was thinking of such things and can only conclude 'tis the poppy talking."

Except the frightening truth was, she didn't believe that. Afi's mind hadn't been wandering and his wishes had been more than coherent. He knew exactly what he'd said and had meant every word.

She could hardly tell Alasdair that. It was clear the poor man already felt trapped enough.

Do I feel trapped?

"Freyja," he said for the third time, and it finally occurred to her that he was trying to tell her something but was obviously having trouble finding the right words. She should make it easy for him by stepping back and telling him that of course they should not wed.

Why hadn't she done that already?

Do I want to marry him?

Her cheeks burned but there was nowhere to hide from Alasdair's penetrating gaze. What a question. Of course she didn't.

Are ye sure about that?

"Are ye all right?"

His solicitous question pulled her forcibly back to the present, and the fact that far from sounding irked by the position Afi had put him in, Alasdair instead seemed concerned for her feelings, somehow eased her embarrassment.

"'Twas a shock, I'll not deny. But I'm all right." He still cradled her face between one finger and his thumb, and she really should break contact before she melted into a puddle at his feet. But since this was undoubtedly the last time she'd ever feel his touch, she couldn't bring herself to end it. "Are ye?"

ALASDAIR GAZED INTO Freyja's anxious blue eyes and her question thundered around his head.

Was he all right?

When Ranulph made his announcement, Alasdair was certain he was about to be denounced. He'd braced himself for Freyja's scorn, but Ranulph had said nothing of the earl's desire to unite their clans.

He'd spoken as though the idea was his own. What in the name of God had happened to change his mind?

And Freyja still waited for his answer.

He exhaled a long breath and stroked his thumb along the line of her jaw. Her cheeks were flushed a fascinating shade of rose and she gripped the edges of her shawl as though her life depended on it. One of the biggest obstacles that had stood between him claiming her for his bride had just handed her to him on a silver platter, yet he couldn't find the words to press his advantage.

But he had to reassure her all was well.

"I'm fine. And there's no need to apologize, Freyja. 'Tis an honor that Ranulph would even consider me worthy to take ye as my bride."

"Ah." She shook her head, but a small smile chased the worry from her face. "Ye cannot help but flirt, can ye, Alasdair? But I thank ye for it, and for not taking offense."

"'Tis the truth." He wasn't sure why it rubbed him the wrong way whenever she accused him of flirting. But that was nothing compared to the thread of guilt that stirred deep inside at how she believed the original idea for them to wed came from her grandfather.

What was he thinking? Surely, now victory was within his grasp, he wasn't seriously considering ruining it all by confessing to his part in it?

No. It would amount to little more than betrayal against the earl, and he'd never do that. And yet disquiet gnawed through him like a canker. It didn't sit right with him to let her believe Ranulph's edict came as a bolt from the blue to him.

Unable to help himself, he cradled her face with both hands. She looked up at him with such trust, and his gaze lingered on her lips as he recalled how sweet she tasted.

God, he wanted her. Wanted the right to call her his wife, to make her mistress of Dunochty Castle. Most of all, he didn't want to risk losing this intriguing connection between them. And if he knew one thing about Freyja MacDonald, it was that she'd never forgive him for keeping the real reason of why he'd traveled to Rum from her.

"Are ye so set against the idea of a marriage between us, Freyja?"

Her smile froze. He doubted that was a good sign. "What?"

"Ranulph has set his mind on it." That was the truth, however unexpected it was.

"He has, and it's true he's taken a shine to ye. But ye mustn't think any of us would hold ye to such an outlandish decree. Ye're free to leave whenever ye wish."

"Do ye want me to leave?" Christ, what was wrong with him? Why was he giving her the opportunity to tell him to go? Because if she did, where did that leave his plans?

"I . . ." she hesitated before releasing her death grip on her shawl and pressing her hands over his, their fingers interlocking. "No, I don't. But I can't expect ye to stay after this."

He bent his head, so their breaths mingled. It wasn't the best idea he'd had, since now all he could think about was kissing her again, when he needed a clear head to persuade her of the merits of Ranulph's wishes.

The elusive scent of roses and rain that would forever conjure up the image of her in his mind swirled about them and he tossed caution to the wind as his mouth captured hers.

Her sigh rocked through him, and he teased the seam of her lips with his tongue, until she opened for him. He pushed inside her welcoming heat, and her tongue stroked his in a tantalizing invitation.

She tasted of mint and honey. And tempting, forbidden promises.

Somehow, he managed to tear free before he completely lost his mind. Panting, he stared into her passion-clouded eyes and traced the pad of his thumb over her warm cheek.

"Do ye think I want to leave, after this?"

Her uneven breath dusted his jaw. It was an insubstantial caress and yet it fired his blood with alluring visions of how Freyja would gasp when he finally made her his.

He swallowed a groan and held grimly onto his unraveling threads of self-control. Now wasn't the time to indulge in those fantasies. First, he had to win her.

"But we're talking of marriage." Her voice was sultry and addictive, and his cock thickened further, driving him to the edge. He was so damn hard he feared even his plaid could not disguise how much he wanted her. "And that's forever."

"Aye." The word rasped his throat, and he speared his fingers into her glorious hair. Her hands slid to his wrists, but she didn't try and push him away. She clung onto him, as though she never wanted to let him go. "Can ye do forever with me?"

"Ye would wed me to please Ranulph?" She sounded scandalized, but fascination glowed in her eyes and her fingers tightened around his wrists.

"'Tis nothing to do with Ranulph. I'd wed ye because I need a wife, and I've never met a woman like ye, Freyja. Ye've bewitched me, and that's a fact. Even if Ranulph hadn't said anything, I believe I would've asked ye before I left Rum."

And he meant every damn word.

"But we scarcely know each other."

"We have the rest of our lives to get to know each other. Is that yer only objection?"

"It's not an objection." She released his wrists and flattened her hands against his chest. "I can scarcely think straight. I've never put my mind to marriage before."

"Neither have I. But there's no one I'd rather wed, and I'm glad to know Ranulph would give his blessing if ye're of like mind."

"Oh." She closed her eyes and a shudder wracked her. Instinctively, he wrapped his arms around her and tugged her close, and she laid her head against his chest where his heart thundered like a wild beast. "I don't understand what possessed him. But I don't want him fretting over it." She heaved a great sigh. "Truly, I thought ye would run for the nearest ship as soon as we left his chamber."

"Why would ye think that? Ye're a prize fit for a prince." And he was far from a prince. He was merely the bastard son of the late earl, who'd scarcely acknowledged his existence.

He'd never tell her that. Let her believe he'd always been a part of the earl's inner circle. It was better than the truth, that he'd been nothing but a thorn in the side of his family.

"A prince?" She gave a silent laugh that caused a strange warmth to encase his chest. "I doubt there's a prince alive who'd want me, and why would I want to live that kind of life, with all its rules and protocols? It would drive me mad, I'm certain of it."

From nowhere, the sound of Ranulph's voice filled his head.

"Her light must never be dimmed. Ye must promise me that."

Ranulph hadn't wanted her tricked into marriage, and he wanted her to be happy. Well, so did he.

"Then ye'll be pleased to know the Queen barely knows I exist, and we'll never be expected to spend time in her court. Ye'll be mistress of yer own castle, and free to make yer own rules and protocols."

"The prospect sounds tempting, I'll not deny. I always believed you were often welcomed at the queen's court." Then she pulled back and looked him in the face, as her smile faded. "Yer fine castle is in the Highlands, is it not?"

"Dunochty is half a day's ride from Oban." He'd been inside the castle only once, more than a year ago, but had never thought he might one day be the master of such a grand estate. He was certain Freyja would admire the castle as soon as she saw it.

"But I'm bound to the Isle of Eigg, Alasdair. I cannot leave."

Goddamn it. He'd been so sure Freyja was close to agreeing to wed him, but now an obstacle he'd barely considered smacked him in the face. The day after they'd met, she told him she'd never wed a man not of the isles. He'd been intrigued, but the truth was, he'd not seriously believed it. But there was no hint of a smile on her face now, and belatedly he realized his error.

What had Ranulph said, before he had even met Freyja?

"'Tis the love of her foremothers that guides her. Best not to forget that."

But he had. Even when her grandfather had invoked the bloodline of her ancestors to elicit a promise from her when they'd been in his bedchamber just now, the implication hadn't hit him.

And Freyja hadn't given Ranulph her word, either.

He wouldn't give up. And not simply because of the earl's edict.

"What is this legacy that makes yer foremothers so against ye wedding a man not from the Small Isles? Is there a curse upon yer bloodline, that if ye decide to leave Eigg ye'll be compelled to follow strange lights on the sea and drown?"

As he had hoped, she smiled at his ridiculous comment. "I told ye the dancing lights are nonsense, and there's no curse. Just the pledge handed down from mother to daughter that we must protect the Isle at all costs."

"Protect it from what? The Campbells of Argyll?"

"If a Campbell made his home at Sgur, there would be no problem with that."

He sighed and tenderly tucked an errant curl, that had fallen across her cheek, behind her ear. "I cannot leave my manor forever, Freyja." Or the castle that would be his, once she became his bride. With a reluctance that didn't make sense, he forced himself to add, "Or Dunochty."

"Are ye certain?" There was such a wistful note in her voice he was almost tempted to say he'd consider it. But he wouldn't lie to her. He'd never make his home on the Small Isles, not when the earl entrusted him with more responsibility each year and the coveted barony inched ever closer.

"I'm the only family my mother has left." And even if she'd never wanted him or had seemingly forgotten he was alive when he was a bairn, she was still the only mother he had and he wouldn't abandon her. "She doesn't put much trust in our steward to oversee the manor, even though the man is more than capable."

"I understand." There was a despairing note in her voice. "I'm not certain we can ever resolve this, Alasdair, when we're both committed to our own land."

The hell they couldn't resolve it. "Don't say that. We—"

"Freyja." The commanding voice of Lady Helga cut through the courtyard, and he swallowed the curse that hovered on his tongue at the interruption. Freyja turned to her grandmother as the old lady approached them, and belatedly he realized he still had his arms around her. It was harder than it should have been to release her.

Lady Helga paused some distance from them and gave him a scrutinizing glance before returning her attention to Freyja. "We have things to discuss."

Freyja gave him a doleful smile. "Ye'll not leave yet, will ye?"

"No. I'll be here when Lady Helga is done with ye. We still have things to discuss, also."

As he watched her walk off with her grandmother, only one thought pounded through his head. No matter what it took, he intended to wed Freyja and take her to Dunochty.

Chapter Thirteen

As Freyja walked with her grandmother in the direction of the stables, she told herself not to glance over her shoulder at Alasdair. But she couldn't help herself.

He stood where she had left him, watching her, a brooding expression on his face, which lightened when their gazes meshed.

Her heart squeezed in her chest, which was absurd nonsense since a heart could do no such thing, and yet there was no denying that was exactly how it felt. Her heart hurt because she could see no way forward where she and Alasdair could possibly be together.

Unless she turned her back on the Deep Knowing.

She stumbled on the uneven path and hastily returned her attention to where they were going before she fell and broke her ankle. That was all she needed, on top of everything else. If she believed in such things, she'd almost think it was a warning from their Pict queen foremother, for daring to even consider leaving Eigg.

For wishing, deep in her heart, that she could wed Alasdair Campbell.

"This is a great shock to all of us." Amma's voice was low as she paused beside the stables, out of sight of Alasdair. "Tell me what ye are thinking, Freyja."

"What does it matter what I'm thinking? It cannot be, can it? Alasdair has told me plainly he won't leave his castle and live at Sgur."

"It matters to me, and that's why I asked the question."

Freyja swung about and gazed at the mighty stronghold, where its stone walls had weathered the fierce elements and harsh sea air for over three hundred years. She loved Kilvenie Tower almost as much as she loved Sgur Castle, but she'd never planned on living here on Rum when her grandfather passed. It was one thing to visit, but she belonged on Eigg.

Yet Alasdair had asked her to go with him to the Highlands. And part of her wished desperately to go, in a way she had never wanted to live on Rum.

But her feelings had nothing to do with the place, did they? It was Alasdair she wanted to be with, and Eir help her, she'd even want to be with him if he decided to make his home in England.

"I'm thinking this is an impossible choice." She took a deep breath and once again faced her grandmother. "Afi wants me to break the sacred pledge of the Deep Knowing."

"In fairness, Ranulph doesn't know of the Deep Knowing." Amma sighed deeply. "Nor did yer father. 'Tis not a thing for men to know."

"That's not what I meant." Of course she knew only the women of their line were aware of the covenant the Pict queen had bequeathed to her descendants.

The bloodline of the Isle must prevail beyond quietus.

She pushed the familiar words, that now sounded ominously like a threat, to the back of her mind. "But he knows the daughters of Sgur are committed to Eigg. Yet he wants me to break that promise for him."

But it wasn't Afi's insistence that she wed Alasdair that troubled her so. It was because she wanted to wed him, even though it meant she'd be turning her back on the Deep Knowing.

"We are in agreement in this. But ye still haven't told me what I need to hear. What are ye thoughts on Alasdair Campbell, Freyja? Is he a man ye can see yerself spending yer life with?"

Stupefied, she stared at Amma. Had she heard right? Of all the things her grandmother might have said, she would never have imagined her asking such a thing.

Amma was committed to ensuring their lineage continued, the way it had for the last nine hundred years. The Deep Knowing was crystal clear. If the daughters of Sgur abandoned the Isle, their bloodline would die.

But that still left the question of Isolde.

Not only had she wed the man she loved and gone to live in the Highlands, but it had been their own grandmother who had hatched the plan years before. It had gone against everything Amma had taught herself and her sisters, and yet here her grandmother was, asking if she could envisage a future with Alasdair.

Away from Sgur Castle.

She pulled her stunted thoughts together. "I confess the idea of wedding him is quite intriguing." Well, she certainly wasn't going to tell Amma she couldn't wrap her mind around the thought of Alasdair being her husband. Until a short while ago, she'd not had thoughts of taking a husband at all, and now it seemed both of her grandparents were hellbent on marrying her off.

'Twas more than that, though. Of all the men she'd met, Alasdair was the only one who had captured her interest. Right from the first moment he'd strolled into the stables while Ban had birthed her puppies.

Hadn't she secretly known in her heart that he was the only one for her?

Amma shuddered, and Freyja shot her a look of alarm. For a moment, her grandmother had seemed so frail, as though everything had briefly become too much for her. But Amma was the strongest woman she knew. The thought of her breaking under pressure was something she couldn't bear to even consider.

"What is it?" Her voice was hushed as she took Amma's hand.

Amma straightened her shoulders and gave her familiar smile, the one that had reassured her all was well from the time she was a small child.

"My heart doesn't want ye to leave, Freyja. My heart didn't want Isolde to leave, either, despite what ye may think of the circumstances. But it's not always possible to follow one's heart."

Unease gripped her deep inside. "Ye're speaking in riddles, Amma. I'm not like Roisin, who understands such vagaries. Tell me plainly what ye mean."

Her grandmother's smile was sad. "Ye're so like yer mama. She had no time for my—" She cut herself off and shook her head. "Never mind. Ye recall the reason why I arranged for Isolde to wed William Campbell?"

Of course she did. Because, inexplicably, her grandmother had decided she needed to act on the strength of a few wild dreams she'd suffered over the years.

Freyja had thought the whole thing madness last year, and she hadn't changed her mind. It was simply fortunate her sister and William had fallen in love regardless.

But she didn't want to risk upsetting her grandmother by reminding her of her skepticism, so she merely nodded. "I do."

"Those visions are not the only ones I've had."

Visions?

Since when did disturbing dreams become *visions*?

And then Amma's meaning hit her.

"Ye've had dreams that I must leave Sgur?" Her voice was hushed. Maybe she'd misunderstood, but she knew she was right. Why else would Amma have mentioned it?

"They started once Isolde left the Isle. I refused to think of them. I didn't want to lose another granddaughter to the Highlands. But as ye see, some things cannot be ignored."

"Ye had these dreams for more than half a year? Amma, maybe ye simply need a soothing remedy to help ye sleep more easily."

"Ah, Freyja." Tenderly, her grandmother stroked her cheek. "If only everything could be solved by a healing elixir. But the moment I laid eyes on Alasdair Campbell, I knew he was yer destiny. And then yer grandfather, who knows nothing of the gift

I inherited from our foremothers, tells me ye must wed the Campbell for yer own safety."

"But . . ." Her voice trailed away as her grandmother's revelations thundered through her mind. She believed in the evidence of her own eyes, not airy-fae dreams that foretold the future. And it was the first she'd ever heard that their foremothers had possessed any such thing, let alone that Amma believed she'd inherited it. "What of our bloodline, Amma? Must its continuation fall to Roisin to keep the Deep Knowing alive?"

"Sgur needs only one daughter to remain to fulfil the queen's will. Perhaps that is why two of ye must leave." Amma gripped her hand and there was no trace of the vulnerability that had fleetingly clouded her eyes. "I understand this is hard for ye to accept. It's a part of me I don't often share. As ye know, so many of the ancient ways and beliefs aren't always accepted now."

Well, that was true enough, although thankfully the power of the poppy was slowly being rediscovered. But that was medicine, and her grandmother spoke of things that could never be proved.

"I don't know what to think." She shook her head and took a deep breath. "Ye're saying I should turn my back on the Deep Knowing and agree to Afi's request?"

"I'm saying the Deep Knowing and my visions are entwined, Freyja."

Unnerved by that surreal remark, Freyja had the urge to pull her hand free and step back, but she was frozen in place. How could leaving Sgur and abiding by their Pict queen foremother's dying wish possibly be anything but incompatible?

But if it was true, it meant she could truly consider the possibility of wedding Alasdair without guilt eating her alive.

To be sure, marriage wasn't something she'd ever craved, like some lasses she knew. But she couldn't lie to herself. Hadn't Alasdair caused her to rethink everything she'd ever believed in from the moment they'd met?

He even respected her healing skills, and that wasn't something to be taken lightly. But would he mind his bride continuing her calling, or would he expect her to devote all her time to more conventional duties as befit the wife of a grand laird?

And then shame burned through her as she realized what she'd so unforgivably forgotten. "I cannot leave my patients, Amma."

"Ye've been teaching Laoise. Yer patients will be in good hands."

"But—"

"Do ye not trust her?"

The question took her aback. "I do. She's meticulous. But . . ." Her voice trailed off. For so long she'd been the only one among the healers on the Small Isles who knew the medicinal secrets of the poppy. But now Laoise understood its properties, some of the others might be willing to learn of its wonders, too.

"I don't know why Ranulph is so fixed on ye wedding Alasdair Campbell," her grandmother said. "Whatever the reason, he's certain this is the right course. And I'm certain the Campbell came to Rum to fulfil our foremothers' purpose."

Freyja didn't believe for a moment their foremothers had anything to do with bringing Alasdair to Rum. To be sure, she honored the legacy that had been handed down from mother to daughter for generations, but that was different. It was a sacred promise, a way to ensure their foremothers were never forgotten. But Amma was seeing hidden signs in disturbing dreams, where there were none.

Besides, Alasdair had told her himself the earl had sent him to pay his respects to Ranulph. And now he was in the middle of a bizarre family upset and instead of fleeing, he wanted to wed her.

Illicit thrills raced through her, converging between her thighs in a delightful cascade, which was most inconvenient when her grandmother gazed at her with such unblinking focus. But she couldn't deny, even if she wanted to, that the idea of marrying Alasdair Campbell captivated her in ways she'd never imagined possible before meeting him.

Could she truly leave everything she'd ever known and embark on a strange new future with a man who'd managed to addle her good sense without even trying? A man who had promised she could make her own rules and protocols in his castle? But maybe the real question was, how could she not entrust her future with him?

ALASDAIR WATCHED FREYJA and Lady Helga until they vanished from sight around the side of the stables, and he exhaled a deep breath. Until he'd met Freyja, he'd not imagined proposing to a woman would be so fraught.

In his experience, a woman wed whomever her guardian told her to. But then, he'd known before he'd ever set foot on Rum that Freyja MacDonald was unlikely to obey any such command from her grandfather. And while her fierce love for her land and her formidable foremothers was admirable, he wished she wasn't so convinced her future was embedded in Eigg. He wanted her to look forward to their new life together. Not be unhappy because she was leaving her beloved Sgur Castle.

"Campbell."

The gruff voice from the direction of the stronghold had him swinging about as Miles approached, and alarm spiked through him.

"Is Ranulph . . ." He left his words hanging, unwilling to voice the real possibility that the old man had died.

"He's sleeping." Miles narrowed his eyes in the direction of the stables, as though he could see through the walls to wherever Freyja and her grandmother had walked to. After an uneasy silence, Miles returned his attention to him. "I've known Lady Freyja since she was born. I want the best for her."

"As do I."

"Aye. Ranulph trusts ye, and that should be enough for me. But listen well, Alasdair Campbell. If word reaches me that ye've made her unhappy, I'll come for ye, so help me God."

"I'd expect nothing less."

Miles grunted. Alasdair couldn't tell whether it was in disgust or approval at his response. Only one thing was certain: Miles expected Freyja to accept Ranulph's command. He could only hope Freyja herself would reach the same conclusion.

"All right, then. So long as we're clear about it." With a menacing frown, as though he was acting against his better judgement, he handed Alasdair an envelope. "Ranulph's set out the terms concerning Kilvenie Tower after ye're wed so there's no misunderstanding."

"Ranulph is very certain Lady Freyja will obey his will."

Miles' smile was grim. "Lady Freyja will follow her heart. Ensure ye treasure it, Campbell."

It was an intriguing notion to suppose he'd managed to ensnare her heart. It had, after all, been his original intention to make Freyja MacDonald fall in love with him, so that she'd wed him without question.

And then he'd met her, and all his presupposed ideas about her had turned to ash at his feet.

He realized Miles was waiting for a response. Although he didn't like the sensation of being on trial, he appreciated the sentiment behind it. Miles cared for Freyja as though she were his own granddaughter.

He could scarcely imagine what that was like. The only close blood relative who'd ever cared if he lived or died was Archibald. Not that he was complaining. Thank God he'd found his own family with William and Hugh.

"If I'm fortunate enough to win her heart, ye can be sure I'll cherish it with my life."

"'Tis the only way I see her leaving her beloved Sgur. And time runs short." He gave a brusque nod and Alasdair turned to see Freyja and Lady Helga making their way back from the stables.

What a fine sight she was in her green gown and russet

shawl, as the late spring breeze ruffled her glorious hair. It took him a full moment before he realized he was smiling at her like a besotted fool, yet he couldn't help himself.

It was only when she raised her hand in greeting that he recalled he still held the letter Miles had given him. Hastily, he stuffed it into the leather pouch that hung from his belt before returning her wave. The last thing he wanted was for her to ask why her grandfather had written him a letter.

That was a whole conversation he had no intention of starting before she was his bride and it was too late for her to change her mind about him.

Chapter Fourteen

Lady Helga and Miles returned to the stronghold, but Freyja remained, which Alasdair took as a good sign. If her grandmother disapproved of Ranulph's wish, he had no doubt she'd do everything in her considerable power to prevent it, which wouldn't include allowing her granddaughter to spend unchaperoned time with him.

"Ye waited," she said, by way of greeting.

"I said I would. I'm a man of my word, Freyja."

"What did Miles want?" She glanced over her shoulder, as the steward followed Lady Helga inside.

Hellfire. For a moment, all his mind conjured up was the letter from Ranulph, but he had no intention of telling her about that, yet.

Freyja turned her curious gaze to him, and he released a harsh breath. Since he had no intention of lying to her, he might as well tell her the truth. "He threatened to come for me if I ever made ye unhappy."

"Ye poor man. Ye're truly having a day of it, aren't ye?" She shook her head. "I apologize on his behalf. But also ye should know if there's any threatening to be done, I'm more than able to do that myself."

He returned her smile, since she clearly expected it, but unease stirred deep inside. He knew damn well why Miles had spoken to him. Ranulph had certainly shared with his friend the true reason why Alasdair had traveled to Rum, and this was

Miles' way of letting him know he knew the truth.

"Don't apologize." His voice was gruff. "He cares for ye, and that's a grand thing."

Her smile faded. "Aye, he does. And I love him dearly. Maybe it's a strange thing for a Highlander to understand, but I've never thought about leaving the Small Isles or the people that live here. I always took it for granted I'd live and die at Sgur, the way my foremothers have for generations."

He took her hand, and her fingers clasped his. Such a small gesture, yet it touched something deep inside his chest that he'd scarcely even known existed until now. "Leaving Sgur doesn't mean ye'll never return to visit, Freyja. I know 'tis not the same, but ye speak as though should ye agree to be my wife, ye'll never see yer loved ones again."

"Ye're right. It won't be the same."

"I've heard 'tis good to try new things."

"Have ye, now? It seems to me if we go ahead with this, it is I who will be doing all the new things."

"Not so. I've never been wed before, and the prospect is daunting."

"Daunting?" There was a thread of amusement in her voice. "Am I that formidable, then?"

"Without doubt, ye're the most formidable woman I've ever met. Although I confess, Lady Helga is a close second."

She laughed at that, and the traces of worry that had clouded her face since Ranulph's collapse momentarily faded. "'Tis true, the women of Sgur are renowned for it."

"I'm confident I can handle anything ye throw at me." Although he grinned at her, disquiet whispered in the back of his mind. How would he handle it when she discovered the truth of why Ranulph had made the decision to choose him as her intended husband, and threw that in his face?

"I'm sure ye are." Then her smile faded into a frown. "'Tis just occurred to me that ye might not be aware, but Kilvenie Tower will come to me when Afi passes. He had only one son, and when my father died, Afi told me I would be the next custodian of his estate. Isolde was always going to inherit Sgur Castle, although now I'm not certain what will happen." Her voice trailed away, and she bit her lip as uncertainty glazed her eyes.

He didn't want her to think he was in ignorance of her inheritance. "Freyja, I—"

"Frey." Lady Roisin's urgent call cut him off, and he and Freyja turned to see her younger sister rushing towards them. Freyja sucked in a sharp breath and as Lady Roisin halted in front of them, she took her sister's hands. Tears filled Lady Roisin's eyes as she gasped, "Ye must come quickly."

Freyja glanced at him and the inevitability he saw in her eyes pierced through him like a blade. "Do ye want me to come with ye?"

She gave a brief nod before wrapping her arm around her sister's shoulders, and they made their way back to the stronghold.

They entered Ranulph's chamber. Lady Helga and Miles stood on one side of the bed, and on the other side of the bed stood the chaplain. In the corner of the chamber Lamont loomed, a stony expression on his face.

Ranulph lay in the bed, his hands folded on his chest, unmoving. God, he hoped they weren't too late. Freyja would never forgive herself if she wasn't by her grandfather's side at the end.

"Afi." Her voice was hushed, and before he could think better of it, he stroked his fingers over her shoulder in a comforting gesture. If only there was something more he could do.

Ranulph's fingers twitched, and he opened his eyes. "Freyja."

Freyja shuddered before she released her sister and went over to the bed and gently placed her hand over his. "I'm here, Afi."

"Promise me." His rasping voice scraped along Alasdair's senses. He shouldn't be here at this private time, and yet he could hardly leave when it seemed both Freyja and Ranulph wanted him here.

"Afi, please." Tears choked Freyja's words, and he had to forcibly stop himself from going to her. Now wasn't the time. But God, he couldn't bear to see her so distressed.

"Ye must give me yer word that ye'll wed Alasdair Campbell."

He was so close to achieving the earl's objective in sending him to Rum. Why then did he have the disquieting urge to sink through the floor?

"I'm—"

"No." Ranulph's surprisingly strong denial echoed around the chamber. "I must have peace, Freyja. I must know ye are going to be safe. Promise me on the bloodline of yer foremothers that ye'll wed Alasdair as soon as it can be arranged."

"I promise," she whispered, and the words thundered around his mind, gaining momentum as though he was in a vast, echoing cave. Yet it wasn't triumph that clutched his heart. It was an overwhelming sensation of suffocation, of something off-kilter.

He didn't want Freyja forced into this marriage. Even though, after speaking with her grandmother, she had seemed more open to the idea she hadn't categorically accepted the proposal. Without Ranulph forcing the issue, how else would he win her?

Ranulph released a wheezing breath, and his shaking fingers cupped her cheek. "Never let yer light dim, my sweet lass. Ye filled my heart with sunlight from the day ye were born." He reached out to Lady Roisin, who took his hand as he transferred his gaze to her. "All of my bonny lasses. My three pearls." And then he once again looked at Freyja. "Don't weep for me. 'Tis my time to go and I'm content. God bless ye, my clever bairn."

It wasn't the first time Alasdair had been in the presence of death. Several times during the last few years he'd fought for the earl against the MacGregors, clan Campbell's sworn enemies, and in the haze of blood and mud it was a case of kill or be killed.

He'd never experienced anything like this, though. His stepfather had died two years ago when Alasdair had been accompanying the earl while he surveyed his many castles and fortifications throughout Argyll. A messenger had eventually conveyed the news to him, and upon his return to the manor, his mother's only concern was that Alasdair might now ensure the roof was repaired.

But here, in this chamber, a deep sense of grief wrapped around him as Freyja and Lady Roisin lay their heads on Ranulph's chest in a gesture that conveyed, more than words ever could, how dearly they loved him. Lady Helga clasped her hands together and bowed her head as the chaplain murmured prayers, and Ranulph's hound, Ban, let out a mournful howl.

Unobtrusively, he tried to clear the obstruction in his throat. Goddamn it. He'd only known the man for a matter of days, and yet his death affected him more than his own stepfather's had, and he'd known him all his life.

But then, Ranulph had never thrown him against a wall in a drunken rage or made him sleep in a broken-down barn in the depths of winter when he'd been a small lad, had he?

Brutally, he pushed the unwelcome memories to the darkest corner of his mind, where they belonged. He'd never be that fearful bairn again. Not now he was one of the earl's most trusted warriors. Not when he was soon to be master of Dunochty Castle, with Freyja as his incomparable bride.

Not when he could glimpse his barony on the far horizon.

Miles came to his side, sorrow wreathing his features.

"Out." Miles' voice was gruff, and after glancing at Freyja, who still clasped her grandfather's hand as though she would never let him go, he bowed his head and followed Miles from the chamber.

Lamont brought up the rear and closed the door behind them. Unease shifted through him, and he turned to Miles. "I should be with Lady Freyja."

"'Tis the women's time," Miles said. "Lady Freyja will find ye when she needs ye."

He understood. There were rituals that needed to be done now Ranulph had died, and there was no place for an outsider such as himself. Yet he couldn't shift the feeling he'd abandoned Freyja when she needed him the most.

With a brusque nod, he went downstairs and left the stronghold. As he stood in the courtyard and sucked air into his lungs, Freyja's response to Ranulph's insistence that she wed as soon as possible thundered around his mind.

"*I promise.*"

They were betrothed. He should send word to the earl to let him know his mission had been accomplished. But somehow that was less important than seeing Freyja again, to make sure that this was what she wanted.

He shook his head, but it didn't help clear his fogged mind. Ahead of him were the stables, and inexplicably he had the urge to enter them, to be in the place where he had first met her, before he even knew who she was.

As he pushed open the doors the familiar scent of hay and horse surrounded him in a comforting wave and he breathed in deep, the soft whickers of the horses calming his mind.

This was what Freyja wanted. She'd all but told him herself. The promise Ranulph had elicited from her was simply her official agreement to seal their alliance.

The sound of the kirk bells peeling tore him from his ruminations and he gave a heavy sigh. Everyone on Rum would now know their laird was dead, and it wouldn't be long before all the people of the Small Isles learned of it.

And then he recalled the letter Miles had given him from Ranulph. He pulled it out and broke the seal and ran his gaze over the brief message.

It was straight to the point and witnessed by Miles' signature. Once he and Freyja were married, Kilvenie Tower was his.

But there was a second letter tucked inside the first, and he hesitated before breaking the seal, feeling that somehow, in this missive, Ranulph would condemn him. But he didn't. It was personal, and one line leaped from the page and hammered inside his mind.

I've watched ye with her and I see how ye care for her, perhaps more than ye realize yerself.

He exhaled a long breath before once again reading the final line.

Look after my lass, Alasdair.

Aye, he would. With his life. He pushed both letters back into his leather pouch just as a shadow fell across him and for a wild heartbeat he thought it might be Freyja who had found him. But it wasn't. Lamont strolled into the stables, a pinched expression on his face as though a foul smell offended his nostrils.

"I offer ye my congratulations, Campbell." Lamont's smile didn't reach his eyes, and Alasdair grunted in response, since he doubted the physician meant a word of it. Since the peace of the stables was shattered, he prepared to leave. But it appeared Lamont hadn't finished. "And my commiserations. Lady Freyja will not be an easy bride, and that's a fact."

Alasdair swung about, irritation at the man's tone scorching through him. "What's that?"

"Ye've seen for yerself how willful she is, and alas she has been pandered to in these matters her entire life." Frustration edged Lamont's words, as though he'd harbored a grudge against Freyja for years.

Alasdair inhaled a long breath. *Easy.* While every muscle he possessed ached to defend Freyja's honor, he'd not disrespect Ranulph's memory by punching his former physician to the straw covered floor. However much he wanted to.

"Is that so." There was a deadly note in his voice which the older man appeared not to notice, since instead of beating a hasty retreat, he gave a disgruntled sniff and folded his arms.

"Aye. Ye'd be wise to curtail her wild ways once ye are wed, lest she tries using her arcane methods on ye or yer kin and ends up killing them, the way she has Ranulph. There's a word for women like her, but I'll not sully the—"

Alasdair forgot about honoring Ranulph's memory as white-hot fury boiled through him. He grabbed the man's robes in his fists, the way he'd wanted to from the first time he'd heard him speak to Freyja and shoved him roughly against the wall. How dare this misbegotten turd disparage Freyja so blatantly?

Lamont gasped in outrage, his insults forgotten, as he clawed Alasdair's hands in a futile attempt to escape.

"Don't ye ever speak of Lady Freyja in such a manner again, do ye hear me? Ye're not fit to wipe her boots, let alone pass judgement on her healing skills."

"Unhand me, Campbell, ye scheming knave. Ye may have fooled Ranulph, God rest his soul, but ye cannot fool me. I hope ye get what ye deserve from yer subterfuge and live long enough to regret it."

Alasdair's fists tightened on Lamont's robe before he released him and stepped back, disgust burning through his blood. The physician straightened his crumpled robes and threw him a glare of loathing, obviously believing he'd had the last word.

To hell with that.

"Ranulph was no fool, and if ye believe otherwise, then ye're a bigger arse than I thought ye were." And then he couldn't stop himself and took a menacing step closer. Lamont instantly stopped brushing his robes and for the first time, fear flickered over his face. "Stay away from Lady Freyja, if ye know what's good for ye."

Lamont edged along the wall until he was free of Alasdair's shadow. The physician's gaze darted to the stable doors, and he sucked in a harsh breath before pushing himself from the walk and stalking away.

"My condolences, Lady Freyja." Lamont's voice was cold.

Alasdair swung about and his heart slammed against his ribs at the sight of Freyja standing by the open door. Her face was ashen, and she clutched her shawl as though it was a shield against the world as Lamont swept by her. Dread gripped his gut as she refused to meet his gaze, and he could think of only one reason why. Had she heard Lamont accuse him of subterfuge?

Chapter Fifteen

There's a word for women like her.

Freyja shuddered as Lamont's scathing words haunted her. She knew only too well what word he meant, and even thinking it chilled her to the marrow of her bones.

Witch.

"Freyja." The concern in Alasdair's voice dragged her back to the present, but it still took everything she had to meet his dark gaze. Did he secretly think she practiced witchcraft?

No. She wouldn't believe it. He'd defended her, and for that alone she knew she'd made the right decision in promising to marry him.

She smiled at him, but it hurt her face, and she had the terrible conviction she was about to weep. And not just for the loss of her beloved Afi.

It was because Alasdair had championed her healing skills.

"God, Freyja." Roughly, he pulled her into his arms, and she pressed her cheek against his chest as he awkwardly patted her back as though he thought that would comfort her. Didn't he know just being here with him gave her all the comfort she needed? "I'm sorry ye heard any of that." He stopped patting her and his arms tightened around her until she could scarcely breathe. It was oddly soothing. "It's not what ye think, Freyja."

It was exactly what she thought, and she had to make him see that. "Lamont has always resented me, Alasdair. His father and grandfather were physicians of Kilvenie, and their word has always been absolute. He's never understood why Afi would listen to me, let alone respect my advice. But..." Her voice trailed away. This was far harder than she'd imagined. No one spoke that taboo word aloud. It was foolish, she knew. A word itself didn't hold power. It was those who would use the word against her, and their power resided in the Witchcraft Act that had been passed just a few years ago.

How Lamont had gloated when he'd told of it. As if he'd expected her to instantly turn her back on all the learning that generations of her foremothers had painstakingly gathered.

"Lamont." There was a vicious undertone in Alasdair's voice as he pulled back just enough to catch her gaze. "Ye mustn't think twice about him. But what he said—"

"I know I didn't kill Afi." She was grieved he had died, but he'd been beyond any help, and she'd always known it deep in her heart. "I eased his pain, and that's all I could do. And I must thank ye for defending my healing arts against Lamont's—his insinuations."

An odd expression flashed over Alasdair's face, as if her remark had taken him aback. She couldn't think why he was surprised that she was grateful for how he'd stood up against another man for her right to practice her medical skills. Maybe he didn't realize what a rare thing that was.

"I'll always defend ye against anyone. Ye can always count on that. But that man makes my skin crawl, and that's a fact." He shook his head and tenderly cradled her face. "Why are we even discussing him? He's not important. Ye're the only one that matters. How are ye, Freyja? Is there anything I can do?"

She'd always thought the phrase *my heart melted* was foolish romantic nonsense. And yet here she was, with her heart seemingly melting into a puddle in her chest. What remarkable tricks the body played, but she was too weary to fight it with logic.

The truth was, she didn't even want to. There was no need to protect herself from his charm anymore for fear of falling too hard. When Alasdair returned to the Highlands, there'd be no wounded heart to mend, for she'd be accompanying him.

But first she needed to marry him.

Good Lord. How could she put her mind to organizing a wedding when Afi had yet to be buried?

She squeezed her eyes shut, but Afi's face swam into view, reminding her that she'd never see him smile or hear him laugh again. Grief clutched her heart, and she wound her arms around Alasdair, his unyielding strength her anchor in this uncharted storm.

"Just hold me." Her voice was husky with the tears that clogged her throat and without a word he wrapped his arms around her, his biceps a living wall of muscle keeping the outside world at bay.

Such foolish thoughts. Yet she couldn't help the way he made her feel. His now-familiar scent of worn leather and untamed woodlands filled every breath she took, sinking into her senses as though they were spices from the Far East, and tiny flames licked through her blood.

He buried his face in her hair, his hot breath causing tremors to dance across her head. Shivers skittered along her arms, and she pressed herself even closer to his hard body.

His groan vibrated through her, as sensual as a physical caress, and sharp darts of pleasure collided between her thighs. She gasped and tilted her head, and his dark gaze scorched her with trammeled desire.

"I should escort ye back to the stronghold." His hoarse voice stoked the smoldering fire in her veins, and she dug her nails into his shirt-clad back. "Before I do something I'll regret."

"Would ye regret it, Alasdair?" Her fingers tangled in his wonderful hair, the silken threads like nothing she'd felt before. Caution unraveled and vanished, like wisps of early morning mist in the forests and she rolled onto her toes, until she was only a hairsbreadth from stealing a kiss. "For I wouldn't."

"I won't compromise ye." He sounded tortured as raw passion blazed in his eyes. "I'll not trick ye into marriage, Freyja."

It was hard to think clearly when he said such noble things, and when the erratic thunder of his heart next to hers told such a different tale. His hands roamed over her back before cradling her bottom, and need spiked through her like trapped lightning.

"There's no trickery," she gasped. "Ye cannot compromise me, now we're betrothed."

Blessed Eir, what was she saying? There was a madness in her blood, for surely otherwise she'd not lose her good sense so utterly. But this wasn't wrong. Nothing had ever seemed so right, and she knew Alasdair felt it too.

He sucked in a harsh breath between his teeth. "Is that what ye want, Freyja? To wed me? Not just because Ranulph commanded it?"

She gave a breathless laugh. How honorable of him to ask her, and now of all times. "How can ye doubt it? Ye're the only man I've met who's made me even think about marriage. If either of us should be asking that question, 'tis I of ye. I should so hate to think ye feel trapped, Alasdair—"

He growled low in his throat, a primal sound that thrilled her to her core, and when he claimed her lips in a savage kiss, her knees had the alarming urge to collapse. She clung onto his shoulders as he ruthlessly explored her mouth, his tongue teasing and stroking until she could think of nothing but the pleasure sparking through every particle of her body.

He tore his mouth from hers, and panted in her face, a wild gleam in his eyes. "Do ye think that's how a trapped man would kiss ye, Freyja? Don't ever think that again. I'm here because I want ye, ye hear me?"

She believed him. He could have left Rum at any time since her grandfather's unexpected request, but he'd chosen to stay. And he'd made that decision before she'd told him she would inherit Kilvenie Tower, so he wasn't even motivated by the thought of her dowry.

Not that Kilvenie would go to her husband. Long ago, Afi had told her the stronghold would be hers, regardless of whether she married or not. But Alasdair didn't know that.

"I hear ye," she whispered. "And I want ye too."

He shuddered before trailing burning kisses along the line of her jaw. Her head tipped back, and his teeth grazed the column of her throat. She clawed his shoulders before plunging her fingers through his hair and clutching him in a death-defying grip.

"Tell me to go." The tip of his tongue teased her earlobe, and she scarcely heard his words let alone retained the wit to respond to him. All she knew was she never wanted him to stop. "Before it's too late."

"It's too late." She barely recognized her own voice. Her words were slurred, as though she'd over-indulged in the finest French wine. "I need ye, Alasdair."

Ah, how she needed him to quench this fire that burned like a furnace and turned all her thoughts to smoldering ash. She had the fierce urge to wrap her legs around his waist and crush him against the wall until the madness consuming her vaporized.

Without warning, he grasped her bottom and hauled her up and her fantasy became a reality as she wound her legs around him and her skirts bunched around her knees. With a startled gasp she clung onto him as he strode into the nearest vacant stall and backed her against the wall.

"I've wanted ye since the moment I saw ye kneeling in the straw." His fingers tenderly stroked her face before trailing with seductive intent over her shoulder and cupping her breast. Her breath stuttered in her throat as the warmth from his palm seeped through her gown and scorched her sensitized flesh. "Yer first time shouldn't be in a stable, but God help me, ye're too hard to resist."

"I'd rather be here with ye now than in the finest castle."

She meant every word. Here, with only the muffled sounds of the neighboring horses and the scent of hay surrounding them, they were in their own world, a moment out of time, a special memory she'd cherish forever.

Unlike the marriage bed, this had nothing to do with alliances or duty.

He lowered his head as his fingers tugged open her bodice, and dizzying exhilaration spun through her when his mouth branded her naked breast. Feverishly, she grasped his shirt, desperate to feel his skin beneath her exploring fingers, but the linen seemed to go on forever and his plaid hampered her best efforts.

"Eir, damn it." Curses. Had she said the Norse goddess' name out loud? Thankfully, Alasdair didn't appear to notice, which was just as well since she was in no condition to rectify her mistake.

He shoved her more securely against the rough wall and his hand slid beneath her skirts, caressing her thigh in ever-increasing circles as his passion-filled gaze caught hers. She panted in his face, her mission of ripping his shirt from his back forgotten, as his fingers edged closer to her throbbing clit.

Her fingers dug into his shoulders, and she crossed her ankles, locking him in place, just in case he had the unthinkable urge to pull back. His grin was tortured, and he shook his head, almost as if he could read her mind.

"I'm not going anywhere." His smoky promise sent shivers of awareness across her cheek, and she leaned forward and captured his mouth in a kiss that seared her reason. His fingers teased her folds, and a groan scorched her throat as liquid heat bloomed, and when he broke their kiss primitive satisfaction carved his features. "Does that please ye, mo leannan?"

She wasn't certain whether it was his intoxicating touch or his whispered endearment that thrilled her more. And it didn't matter, for both were entwined within this ephemeral cocoon they'd woven about themselves.

My sweetheart.

"It does," she breathed, and her head fell back against the wall as his finger dipped inside her, stroking her slick flesh and swollen clit until all rational thought fled her mind. Only one thing filled her world. "Alasdair."

"Aye, I'm here, my beautiful Freyja." He rained kisses along her throat and pleasure spiked through her, sucking the air from her lungs as she bucked helplessly against his unyielding palm.

Beyond the pounding of her heart, she heard Alasdair give a primal growl as he shifted position. She gasped mindlessly, scarcely aware of what he was doing, until the head of his cock pressed against her tender flesh.

"Christ, Freyja." His hot breath was a sensual caress across her cheek. "I must have ye, my sweet bride, and make ye mine."

His mouth crashed down on hers and he nipped her lip, the sharp sting arrowing through her in a shocking blaze of delight. As she wound her arms tighter around his shoulders, he pushed into her, and a fleeting burn had her gasping in shock inside his mouth.

He stilled, breaking their kiss although their lips still touched, and slowly her tense muscles relaxed as her body stretched to accommodate him. Tremors licked through her, and she stirred restlessly, needing more. Needing *him*.

"Are ye all right?" He sounded tortured. "Did I hurt ye, leannan?"

Words were beyond her and she shook her head, spearing her fingers in his nape in silent encouragement. The worry faded from his eyes, and he pushed her hair back from her cheek before grasping her naked bottom with both hands and thrusting inside her with a suddenness that drove the air from her lungs.

"My Freyja." He whispered her name, again and again, and each time he did, ripples of pleasure swirled through her. He filled her so completely, like nothing she had imagined before, and instinctively she squeezed her muscles around him.

He sucked in a sharp breath and his jaw clenched. Enthralled, she did it again and his agonized groan echoed around the stall.

"Ye're killing me, so ye are." His grin was feral. "'Tis a good thing ye're a healer."

"Don't get yer hopes up. This is outside my scope of knowledge."

"Then I'm happy to teach ye."

Her laugh turned into a heady moan as his restraint vanished and a wild gleam filled his eyes. He rammed into her, shoving her roughly against the wall with every frenzied thrust, and the lingering remnants of passion in her blood once more ignited.

She ground her hips against him, taking everything he offered, and demanding more. With a stifled hiss, he went rigid and spilled his hot seed inside her, and she shattered around him.

Chapter Sixteen

ALASDAIR PRESSED HIS forehead against Freyja's as he sucked elusive air into his lungs. All he could hear was the frenzied hammer of his heart in his ears, as Freyja clung to him as though he was her everything.

Fierce possessiveness burned through him, and he dropped a kiss against her temple. It was only right he was her everything, for she was his, now, and nothing on God's earth would take her from him.

His Freyja. *His bride.*

She shuddered, dragging him sharply back to the present. And the precarious position they were in. With more reluctance than the situation warranted, he withdrew from her silken heat, and he swallowed the groan that razed his throat.

He shouldn't have taken her here in the stables, where anyone might have discovered them. But he didn't regret it. She was so much more than any of his midnight fantasies had promised, and their marriage couldn't come soon enough.

I hope ye get what ye deserve from yer subterfuge.

Lamont's vindictive snarl scraped through his head like the rusted squeal of the door from the old barn where he'd spent bitter winter nights during his childhood. He'd braced himself against Freyja's inevitable questions, but thank God, she hadn't mentioned it.

Her legs slid from around his waist, and as her feet hit the floor she swayed, as though she was on the deck of a ship. He took her hand and pressed it against his chest, and she offered him a small smile. Her hair was disheveled, her lips swollen from his kisses and a bewitching blush heated her cheeks. Never in his life had he seen a more captivating sight.

"Are ye all right?" Tenderly, he cradled her face. "Can ye walk?"

"I'm certain I haven't lost the power to walk, Alasdair Campbell."

"I have the need to sweep ye into my arms and carry ye back to the stronghold." He was only half jesting, too.

"Aye, that would raise a few eyebrows." Then her smile faded. "It feels wrong, feeling like this."

Hellfire, the last thing he wanted was for her to regret this. "It wasn't wrong, Freyja. We are to be wed. Ye're my bride in all but name and we'll deal with that soon enough."

Gently, she traced her fingertips over his face. How could such a fleeing touch arouse him so? It took all his willpower not to pull her into his arms and kiss her once again.

"Not that." Her voice was soft. "Being with ye makes me happy, Alasdair, yet my heart weeps for Afi. It feels wrong to be here with ye, when I'm so sad."

Relief that she didn't regret giving herself to him made him strangely lightheaded. He drew in a steadying breath and attempted to straighten her shawl. "If I know anything about Ranulph, it was that he wanted yer happiness above all else."

It was true. He believed that. But he was also certain Ranulph wouldn't have approved of what had just occurred. He'd be sure to think Alasdair had taken advantage of Freyja.

But he hadn't. And neither had he tricked her. His conscience was clear, so why then did a thread of unease lurk in the back of his mind?

"I know he did," Freyja said, and it took him a moment to understand what she was talking about. "And I know we always grasp onto life when death's shadow touches us. I've seen it many times. And yet . . ." Her voice trailed away, and Alasdair stared at her as an unsavory possibility crawled through his mind.

Had Freyja only responded to his touch as a way to dull the edges of her grief?

"It's not that."

"Not what?" God, he didn't mean to sound so harsh, but this wasn't how he'd imagined the aftermath of their first time together would unfold.

She cocked her head as though his response made no sense. "Afi's loss didn't make me fall into yer arms, Alasdair. I wanted this, with ye."

He dragged in a long breath and tried to clear his head. Curse the devil, what was wrong with him? Freyja was irrevocably his, and her gasps of pleasure still echoed in his ears. Yet even the fleeting suspicion that she'd not been in full possession of her senses when he'd taken her scraped along his nerves like poisoned thorns.

But his concerns were unfounded. She'd told him so herself. He shook his head at his folly and tucked a curl behind her ear. "I'm glad to hear it. We must make arrangements to wed as soon as possible."

Concern clouded her eyes. "I know that's what Afi wanted, but I can't think of that when we must first put him to rest."

Her bottom lip wobbled, and he didn't want to press her, but surely she understood the urgency that they wed without delay. Suppose she'd conceived his bairn?

He wouldn't risk tarnishing her honor with a delayed marriage. She was a skilled healer, not an ignorant lass, so why hadn't that possibility occurred to her already?

"I understand," he assured her. "But Freyja, we—"

The words locked in his throat at the sound of the stable doors creaking open. Freyja darted him an alarmed glance before hastily pulling her shawl over her head, hiding her tangled hair.

Hellfire. He swung about, putting some distance between them, although the very fact they were together in a stall was damning enough. Maybe he could divert whoever had entered before they saw Freyja, and he marched from the stall, almost tripping over Dubh, only to come face-to-face with Lady Roisin.

She gazed at him, and he had the uncanny certainty she knew exactly what had just transpired between himself and her sister, even though Freyja was out of sight. He cleared his throat and bowed his head. "My lady."

"I'm looking for my sister. Have ye seen her?"

It was on the tip of his tongue to say he hadn't, when Freyja, with Dubh at her feet, emerged from the stall behind him. Goddamn it, did she have no care for her reputation?

"I'm here, Roisin. Are ye all right?"

Lady Roisin glanced between him and Freyja. With difficulty, he refrained from looking at Freyja himself, in the vain hope that might somehow prove he'd not just taken her maidenhead.

Curse the devil. That was the wrong thing to recall while her sister stood in front of them, no doubt silently judging the pair of them.

"I am." Lady Roisin shook her head. "I was troubled and needed to find ye."

"I'm sorry." Freyja sounded contrite and took her sister's hands. Should he leave? He felt he should, but he appeared rooted to the spot. It seemed he'd done nothing but intrude in the MacDonalds of Sgur's private moments of late.

"No, Frey, I'm not troubled for myself. I saw Lamont a while back, and he was deeply affronted, the odious creature."

Alasdair shot her a startled glance. She'd scarcely spoken a dozen words in his presence before now, and although he barely knew her, he'd not imagined she'd ever voice such a derogatory opinion about anyone out loud, least of all a physician. But then, after all, she was Freyja's sister.

"He'll be gone from Kilvenie soon enough." A thread of bitterness heated Freyja's voice. "Don't worry about that."

"I'm not. And he won't give ye the chance to dispense with his services, Frey. He's leaving Rum this very day."

"Good. No one will weep for his loss. I'll find a better replacement, and God knows that shouldn't be too difficult."

"Aye, but Frey . . ." Lady Roisin's voice trailed away, and she gave him an anxious glance. He wasn't sure whether to give her a reassuring smile or pretend he was oblivious to the sisters' conversation. Thankfully, she didn't give him the chance to make a choice as she returned her attention to Freyja. "His anger frightens me."

Freyja wrapped her arm around Lady Roisin's shoulders. "Ye've no need to be afraid of him. He'll not dare hurt ye. But we'll warn our people of him, nonetheless."

"No, ye don't understand." Lady Roisin twisted her hands together in clear distress. "'Tis not myself that I'm afraid for. 'Tis ye. I fear what he may do in his anger that Afi chose ye over him."

"Have no fear of that, Lady Roisin," he said, unable to remain silent any longer. "I'll protect Lady Freyja with my life, and ye can rest assured if Lamont threatens her, it will be the last thing he ever does."

"Lamont won't do anything." Freyja dismissed the notion with an expressive wave of her hand. "He's full of bilious wind and nothing more." She gave her sister a little shake. "Ye must promise me ye'll think no more of this, ye hear? And besides, we both know I can take care of myself should the need arise."

"The need won't arise," he said. "When we are wed, I shall take care of ye and let no one harm ye."

"Ye have decided then?" Lady Roisin sounded doleful. "I wasn't certain, even though Afi wanted it so badly."

Freyja gave him an exasperated look, which took him aback. Why was she irked he'd confirmed their betrothal to Lady Roisin? There was no doubt about it. She'd not only given her word to her grandfather.

She'd given it to him.

"We have," Freyja confirmed, and he exhaled a relieved breath. For a moment he'd not been certain of her answer. But now she'd told her sister there was surely no way she'd change her mind.

If not for Ranulph's demise, and the faint threat of Lamont's wounded pride in some way injuring Freyja, the situation would be amusing. Who would've thought a noblewoman would give him such a headache over a simple marriage alliance?

"Ye'll be leaving the Small Isles?"

"Alasdair cannot leave his fine castle." She gave him a smile, but it was filled with sadness, and a cursed glimmer of guilt ate through him. He didn't know why he felt so wrong-footed whenever this subject was broached. Women always left their home when they wed. It wasn't as though he expected anything outrageous from her, and yet the guilt sat there, like a condemning toad in the back of his mind.

"I know this is yer destiny," Lady Roisin whispered, and Freyja's smile vanished.

"What did ye say?" There was a sharp note in her voice, but her sister didn't appear to notice, or even acknowledge the question.

"But it still grieves me that ye must leave. I don't know what I'll do without ye and Isolde."

"Have ye been discussing this with Amma?"

"No, but there's nothing to discuss, is there, Frey?"

Freyja tugged her sister close and kissed her forehead, but her gaze clashed with his, and he saw the confusion in her eyes. "I don't know," she said. "I've promised to wed Alasdair and I'll not go back on my word, but how is this following the will of our foremothers?"

"I can't tell ye things I don't know. I only feel in my heart ye and Isolde are following the path laid down for ye."

An eerie shudder inched along his arms. He didn't know what Lady Roisin was talking about, and he didn't want to. All he knew was the memory of their foremothers retained a daunting hold over the MacDonalds of Sgur, and although Freyja had likened it to the pride that caused men to fight to the death to preserve the legacy of their forefathers, he still didn't see it.

Although he was the reason why Freyja was leaving her beloved Isle, he didn't want to be painted as the enemy. "My lady," he said to Roisin, "I hope ye know ye and Lady Helga will always be more than welcome at Dunochty. 'Tis not my intention to steal Lady Freyja away from her kin. The Highlands are not so very far from here, after all."

Freyja smiled at him, but her sister gave a ragged sigh.

"They are far away enough," Lady Roisin said. She pulled back from Freyja's embrace and gazed at her sister. "At least ye'll be close to Isolde on the mainland."

This time he kept his mouth shut. To be sure, Dunochty Castle was closer to William and Isolde than Sgur Castle was, but it was still a good day's ride between them.

"That's right," Freyja said. "And when ye visit, we'll all be together again. It will not be so bad, Roisin, ye'll see."

Lady Roisin nodded and Freyja smiled, but Alasdair had the sobering notion that she was trying to persuade herself, more than her sister, of that bright future.

Freyja drew in a great breath and then turned to him. "I must return to the stronghold, Alasdair, and assist Amma. But ye're right. Once we've laid Afi to rest, we'll arrange our wedding without delay."

He took her hand and pressed his lips against her knuckles. Their eyes locked for an eternal moment and frustrated lust throbbed through his blood, an inconvenient reminder that he'd have to wait God only knew how long before he could welcome her into his bed.

"I'll see ye shortly," he said, and watched as they left the stables.

They couldn't wed until after Ranulph's burial. But he had no intention of waiting even a few days before starting the process. First, he needed to send a message to the earl on the next ship to the mainland, to let him know he and Freyja were betrothed.

And then he'd visit the kirk, to arrange their marriage.

Chapter Seventeen

It was late that night before Freyja escaped to the bedchamber she shared with Roisin, and she sank onto the bed and buried her face in her hands. Roisin sat beside her and wrapped her arm around her shoulders, and silence enveloped them in a grief-streaked cocoon.

After leaving Alasdair in the stables, she'd returned to the stronghold, and in the hours since, she hadn't had the chance to share even a single word with him. Amma had kept her close, supervising all that needed to be done, but ultimately every decision needed her approval.

Even during supper, there had been no respite. She hadn't been hungry but had forced herself to eat because that was expected of her. What a relief it was now, not to have all the eyes of Kilvenie follow her everywhere she went, or surreptitiously attempt to listen to anything she said. Her grandfather had made no secret that his estate would pass onto her, and now the populace of Rum waited for her next move.

She shuddered, pushed her hair from her face, and straightened. Aye, she was glad to be in her own chamber with her sister where she didn't need to keep up the pretense that she was in complete control of her weeping heart. But how she wished Alasdair was with her instead.

It felt disloyal. Until she'd met Alasdair, her sisters were everything to her. But now she was torn. Had Isolde felt this way, before she'd started her new life with William?

"Do ye want me to send for a hot drink?" Roisin's voice was hushed, and she gave her sister a tired smile.

"I should be asking that of ye." She was, after all, the elder sister.

"Ye have enough on yer mind and I'm not a bairn, despite what ye and Isolde think." Roisin took her hand. "When ye wed Alasdair and leave for his castle, I'll be the only daughter of Sgur to continue the legacy. I'll not be able to hide behind either of ye again. I'll one day inherit all of Amma's duties."

Guilt stabbed through her at the knowledge Roisin was right. "I'm sorry, Roisin. 'Tis unfair the burden of running Sgur Castle falls upon yer shoulders, when ye are the youngest and have never wanted it."

"I'll be all right." Roisin squeezed her fingers as if to emphasize that point. "And Amma is convinced that by leaving Eigg, both ye and Isolde are still abiding by the Deep Knowing. It is just, I shall miss ye so."

"Ah, come here." She hugged her sister tight, blinking back tears, but the thread of unease that had haunted her all day wouldn't fade.

The Deep Knowing was clear. If the daughters of Sgur left the Isle, their bloodline would die.

But in this generation, for the first time in nine hundred years, there were three daughters of Sgur. Their bloodline would not die, so long as Roisin remained to continue their legacy.

It was a logical explanation. Why then did she have the certainty that she was missing something vital?

AFTER A RESTLESS night, where sleep eluded her and Alasdair's face haunted every waking moment and fragmented dream, she finally left the bed she shared with Roisin and opened the shutter on the window to breathe in the fresh, early morning sea air.

Across the mist-shrouded water, she could see her beloved Isle, and another wave of sadness rolled through her. Was Dunochty near the coast? The view wouldn't be the same, of course, but how she hoped the castle wasn't landlocked.

Roisin came to her side. "Ye dreamed of Alasdair Campbell last night."

Startled, Freyja turned to her sister. "What?"

Roisin gave a faint smile. "Ye whispered his name. Several times."

"I did?" Blood heated her face. Good Eir, what else had she whispered aloud?

"'Twas quite romantic. Do not fear, ye said nothing incriminating."

Furtively, she glanced over her shoulder, but thankfully Grear was busy sorting out their gowns and was too far away to eavesdrop. On the other hand, she slept at the end of their bed, so doubtless had also overheard whatever Roisin had.

She should leave it well alone but couldn't help herself. "What else did I say?"

"Ye weren't clear," Roisin said, to her relief. "But ye sounded happy, which is all that matters."

"Hmm." She focused on the mighty ridge that defined the landscape of her beloved Eigg before sighing and shaking her head. Who was she trying to fool? She wanted to confide in Roisin while she still could. Lord, who would she share her secrets with when she was the mistress of Dunochty, and her sisters were hours away from her?

She leaned against the wall and tugged her shawl about her. "I believe I will be happy. I wouldn't have promised to wed Alasdair if I thought otherwise."

"When he thinks no one is aware, he looks at ye the way William looked at Isolde last year."

"Does he indeed?" She smiled, as warmth unfurled deep inside, causing flickers of need to heat her blood.

"Aye. I truly think he fell for ye from the moment he first saw ye. Just as William fell for Isolde."

She smiled at Roisin, who was an avid believer of love at first sight and all that entailed. There was no such thing, of course. But since meeting Alasdair, her skepticism of such airy-fae romanticism had significantly dwindled. "The first time he saw me I was elbows deep helping Ban birth her pups. I doubt he fell for me then."

Did she doubt it, though? He had certainly managed to instantly intrigue her more than any other man she'd ever met, despite what she'd been doing. It was entirely possible that Roisin was right.

"Well, he is certainly eager to wed ye as soon as possible."

It wasn't a question, but Freyja knew her sister, and understood what she hadn't asked.

"Don't worry," she whispered. "Alasdair did nothing that I didn't want him to do. He wants us to marry as soon as possible so he can return to his castle, but that is the only reason for haste." She paused, as something belatedly occurred to her. Since Afi's unexpected request, Alasdair had been most accommodating with his wishes for a speedy wedding. But was his insistence on arranging their marriage as soon as possible now colored by the possibility she'd conceived his bairn?

It wasn't possible, since she was in the moon phase where her body was not receptive to a man's seed. Sacred knowledge had been passed down from her foremothers of the mysteries of fertility, and they weren't mysterious at all once one recognized the patterns. But that, along with the secrets of the herbs that helped to regulate a woman's monthly cycles, wasn't knowledge shared with men.

Even though she was quite certain Alasdair wouldn't fault her for the knowledge, it was powerful nonetheless, and alas, there were too many men like Lamont who'd condemn her for it.

It was always best to keep one's counsel in such matters.

She eyed her sister. Both Roisin and Isolde had learned of the old ways and another stab of regret pierced her. Would there be anyone in her new home with whom she could discuss her medical learning with?

But for now, she needed to reassure Roisin.

"I do not need to wed him for any reason other than I want to honor Afi's wishes, and well, I want to for myself."

Roisin nodded. "I know. And he is not only a favored half-brother of the Earl of Argyll, but a friend of William. Ye're sure to see Isolde quite often."

There was a wistful note in her sister's voice that pierced her heart. "Well, look," she said. "Ye know full well ye can come and stay with us for however long ye wish, whenever ye want." To be sure, she wasn't certain extended stays had been what Alasdair had meant when he'd made his offer, but that was neither here nor there. Roisin was her younger sister, and if she wanted to spend half her year at Dunochty Castle, then Freyja would ensure it happened.

"It might be the only way I'll see Hugh Campbell again." Roisin offered her a sad smile and Freyja had to concede she was likely right.

"'Tis possible." And before that happened, she'd make sure Hugh was under no illusion that he could toy with Roisin's affections if he knew what was good for him.

"Except nothing can come of it, since I'm certain he, like William and Alasdair, would never consent to spending his life at Sgur."

There was nothing she could offer to counter that. What was it with these Campbell men that made them so stubborn? She sighed and once again gazed out of the window.

Her father hadn't minded moving from Kilvenie to Sgur when he'd married her mother. But then, he had been a MacDonald of the Isles and had always known the women of Sgur didn't leave their home.

And, in fairness, Rum was only a short trip from Eigg by boat and could be easily seen on a clear day.

But still, it was perplexing that both Isolde and she were

committed to men who had plainly stated they wouldn't consider uprooting themselves, when all their lives she and her sisters had been so sure the Deep Knowing demanded they remain on their Isle.

It was almost as though something fundamental in their legacy had changed. Except that was nonsense. She believed in the Deep Knowing because it had been handed down from mother to daughter in an unbroken line, and in her mind it was a tangible thing. But to even consider the message had somehow shifted implied unseen forces were at work.

And that was something she couldn't believe, since it balanced precariously on the edge of magic.

No. She was trying to read too much into this because she felt guilty about leaving Roisin. The truth was simple. The legacy could only be handed down to one daughter, not three. Why hadn't any of them considered that before? Yet until now, it hadn't crossed her mind that two of them needed to leave Sgur so that the third sister could fulfil the legacy.

She recalled her grandmother's strange dreams and finally understood. They weren't disturbing visions, as Amma believed. It was simply her mind telling her the same thing: That two daughters needed to leave, so only one remained.

Relief washed through her that she'd managed to unravel that mystery, and she took Roisin's hand. "Come," she said. "I need ye by my side to face the day."

Because today she had to make the arrangements for Afi's burial.

ALASDAIR STOOD ON the same beach where just days ago he'd watched Freyja return to Eigg, before Ranulph had fallen into his final decline. It had been three days since he'd last been alone with her, and God help him, but if he didn't speak to her soon, he'd shatter every protocol known to man and storm her damn bedchamber.

He exhaled a harsh sigh and raked his fingers through his hair. Yesterday they had put Ranulph to rest, and he'd intended to stand by Freyja's side. But Lady Helga had stood between them, an insurmountable obstacle despite her slight stature, and afterwards she hadn't allowed Freyja out of her sight.

It was almost as though she knew what had happened in the stables and was determined there would be no opportunity to repeat it.

But that was madness. If she suspected such a thing, surely she would have confronted him? And far from all but ostracizing him, wouldn't she be pressing for an early wedding to save her granddaughter's reputation?

Goddamn it, the women of Sgur were a mystery. And just because Freyja's independent spirit that so entranced him had clearly been inherited from her grandmother, it didn't mean he had to appreciate Lady Helga's actions now.

The sea wind buffeted him, and he welcomed it, but it didn't help clear his mind. Or cool the fire in his blood that had relentlessly burned since the day he'd made Freyja his.

He swallowed a groan but despite his best efforts couldn't quell the images of Freyja in his arms that flooded his brain. Thank God their wedding was arranged for the end of the week.

Now all that remained was to let her know.

He swung on his heel and made his way back to the stronghold, but the thread of unease that had remained with him since he'd first spoken to the minister of the kirk wouldn't fade. He'd fully expected the minister to tell Freyja of his plans two days ago. In fact, he'd been banking on it, since it seemed she was in no hurry to escape her grandmother's watchful eye, but surely that news would've ensured she found a way to speak with him privately.

Even if only to berate him for going behind her back.

He couldn't wait any longer. If confronting Lady Helga and

requesting a formal meeting with Freyja was the only way to speak with her, then that's what he'd do.

The message of his impending nuptials had already been sent to the earl, and he'd also sent word to his mother. Not that he intended to stop at the manor to introduce Freyja. He doubted his prestigious marriage would change her mind about him, and his pride balked at the prospect of Freyja witnessing how little his mother regarded him.

His priority was to take his bride to her new home.

Their new home. A castle fit for a MacDonald of Sgur.

He strode across the courtyard and then stopped dead as Lady Helga emerged from the stronghold, her unwavering gaze fixed on him as though she'd somehow summoned him. Was there something in the air that surrounded the Small Isles that gave him such bizarre thoughts? He shoved the absurd notion aside and bowed his head in greeting. "Lady Helga."

"Alasdair."

He waited a heartbeat, fully expecting her to say more, but when it became apparent that she was waiting for him, he wasted no time on pretty compliments.

"My lady, I must see Lady Freyja without delay."

"Allow me to put yer mind at rest. Lady Freyja hasn't been avoiding ye. But she needed time to make arrangements for the stronghold's security and ongoing upkeep, as I'm certain ye'll understand."

He did understand, but even as he nodded his assent, a dark twist of guilt ate through him. Once they were wed, Kilvenie Tower would come to him, and when they returned to Argyll, he was duty bound to pass it onto the earl.

None of which he intended to share with Lady Helga, even if he'd been at liberty to do so.

"I'd be honored to assist Lady Freyja in any way to lessen her burden."

"Aye. Like the way ye arranged the wedding without first discussing it with us."

So the minister had informed them. "I meant no disrespect, my lady. But I can't remain in Rum much longer. I must return to Argyll and to my responsibilities."

Lady Helga inclined her head. "My granddaughter awaits ye in the solar."

Anticipation thudded through him as he made his way to the solar. It was disconcerting how much he'd missed Freyja these last three days, and he had the uneasy suspicion it wasn't normal for a man to crave a woman's company so badly.

Doubtless, once they were wed, he'd settle into more conventional habits where she was only on his mind when they were in each other's presence. Wasn't that how other marriages worked?

It was certainly true of his mother and stepfather, who had scarcely acknowledged each other during the last few years before his stepfather's death. And besides William, who admittedly couldn't take his eyes off Isolde whenever she was around, none of his friends were wed for comparison.

The only one of his generation who had been married for years was his half-brother, the earl. And Archibald rarely shared the same roof as his wife, never mind utter her name in company.

He paused outside the door to the solar. Was that really the kind of marriage he wanted? One where Freyja lived in the castle, and he lived elsewhere because they were both happier that way?

It didn't appeal. He thrust the disconcerting thoughts from his head and knocked on the door before entering.

Freyja and Lady Roisin sat behind a desk that was covered in piles of documents. Freyja smiled and made her way across the solar to him as Dubh sniffed his boots, and he gave the dog a quick scratch behind his ears.

She stood before him, and he straightened before taking her hands. Did he dare kiss her, with her sister looking on? He reined in his lust and dropped a chaste kiss upon the back of her hand instead of her lips.

"'Tis good to see ye," she said. "I've missed ye."

"I confess, I half wondered if ye were trying to avoid me."

"Never. But there was so much to do." Then she sighed and glanced over her shoulder at her sister before returning her attention to him. "Amma wanted everything to be clear in how Kilvenie continues to function, so there's no misunderstanding when I leave. The villagers rely on the stronghold, and we cannot give them any cause to worry about their livelihoods."

The damned guilt burned through him once again. If he told her the truth, that Ranulph had bequeathed the stronghold to him upon his marriage to her, he risked her refusing to go through with it. But that wouldn't ensure she remained in possession of Kilvenie Tower, since the earl had made it very clear he wanted the stronghold by whatever means necessary.

The prospect of Freyja being humiliated should a battle ensue for Kilvenie turned his guts. Blood would spill, old resentments would resurface, and the end would still be the same.

She'd lose the stronghold.

Belatedly, another thought struck him. He wouldn't secure Dunochty Castle, either.

"I'll give ye some privacy," Lady Roisin said to Freyja, before she gave him a shy smile and left the solar.

The door remained ajar, and much as he wanted to shut it and give them real privacy, he wouldn't give any cause for gossip to flourish. He'd risked her reputation once, and he'd wait a few more days for her. Even if it killed him.

"Alasdair?" There was a questioning note in her voice, and he sucked in a deep breath. She was clearly waiting for him to respond to her.

"Ye know I'll help with Kilvenie in any way I can." Aye, it would belong to the earl, but he'd do everything he could to ensure Freyja's wishes and concerns were heard.

"I know." Her smile was gentle as she pressed a hand against his heart, and his guilt ate deeper. But he was certain she'd understand why he'd kept his counsel when he explained everything to her after they were wed. He was, after all, oath-bound to the earl not to share the mission. But the keeping of such oaths didn't extend to one's own wife.

"Nothing much needs to change." Christ, he hoped the earl didn't intend to bring sweeping changes to Rum.

"Miles will continue as steward," she said. "There's no one better who could ensure Kilvenie will prosper. He knows the stronghold and the people of Rum like no other, and they trust him."

And he'd be sure to recommend the earl continued to allow Miles to remain as steward.

"'Tis a good plan."

"I know Miles will do everything he can, but I should like to visit the stronghold twice a year, so my grandfather's bloodline isn't forgotten."

"I'm certain that can be arranged."

"It will be easy enough, whenever we visit Sgur."

"Aye. Of course." Damn, he had to change the subject. Skirting around the truth wasn't only hard, it made him decidedly uncomfortable. "Is there anything further ye wish me to arrange for our wedding?"

She stared at him. "Anything further? Ye mean meeting with the minister? I'd planned on returning to Eigg tomorrow to speak with him about it, but we could go this very afternoon, if ye wish."

Hellfire. Why hadn't Lady Helga passed on the message from the minister to Freyja? And she expected to wed in Eigg? That hadn't even occurred to him. He'd assumed Ranulph had wanted them to marry here on Rum.

"I've already spoken with the minister, Freyja, and our wedding is in two days in the kirk of Kilvenie."

"What?"

"Ye've been busy dealing with the affairs of the estate. I wouldn't expect ye to arrange our marriage as well."

"But the daughters of Sgur always wed in Eigg, not Rum. Why wouldn't ye discuss this with me before making this decision?"

"These last few days I've barely had the chance to wish ye a good morning, never mind have a serious discussion with ye." He cast a furtive glance over his shoulder at the door, to ensure they were still alone, before turning back to her and dropping his voice. "Ye know as well as I that we cannot delay our marriage."

Comprehension did not sweep across her face and neither did relief at his foresight. She appeared, if anything, irked. "I gave ye my word I'd wed ye, Alasdair. And I've no intention of delaying it. I know ye must return to yer castle, but surely ye could've waited a few more days until we were back on Eigg."

Now he was feeling irked, too. "'Tis nothing to do with me having to return to my castle, Freyja. I won't have ye compromised and that's the end of it."

The irritation on her face slowly faded. "Oh."

Finally, she understood. Although he still couldn't fathom why it had taken her so long. Surely all women had a mind to protecting their reputation?

"'Tis possible ye are pregnant with my bairn. I'll not allow any whisper to surround ye, or our bairn, if that's the case." The way whispers and rumors had plagued him for years. Had the earl acknowledged him, doubtless his childhood would've been different. But he hadn't, and any prestige his father's bloodline may have bestowed upon him had been worthless.

Until Archibald had welcomed him as his half-brother.

Freyja took his hand. There was a soft smile on her face, and although he was glad that she was no longer vexed, there was something baffling about her countenance that he couldn't quite put his finger on.

"Ye're most thoughtful," she whispered. "I understand yer haste, although—" She cut herself off, and then pressed a kiss onto the back of his fingers. Entranced, he lost himself in the endless blue of her eyes as she gave a small nod. "We shall wed in the kirk of Kilvenie. 'Tis a fitting place, since Afi loved Rum so. After all, I'm a daughter of Kilvenie too, as well as Sgur, so our ceremony can bind my legacies together."

He couldn't speak of Kilvenie without the thread of guilt that stirred at every mention of its name. And so he focused on the one aspect she hadn't raised. "When we are wed, ye'll have a new legacy as the mistress of Dunochty Castle." And then he couldn't resist sharing his deepest dream. "And as God's my witness, one day ye'll be the wife of a baron."

Chapter Eighteen

Two days later, as the sun edged towards its zenith, Freyja, with Roisin and their grandmother, walked the short distance from Kilvenie Tower to the kirk. Clouds dotted the sky, but the breeze was warm, and the villagers had gathered along the path to the kirk, just as they had a few days ago when Afi had made his final journey.

She blinked back her tears. This was what her grandfather had wanted, and she wouldn't mar the moment with her grief. After all, marriage to Alasdair was something she wanted, too.

As she entered the small stone kirk that had been a part of Rum for as long as Kilvenie Tower itself, the scent of spring flowers drifted in the air, and she shot Roisin a grateful glance. Her sister had spent most of the previous day gathering wildflowers, and bluebells and primroses filled the nave.

There were not many guests. There hadn't been time to invite the prominent MacDonald clans that were spread across the Western Isles, never mind Isolde and William. But Miles was there, as were her grandfather's faithful servants, as well as those who had accompanied her grandmother from Eigg.

And waiting for her by the altar, smiling at her as though she was the only woman in the world, was Alasdair.

Freyja grasped Roisin's hands in the bedchamber they'd shared for the last week in Kilvenie and squeezed her fingers. "Are ye all right?"

Roisin shook her head. "'Tis *yer* wedding night, Frey. But I won't be asking ye the same question since I know ye will always be all right. And I'm happy for ye, truly I am. Even though everything has happened so fast."

Aye, wasn't that the truth. She could still scarcely believe Alasdair was her husband, but the minister had bound them together and tomorrow they were returning to Eigg before sailing to Oban on the mainland.

Amma kissed her cheek. "Ye chose the right path," she whispered, before straightening and smiling at Roisin. "Come, Roisin. 'Tis time to leave."

Freyja watched her sister and grandmother leave the chamber, taking a reluctant Dubh with them, and when they closed the door behind them a deep silence filled the air. She drew in a calming breath and tugged her shawl about her, even though she wasn't cold, despite wearing only her shift.

It was absurd to feel so nervous about her wedding night. She'd already given Alasdair her maidenhood, so it wasn't trepidation of the unknown that caused the constant flutters in her stomach and jitters in her chest.

Yet here she was, plucking the edges of her shawl and wondering if she should climb into the bed and pull the coverings up to her chin.

It had been a lot easier in the stables, when she hadn't time to think about what she was doing. It had all been so natural, unlike now, when everyone in the stronghold—make that the entire Isle of Rum—knew exactly what was about to happen in this bedchamber tonight.

Did every bride suffer with these thoughts? Or was it just her?

Thankfully, a knock on the door distracted her from her foolish notions and she smiled when Alasdair entered the chamber. How splendid he looked, in a fine saffron shirt that emphasized his magnificent broad shoulders and impressive biceps, with his blond hair pulled back in a black velvet ribbon.

He shut the door and strode across the chamber to where she stood beside the bed, his dark gaze never leaving hers.

"My beautiful bride," he said, as he took her hands. "I can scarcely believe my good fortune."

She laughed, and the nerves that had plagued her all day evaporated as spirals of pleasure warmed her blood. "I'll be certain to remind ye of yer good fortune whenever I irk ye."

"There will be no need. There's nothing ye could do that would cause me even a moment's vexation."

"I thought ye knew me better than that."

He dropped a kiss upon the back of her hand, and shivers of delight raced through her. "I know ye well enough, Freyja MacDonald, and I'd have ye no other way."

"'Tis just as well, since I shall never change."

He released her hand and plucked one of the bluebells Roisin had threaded through her hair that morning and twirled it between his fingers.

"'Tis the same blue as yer eyes." He sounded a little awed and she smiled.

"I don't believe that's the reason why my sister gathered so many bluebells for our wedding. She believes they're flowers of the fae and will bring us great joy."

Roisin also believed both bluebells and primroses signified everlasting love, but she wasn't going to tell Alasdair that. It was all very well for her to gently mock her sister for her rose-hued certainties about how Alasdair really felt about his new bride, but she didn't quite have the nerve to risk him laughing should she mention the notion of *everlasting love* to him.

He trailed the dainty petals along her cheek. "I don't believe in the fae folk," he said. "But I'm willing to believe the bluebells will bring us joy."

"Then I trust the woodlands around yer castle are filled with them every spring."

For a fleeting moment, confusion flashed across his face, as though he had no idea what she was talking about. Then he smiled and the only thing she saw in his eyes was admiration. "That's something to discover for yerself."

She sighed and traced her finger along his throat to where his shirt opened, showing a tantalizing glimpse of his chest. "There are many things for me to discover in my new life."

"Ye're not the only one." He dropped the bluebells onto the bed and cupped her face. "I've yet to discover how exquisite my bride will look when she's lying naked upon the bed, waiting for her husband."

The image burned into her mind, and the breath caught in her throat. "I hope her husband is also naked in this fantasy ye speak of."

"Certainly. But 'tis no fantasy." Laughter filled his voice, but there was an irresistible undertone of lust that ignited sparks of flame deep inside. "And thank God for that. I've dreamed of being with ye since the day we met, and I'm certain I'd have gone mad with wanting ye had we not wed this day."

"Well, to be fair," she was compelled to remind him, "ye've already had me, Alasdair."

"Once. And I've been burning for yer touch again ever since."

She shook her head and tugged on the ties of his shirt. "Yer honeyed tongue is always a source of wonder to me. I don't possess the knack of whispering such sweet nothings in yer ear."

"They're not sweet nothings." There was an odd tone in his voice, as though she'd inadvertently wounded him. Great Eir, maybe she had? Perhaps in the middle of one's wedding night wasn't the right time to say whatever was on her mind? "I mean it, Freyja. There's never been another woman I've wanted for my wife, and that's the truth. One tumble in the stables with ye could never be enough. I know I should regret what happened, but I don't. I never will. And I hope to God ye don't regret it, either."

"Ah, ye foolish man," she said before she could think better of it. "Of course I don't regret it. How could ye even think such a thing? The memory has kept me awake at night for this last week. There, are ye happy now I've bared my soul to ye?"

His grin fairly took her breath away. "Aye. And feel free to bare ye soul—and the rest of yerself—to me whenever the mood takes ye."

"I'll do my best but make no promises."

"Yer best works for me." He tugged her shawl from her shoulders and dropped it to the floor. "I do have one regret about the stables."

"Ye do?"

"Aye. It was too rushed for yer first time. That's my only regret, but I intend to make it up to ye, make no mistake."

"I've no complaints. If I had, I'd share them with ye."

His big body shook with silent laughter. "I've no doubt of that." He unclasped his brooch and placed it on a nearby table before unwinding his plaid. "I trust ye'll have no complaints when I take my time with ye tonight."

Her mouth dried as he finally unwound the last of the material and tossed it across a chair. His shirt hung to his knees, but without his heavy plaid in the way, his arousal was plain to see.

She licked her lips and tried to speak but it appeared her wits had fled. How mortifying. Alasdair wasn't even naked yet. As if he'd heard her thoughts, he grasped the back of his shirt and hauled it over his head.

Good goddess Eir. Her gaze fixed on his breathtaking cock as if she'd never seen one before in her life. To be fair, patients didn't count and despite what had occurred between them in the stables, she'd never had the chance to see Alasdair in all his naked glory.

"Does yer unnatural silence indicate approval?" Alasdair loosened the laces on her bodice while she attempted to locate her voice. "I cannot tell by the expression on yer face."

As he gently tugged her shift over her shoulders she hitched in a ragged breath. "I'm more than adequately impressed."

"I'll take that as a compliment."

"I think ye should."

He gave a grunt of laughter before wrenching her shift along her arms where it floated to the floor in a pool of pale green. His hot gaze devoured her, sweeping from her flushed face to her curling toes, and liquid heat bloomed between her thighs in a molten wave.

"I believe I'm more than adequately impressed also." His voice was rough with desire, and she managed a sardonic smile until he cupped her breasts, and she exhaled a shaky breath instead.

"Being naked has its merits," she conceded, as he bent his head and sucked her nipple into his mouth. She dug her fingers into his hair and her eyes drifted shut as his tongue and lips created sweet havoc with her senses.

Slowly, he inched down her body, his hands gliding over her waist and bottom, leaving ribbons of fire in his wake. His mouth was an instrument of exquisite torture as he licked and nibbled her flesh, causing her to all but collapse beneath his ministrations.

And then he knelt before her, easing her knees apart with one hand as he wrapped his other arm around her hips. His fingers stroked her damp folds, dipping inside her heat and teasing her throbbing clit until every sense she possessed burned for release.

His hot breath was as provocative as an ethereal caress against her sensitized lips and when he pressed an open mouthed kiss on her, she gave a rasping moan. His tongue teased and probed, and an unbearable pressure coiled through her, until she tumbled over the edge as waves of unbridled pleasure consumed her.

He swept her into his arms, swung about, and laid her on the bed. She gave a gasping laugh as he straddled her, before roughly pushing her thighs apart with his knees.

"I need ye, mo leannan." He sounded in agony, but passion burned within the dark depths of his eyes and renewed desire rippled through her blood. "I need to be inside ye again and make ye mine."

"Aye," she breathed, barely aware she even spoke, and she wrapped her legs around him, delighting in how wonderful it was not to be hampered by endless lengths of gown and plaid between them. His muscled chest with its smattering of hair crushed her breasts, and his mouth against her throat pushed her once again to the fiery edge. "Take me again, husband of mine."

With a strangled groan he pushed inside her, and there was no sting of discomfort to distract her from the sensation of being utterly possessed by Alasdair. She panted desperately in his face, but although air eluded her, it was exhilarating, and his feral grin merely stoked her passion.

He rode her hard, slamming her into the mattress. Time lost all meaning as she convulsed around him, again and again, gasping his name with mindless abandon.

"Freyja, leannan." His husky endearment spun through her, and she shuddered uncontrollably as he followed her over the precipice into a pleasure-fueled oblivion.

Chapter Nineteen

Alasdair stole a sideways glance at Freyja as they rode through the town of Oban. They had been wed ten days, and he still couldn't quite believe his luck in winning such an incomparable bride.

After they'd left Rum and returned to Eigg, Freyja had wasted no time in organizing her departure from Sgur Castle. And while he'd expected a wagon or so of her personal possessions, he hadn't expected the two wagon loads of plants she'd insisted she couldn't leave behind.

God knew, he would have agreed to bring anything with them, if it made her happy.

Before they left Eigg he'd sent messages to the mainland, and when they'd disembarked at the port of Oban, a dozen warriors had joined them. He'd known them all for years and trusted them with his life. They would ensure his bride encountered no dangers during the journey to Dunochty. And God knew, he needed men he could count on when he began his new life as laird of the castle.

"I believe I spy yer manor." She turned and smiled at him and even though the prospect of seeing his mother caused a hard knot of dread in the pit of his stomach, he couldn't help smiling back at her.

"Aye." There wasn't much else he could say. It was his manor.

"'Twas kind of yer lady mother to invite us to visit her."

He grunted in response. Ever since the unexpected message had arrived on Eigg four days ago, Freyja had attempted to engage him in conversation about his mother several times, and each time he'd managed to change the subject without arousing her curiosity.

Or so he'd thought. Right up until they'd disembarked at the port of Oban, he'd intended to bypass the manor and take Freyja to Dunochty, but she'd been adamant they couldn't ignore the offer of hospitality. And since he didn't want to dredge up the nonexistent relationship he had with his mother, it had been easier to agree that they'd stop at the manor for refreshments before continuing their journey home.

Home. The prospect of having his own home sent a warm glow through him, but if he had to suffer his mother's barbs to satisfy Freyja's sense of honor, then it was a small price to pay to make his bride content, and so he had sent a messenger ahead to inform her to expect them.

As they entered the small courtyard, he was taken aback to see his mother standing in front of the doors to the manor, along with the steward and the rest of their small staff. He hadn't expected her to make the effort to greet his bride in the manner she deserved.

He dismounted and helped Freyja from her horse. She squeezed his hand as though offering comfort, and he had the strangest notion she wasn't as unaware of how he felt about his mother as he'd assumed.

The knot in his gut tightened. He didn't know how he felt about that. Her family was so different from his own and a part of him had wanted her to believe in the illusion that he shared that same closeness with his mother.

Too late to think about that now. She'd soon discover the truth. From the corner of his eye he saw Clyde, the warrior Lady Helga had assigned for Freyja's protection, take Dubh from one of the wagons where he'd spent the journey in a basket, and the dog instantly shot to Freyja's side.

The rest of his men also dismounted but made no move towards the manor. They knew no invitation would be extended for them to enjoy any refreshments. Thank God they knew him, and his mother, well enough not to take offence.

He came to a halt before his mother. At least she was smiling at Freyja, which was a good sign.

He turned to his bride. "Lady Freyja, may I present my mother, Mistress Campbell. Mistress Campbell, my bride, Lady Freyja MacDonald of Sgur Castle."

"I'm delighted to meet ye, Mistress Campbell. 'Tis most kind of ye to offer us refreshments."

"Not at all, my lady. 'Tis an honor to meet my son's bride. He's a lucky man, and that's a fact."

"'Tis I who am the lucky one, Mistress Campbell. Yer son is an honorable man and I'm proud to be his wife."

Alasdair smiled grimly when his mother shot him a calculating glance. To be sure, it was gratifying Freyja spoke so highly of him. But would she still think him such an honorable man if she knew the real reason why he had traveled to Rum?

"Aye, indeed." His mother nodded sagely. "Allow me to welcome ye to our humble manor, my lady. If ye wish to refresh yerself after the journey, my maid can take ye to the solar."

"I should like that, thank ye."

A maid stepped forward and bobbed a curtsey, and after glancing at him Freyja followed the maid inside the manor.

His mother eyed him. "Ye've done well for yerself, and no mistake."

He had no intention of discussing Freyja with her. For as long as he could remember, whenever his mother said something that could lead to discord, he'd steered her interest in a safer direction. It had never failed him before. There was no reason to think it would now.

"I'm glad our marriage pleases ye. And I must concur with my wife, 'tis good of ye to welcome us at such short notice."

His mother gave a faint smile and the tension that had crackled around her since his arrival faded. "Ye'd best come inside. I trust yer men have their own victuals."

"Aye. Let me tend to the horses first. I'll join ye in the hall."

He watched her disappear into the manor and raked his fingers through his hair. It was a small reprieve, but he couldn't tarry too long. He didn't want his mother cornering Freyja and filling her head with the truth of his childhood.

Freyja believed he'd enjoyed a privileged upbringing as the son of the earl, and that was the way he wanted things to stay.

FREYJA FRESHENED UP in the small solar, where a pitcher of lukewarm water had been left for her on a table, as her serving woman, Morag, tidied her hair. Amma had insisted she take one of her own women with her, and Freyja was grateful for the familiar face, but how she wished she could have brought Laoise.

It was out of the question, of course, and she hadn't even asked her. Laoise had four bairns and her widowed mother to support. Besides, she was the only one left on Eigg who understood the power of the poppy.

As she dried her hands, she glanced around the solar. The manor wasn't quite what she'd been expecting. There was an air of neglect about the place, but perhaps that was because Alasdair spent most of his time in his castle.

Still, a laird should ensure all his properties were maintained.

She frowned as she crouched down to pat Dubh. It felt disloyal to even think that about Alasdair, but she couldn't shift the feeling that something wasn't quite right. He'd told her a few days ago, after she'd pressed him on the matter, that his stepfather had died two years ago. If there was any blame for the lack of upkeep of the manor, it fell squarely at the feet of the late master.

Ah, well. She straightened and adjusted her shawl. Now she was here, she could help ease the burden on Alasdair's shoulders so he could ensure his mother's comfort.

As she left the solar to retrace her steps to the great hall, her mind lingered on Mistress Campbell. When Alasdair had received her invitation to visit them, his expression had given nothing away, and yet she'd been instantly concerned for him. Her suspicions about his mother had grown when he'd dismissed the offer under the pretext he wanted to take his bride straight to Dunochty instead.

And every time she'd raised the subject, he'd deflected the conversation elsewhere. It was glaringly obvious he didn't get along with his mother, and since Alasdair was the kindest man she had ever met, the fault certainly lay with Mistress Campbell.

But apart from the way she hadn't offered Alasdair's men any sustenance, the older woman seemed perfectly amiable. Why then hadn't Alasdair wanted to take her to the manor? Inadvertently, her glance fell upon the damaged wall panels that lined the corridor. Surely it had nothing to do with its sad state of repair?

As she approached the great hall, Mistress Campbell's voice floated into the corridor, and she stopped dead.

"I'll tell ye plainly. I'm agog at how ye managed to snare a Sgur MacDonald." Incredulity thrummed in every word, and Freyja bristled at Mistress Campbell's tone. Why wouldn't she think her own son was worthy of such a match?

"I didn't ensnare her." Alasdair's retort was surprisingly calm, but she heard the underlying affront. She didn't blame him. Even Dubh, standing by her feet, had gone onto alert, as though he also found Mistress Campbell's manner offensive.

Well, she certainly wasn't going to skulk in corners, eavesdropping on conversations that were none of her business, even when it involved her own husband, and she had to battle the urge to leap to his defense. She took a deep breath and had taken a step forward when Mistress Campbell spoke again.

"I cannot help but suspect yer new bride and Dunochty are connected, Alasdair. It seems—"

She marched into the great hall, a smile on her face, even

though inside she was seething. Mistress Campbell snapped her lips together and offered a reciprocating smile that didn't reach her eyes.

"My lady, please take some refreshments." She waved her hand over to the hearth, where a maid was arranging a fine spread upon a table.

Freyja glanced at Alasdair. He had an unreadable expression on his face but the muscles in his jaw and shoulders were taut with suppressed frustration and anger against his mother flared through her.

She didn't know their history, it was true. But Mistress Campbell had disrespected her Alasdair, and she wanted to show him that no matter what, she was on his side. With a regal nod in his direction, she slipped her arm through his, and with a startled glance at her breach in etiquette, he led her after his mother.

IT WAS EARLY afternoon when they left the manor, and when they were some distance from the estate, Freyja leaned across the small space between their horses and briefly grasped Alasdair's forearm. "I'm sorry for insisting we visit Mistress Campbell."

A dark frown slashed his brow. "Did my mother offend ye?"

"No," she said hastily. "She was most pleasant. But I could see it was difficult for ye. I shouldn't have put ye in that position. 'Tis in my nature to pursue something when it occurs to me, and I thought it was right to meet my husband's mother as soon as possible."

He transferred his glower to the path ahead and as the silence stretched between them, she silently sighed. It was obvious he didn't want to discuss the matter further.

She cast her glance from the woodlands to their right, to where glimpses of the sea could be seen on the left. And again she hoped Dunochty would be close to the coast. She should have asked Alasdair about the castle's location before they left Eigg, but it seemed pointless now, when they were merely hours from arriving.

"We were never close," he said, suddenly breaking the silence. "I learned early on she preferred it if I wasn't around."

"That must have been hard." Her own parents had died eleven years ago, and their loss had devastated her. She still missed the long conversations she and her sisters had enjoyed with their mother, and the sound of their father's laugh and the way he'd swung them around in his arms when they'd been small.

She swallowed around the constriction in her throat, and it wasn't entirely caused by the grief of losing her parents when she had been so young, or the recent loss of her beloved Afi.

It was because Alasdair didn't have similar happy memories of when he was a bairn.

Yet he was the son of the late earl, and considering he was clearly a trusted confidant of the current earl, it stood to reason his entire childhood hadn't been one of neglect. Just when he resided at his stepfather's manor.

She dearly hoped he'd spent most of the time with his half-brother.

Alasdair still stared grimly ahead, as though he regretted his confession. But she didn't want him to regret it. She wanted to know everything about him, and it was only now the sobering realization hit her that she actually knew very little.

"I survived," he said, breaking into her reverie, and when he smiled at her, chasing away the cloud that had surrounded him, a warm glow heated her heart. She didn't even chide herself for such a fanciful notion since possible or not, it felt as though a shard of sunlight enfolded her chest.

She reached for him, and he took her hand and kissed her gloved fingers. "I know ye did," she said. "And I'm thankful for it, make no mistake."

He squeezed her fingers before releasing her, but as he turned away she caught a furtive expression on his face. It was gone in an instant and she almost wondered if she'd imagined it.

But she hadn't. Yet what on earth did Alasdair need to feel guilty about?

Chapter Twenty

IT WAS EARLY evening when Dunochty Castle came into view through a gap in the woodlands, and fierce pride stabbed through Alasdair at the knowledge he had a home worthy enough for Freyja. Thank God the earl had seen fit to grant him the castle, for the manor was in no state for a noblewoman such as her.

He'd done his best to maintain the manor during the last two years since it had become his responsibility, but the income from its estate had rendered that task a challenge. But now, with the revenue Dunochty generated, he'd be able to replace the rotting wood and crumbling stonework. To make it a suitable second residence for his wife.

Maybe the repairs would even please his mother, but he wasn't going to count on it. He'd long ago given up on trying to win her favor. And now he didn't even want to. He had Freyja. And every time she glanced at him, he saw only admiration glowing in her bonny blue eyes. Admiration and, aye, affection. And maybe something even more.

"Dunochty is a fine castle indeed."

He turned to Freyja, who was gazing at the magnificent façade of the castle on the summit of the hill, where it commanded impressive views of the surrounding countryside and the coast.

"I'm glad it meets with yer approval."

"And so near to the sea. I was hoping it was. Isolde will be so envious."

Despite his pleasure at her evident delight in her new home, he was compelled to defend his friend. "William's castle is a grand stronghold."

She laughed and shook her head. "I'm sure it is. Isolde couldn't speak highly enough of Creagdoun when we last saw her a few weeks ago. I'm merely jesting with ye, Alasdair. My sister would be happy to live in a cave, so long as William was there with her."

Would Freyja ever say such a thing about him?

It was a moot point. His wife would never want for anything, least of all a roof over her head.

Twilight had fallen when they finally reached the gatehouse with its impressive twin round towers and rode under the mighty portcullis and into the courtyard. Lamps blazed in sconces by the double doors that led into the castle and a sizeable staff stood ready to greet them.

It appeared the earl had entailed a full working complement to him, as well as the castle itself.

After they dismounted, grooms and stable lads took the horses to the stables, and Alasdair led Freyja to the waiting servants as unease gnawed through him. How could he introduce his bride, the mistress of Dunochty, to her servants, when he didn't even know any of them?

A man stepped forward and bowed his head. "Sir, I'm Raso, the new steward of Dunochty Castle sent by the Earl of Argyll. 'Tis an honor to welcome ye and Lady Freyja. Supper will be served shortly."

"Thank ye, Raso." Alasdair held out his arm to Freyja and didn't miss the bemused expression on her face before she quickly masked it with a smile as she hooked her arm through his.

Damn, he didn't want her to think anything was amiss. But clearly Raso's intervention, while relieving him of the embarrassment of not knowing any of his servants' names or their occupations, had strayed so far from protocol that Freyja's curiosity was piqued.

He'd brazen it out. He was good at doing that.

With a purposeful stride, he entered the great hall. Opulent tapestries adorned the walls, and fine lanterns bathed the hall in a warm glow. The castle's chattels were more impressive than he recalled, and there would be no need for him to take anything from the manor to make Dunochty more comfortable for his bride.

As he led the way to the stairs, Freyja whispered in his ear. "Dunochty Castle is grand indeed, Alasdair. Why did ye never tell me? I am quite overawed."

He tugged her closer. "'Tis nothing less than ye deserve. Do whatever ye wish to make the castle more comfortable. I leave it in yer capable hands."

She gave a small laugh as they climbed the stairs. "So long as I have a good garden for my herbs, I shall be content."

"It shall be my first priority in the morning."

They followed Raso along the corridor until he paused and opened a door. "My lady's chambers," he said.

Freyja entered the antechamber and gazed around, clearly impressed by the thick rugs that covered the floor, the vibrant tapestries that kept the chill from penetrating the stone walls, and two richly upholstered chairs that sat before the elegant hearth. A half-open door led to another antechamber that he presumed led, in turn, to the master's chamber.

A subtle hint from Raso, no doubt. The man had already proved his worth.

"I've never seen such splendor." She sounded awed. "Alasdair, I'm not certain I can be the lady this castle demands."

He took her hand and led her into the bedchamber before closing the door behind them, leaving her serving woman and Clyde, who shadowed Freyja everywhere, in the antechamber.

"Ye're exactly the lady this castle needs." He wrapped his arms around her and lifted her into his arms, and she laughed and smacked his shoulder before hugging him close. "I want ye to be happy, Freyja. That's all."

She sighed before trailing kisses along his jaw and a growl burned his throat. Every time she touched him was as potent as the first time. Would he ever get enough of this enchanting woman? "How could I not be happy with an honorable man such as yerself, Alasdair? I do believe ye are single-handedly changing my opinion of the entire Campbell clan."

He laughed at her outrageous remark, even though that damned thread of guilt would not lay down and die. "That's a mighty burden to put on any man's shoulders. I must tell ye, I believe ye're overestimating my worth."

"Never. And I'll not allow another doubting word to escape yer delectable mouth." With that, she kissed him, and he forgot about everything but his bewitching bride.

THE FOLLOWING MORNING, he experienced his first taste of what life would be like, now he was laird of a great estate. Instead of spending time with Freyja, showing her the castle and finding the perfect spot for her garden, Raso approached him as they prepared to make their escape after breakfast.

"A word if I may, sir."

Damn it. He'd hoped the affairs of the estate could wait until this afternoon. He kissed Freyja's hand and walked with Raso until they were out of earshot.

"What is it?"

"There are some disputes that need settling in the village," he said.

"I'll attend to them after dinner."

"Unfortunately, these issues are long outstanding, sir. And after dinner, there's a pressing need to establish that the lairdship of Dunochty is secure. Ye need to be seen about the estate, to quash any rumors that the castle has been abandoned."

He acknowledged the wisdom of Raso's counsel. More than

that, he appreciated how the steward had the tact not to say such things in front of Freyja.

"I'll be with ye directly." He swung about and returned to Freyja. "Alas, duty calls and it seems I cannot get out of it."

She cradled his face, supremely unconcerned by the servants and his men who filled the hall. And why should she be concerned? She was the mistress of Dunochty, and ancient royal blood flowed in her veins.

"Nor should ye," she said. "Do not fret, Alasdair. I'm very capable of investigating my new home by myself. Shall I see ye at dinner?"

"The Queen herself couldn't keep me away."

"I should have words with her if she tried." She smiled, and breaking this moment was the hardest thing he'd ever done. But the earl had bequeathed him one of his grandest properties and he had every intention of ensuring it prospered.

For Freyja.

AFTER ALASDAIR LEFT the hall, Freyja glanced at Morag and then Clyde, who stood with his arms folded and a menacing glare on his face. Good Lord, she couldn't possibly expect to win the trust of her servants if he insisted on shadowing her everywhere and glowering at anyone who dared to look her way.

She went over to him. "Clyde, I wonder if ye might get to know Alasdair's men? And find out the lay of the land."

"Lady Helga's instructions were clear. I'm to protect ye at all times."

"Aye, but I'm certain she didn't mean ye should follow me around once we safely arrived at Dunochty. Besides, I feel bad for ye. There must be a hundred tasks ye'd rather be doing and I'm certain ye could teach these Highlanders a thing or two about—" she couldn't come up with anything specific so added brightly, "everything."

He growled deep in his throat. "'Tis wise to investigate Alasdair's men." He sounded reluctant to admit it.

"I agree. Although I can't imagine anyone that he trusts could be disloyal, but 'tis prudent to be vigilant."

After Clyde marched off, she heaved a silent sigh of relief. Now she needed to find a senior servant who could show her around. It was most odd how Alasdair's steward had ushered them into the castle after they'd arrived yesterday, without any chance of introductions. She was certain the ways of the Highlands couldn't be that far different to those of the Small Isles.

Then again, no castle on any of the Small Isles came close to the grandeur of Dunochty. To be sure, she'd learned from her grandmother how to manage a great stronghold, but she'd never envisaged anything more imposing than Sgur itself.

The trick was to ensure she always looked as though she knew exactly what she was doing, so the servants wouldn't doubt her.

If only she knew where to begin.

"Milady," Morag murmured, nodding her head in a significant manner. Freyja followed her gaze, to where a middle-aged woman stood a respectful distance away. A chatelaine hung from her waist and relief washed through Freyja. Finally, someone who could help her navigate the castle and its inhabitants.

She smiled, and the woman came over to them. "My lady," she said. "My name is Sine. I oversee the domestic arrangements of Dunochty Castle. If ye have any concerns, please let me know."

"Everything has been most agreeable, Sine. I thank ye for yer attentiveness."

Sine inclined her head. "I'm gratified all is to yer satisfaction. Would my lady like to see the kitchens and speak with the cook?"

"I should like that very much."

Sine led the way to the kitchens, which were very well appointed, and the cook appeared most congenial. After discussing various menus, she inspected the larders and butteries, and while stocks were low, there was nothing that couldn't be resolved.

It was late morning before they emerged from the kitchens, and she still hadn't seen the one place she truly wanted to.

"Sine, might I see the kitchen gardens? The laird promised I might enlarge it for my own use."

"Of course, my lady. 'Tis this way." She led the way outside, where a lackluster herb garden was located next to an array of vegetables. Although the gardens were substantial, as befit an estate as grand as Dunochty, they looked untended, and somewhat sparse, considering the number of mouths within the castle that needed to be fed.

As she walked along the paths that separated the gardens into segments, a thread of disquiet gnawed through her. Was Alasdair aware that his kitchen gardens were so woefully underutilized?

Certainly, it wasn't a laird's responsibility to keep his gardens fully stocked. That was the duty of the seneschal, or, in this case, it appeared to fall under Sine's purview.

'Twas most strange. To be sure, she hadn't met every member of the household, but she'd seen many maids about the castle, and the cook had several staff under her. How were they all being fed?

Well, she was here now, and she'd ensure the castle gardens were soon put to rights.

"Sine, we must discuss the replenishing of the kitchen gardens."

"Aye, my lady. Now the castle is occupied again, I took the liberty of rehiring several locals for the menial tasks about Dunochty. We shall increase production of the kitchen gardens as quickly as possible."

But Alasdair had only been gone from his castle for a few weeks. Surely he hadn't dismissed half his staff for such a short absence? Besides, that wouldn't account for how low on stock they were now.

"I see," she said, although she didn't. In fact, it only made sense if the castle had been without a laird for a year or more, and the only occupants had been a handful of the most indispensable servants.

Just how long had Alasdair been laird of Dunochty? Was the reason he'd not made the proper introductions after they'd arrived yesterday because he didn't know any of his staff?

That was madness. What was she thinking?

And then Mistress Campbell's voice echoed in her mind.

"I cannot help but suspect yer new bride and Dunochty are connected, Alasdair."

Unease slithered along her spine, although she couldn't quite pinpoint why. Mistress Campbell's overheard conversation wasn't something she intended to waste any thought on, and yet she couldn't dislodge the feeling she was missing something obvious.

She took a deep breath. She'd ask him about it at dinner. But for now, she intended to find the perfect place where she could recreate her beloved medicinal gardens.

Chapter Twenty-One

It was midday before Alasdair returned to the castle. While he'd frequently been called upon to settle disputes between the manor's villagers since his stepfather's death, the village attached to Dunochty was easily three times the size of the one under the jurisdiction of the manor. And by the longstanding nature of many of the villagers' complaints, it was clear nothing had been done to resolve the grievances for a long time.

Not that he blamed the earl. Archibald had many properties, and each one relied on the integrity of its steward to keep things satisfactory. Maybe that was a reason why the earl had replaced the former steward with Raso.

When he walked into the great hall, two long tables had been set, as well as a smaller table on a raised dais at the far end of the hall. His men were seated, and servants stood behind benches, and he cursed under his breath.

He'd kept Freyja waiting on her first full day as mistress of Dunochty.

He hastened up the stairs and flung open the door to the antechamber. She was at a table, poring over a document, and looked up and smiled at his entrance.

"There ye are. I was thinking of sending a search party out for ye. Ye shouldn't miss dinner, no matter how busy ye are."

He went over to her and kissed her before giving Dubh a scratch behind his ears. "Aye. Time got away from me. But 'twas a good morning's work. How about ye?" He nodded to the documents she'd been looking at before going to the hearth, where a bowl and pitcher sat on a table.

"Likewise," she said. "I've decided where to have my medicinal gardens and have arranged for a wall to be built around it for safety. All being well, I can start replanting within a few days."

He smiled to himself as he poured water into the pitcher so he could wash the dust of the village from his hands. How like Freyja to be more excited about the thought of her medicinal gardens than the stately appeal of Dunochty.

"That's good all is well." He dried his hands and turned back to her, ready to escort her down to the hall, but instead of taking his proffered arm, concern wreathed her face.

"Alasdair, there is one thing that concerns me. The kitchen gardens have been sorely neglected, and it will take a little time to bring them up to a satisfactory standard that a castle the size of Dunochty requires. I'm working with Sine to ensure we build up our reserves as quickly as possible."

He had no idea who Sine was, but that was a minor concern. "Our stocks of nonperishables are low as well?"

Goddamn it, he hadn't expected that. He knew they were well supplied with their own livestock and what could be hunted in the nearby forest, but he hadn't thought beyond that. Yet even if he had, what the hell could he have done about it before formally taking possession of the castle?

Freyja came over to him and took his hand. "I'm not good at pretty words, as ye well know, so I shall come straight to the point. How long have ye been laird of Dunochty, Alasdair?"

The suspicion that she'd one day ask him this had haunted his mind from the moment they'd wed. He'd hoped he was wrong, even knowing he wasn't. Freyja was bound to discover Dunochty was a new acquisition, merely from overhearing servants' unwary gossip, if nothing else. What was more, he'd seen the questions in her eyes when they had arrived yesterday, and Raso had cut short the introductions.

It wasn't something he'd wanted to keep from her, but he

hadn't known how to tell her without her questioning why the earl had suddenly granted him such a prestigious estate.

But now he felt wrongfooted. And had only himself to blame.

He sighed heavily. "Not long. 'Tis a recent acquisition as ye rightly surmised."

"From the earl?"

"Aye." God, he hoped she didn't leap to the obvious conclusion, but there was nothing he could do if she guessed the truth. "I didn't have the opportunity to check the stores before I was sent to Rum. But regardless, this is my fault. I'll sort it out."

She gave his fingers a little squeeze. "Nonsense. How can ye blame yerself for this? But I understand now. Sine said she had rehired some locals, so clearly before ye acquired the castle it was being run on a skeleton staff. That's why the stocks are so low, not because of any bad management, which I confess was my first worry."

"I don't want ye to worry about anything."

She laughed. "I'm not a worrier by nature, but had yer staff been mismanaging yer estate, I would've been most aggrieved."

"God help us," he said with feeling.

"Aye, and don't be fooled by my gentle nature. I can be formidable when I put my mind to it." She gave him a stern glare to underscore her point, but laughter glinted in her beautiful eyes.

"Just so ye know, I do happen to think ye have a gentle nature."

She made a scoffing sound. "Do ye know me at all, Alasdair Campbell? Now come on down to dinner, before all the dishes go cold. And let me tell ye, it's a real feast the cook has prepared. I hope ye're famished."

"I've heard back from Isolde." Freyja came into the stables where he was grooming his favorite horse. To be sure, he had a full complement of grooms and stable lads, but there was nothing as satisfying as doing it himself. He supposed it was a strange thing to miss from his days at the manor, but there he was.

"Let me guess. She can't wait to see ye."

Freyja flapped her letter at him. It had been a week since their conversation when he'd admitted Dunochty had only recently come into his possession, and much to his surprise, she hadn't pressed him for more details. He'd been certain she'd ask questions as to why the earl had granted him the castle, but God knew, he was thankful she hadn't.

"Ye must be a mind reader." Mockery threaded through Freyja's voice. She skimmed her letter. "Ah, here it is. 'I cannot wait to see ye, Frey.'"

He laughed. Since moving to Dunochty, Freyja and her sister had frequently corresponded and decided between themselves that a visit was of paramount importance.

He'd wanted William and Lady Isolde to visit them here, but Freyja had suggested that until their pantries were replenished it would be an unnecessary burden. Besides which, she was eager to see Creagdoun, which her sister appeared to love so dearly.

"Well, it won't be long," he reminded her. "We leave in two days." They were staying for a week, and it was a novel sensation to be visiting his friend as a guest. They'd known each other for so long, there had never been the need for any formal invitations. Even after William had become the laird of Creagdoun, Alasdair had merely turned up at his gatehouse without announcing his intentions and been welcomed.

Everything was different now they were both married. And he wouldn't have it any other way.

THE FOLLOWING AFTERNOON, Freyja was in her medicinal gardens, tending to some of the plants that hadn't taken kindly to their new home. Her precious poppies were currently being pampered in a small disused pantry, which she'd claimed as her apothecary, and she was quietly hopeful that they'd survive and would soon be robust enough to replant.

She wiped her hair off her face with the back of her hand and eyed her handiwork. It would take years before her gardens were as established as those she had at Sgur, but her pang of homesickness was relieved by the knowledge that this time tomorrow she would see Isolde.

How much easier it was to stay in touch when only a day's ride stood between them. Until she'd moved to Dunochty, it had taken several days for a letter to reach Isolde, and then another week before her sister's reply had arrived on Eigg.

She stretched her aching back, and in the distance saw Alasdair coming her way. She smiled, even though he was too far away to see, and waved. Sometimes she wondered if her excitement every time she caught sight of her husband was seemly. And then reminded herself that even if it wasn't, she didn't care.

Alasdair had been true to his word when he'd told her she was free to make her own rules and protocols once she was mistress of Dunochty. Of course, she ensured the castle was run as befit its grand status, but where other ladies might take to their exquisite embroidery, she spent her time in her gardens and apothecary, and working to earn the trust of the villagers.

She was glad she'd asked Alasdair about the castle the other day. The thought of trusted servants allowing his estate to fall into neglect had irked her greatly, but now the only thing that puzzled her was why Alasdair had only so recently acquired a property as befit his status as the recognized son of the previous earl.

'Twas different if the late earl had turned his back on him. But he was close to his half-brother, which indicated Alasdair had been part of the family. And both royalty and nobility were known for bestowing great honors upon their favored bastards.

Ah well. There were likely many reasons why he had only lately acquired the castle, and if he wanted to share them with her, he would. She pulled off her gloves as she stepped over a row of seedlings before opening the gate in the wall that separated her plants from the rest of the kitchen gardens.

"A pleasant surprise," she said as Alasdair took her hand. Although, judging by the expression on his face, he didn't look as though he found this unexpected visit nearly as pleasant.

"Freyja, mo leannan, I'm sorry, but we need to postpone our visit to Creagdoun."

Her happy thoughts fled. "What? Why, what's happened?" Fear gripped her. "Have ye heard from William? Is Isolde ill?"

"Yer sister is fine," he said hastily. "'Tis nothing of that nature. The earl sent word, and I must leave at once."

Bemused, she stared at him. "At once?" she echoed. "Ye mean now?"

Who left to start a long journey in the midafternoon?

"Aye. The earl is to be present at the Queen's confinement and will be leaving for Edinburgh soon, so there's no time to waste."

But we were going to visit Isolde in the morning.

She bit back the words, even though inside she burned with the injustice of needing to bend to the Earl of Argyll's will. On the Small Isles, they were still within his jurisdiction, but it was a nebulous thing. He didn't bother them, and they didn't bother him. As MacDonalds of Sgur, she and her sisters and grandmother had been beholden to no one.

Despite her best intentions, she couldn't stop herself. "I feel the earl should manage his time better. Why couldn't he give ye more notice? Suppose we'd already left for Creagdoun?"

"The earl's a busy man, Freyja. We'll arrange another time to visit yer sister when I return."

Aye, but that wasn't her point. It was also clear Alasdair didn't see her point, either.

"Ye're a busy man too, Alasdair. Don't forget that."

His sudden grin fairly took her breath away and, with it, a good degree of her resentment against the earl. How did he manage to do that, with just one smile?

"I am," he acknowledged. "But I'll always be there whenever the earl needs me. He's my half-brother, and I'll do anything for him. But there's something else, Freyja. I told ye before we wed that one day ye'd be the wife of a baron. And the earl is the only one who can grant me that honor."

"Does a barony mean that much to ye?"

A frown slashed his brow, as though he didn't understand her question. "'Tis security," he said. "No one spits in the face of a baron or his bairns. I'll make ye proud of me, if it's the last thing I do."

Bemused, she shook her head. "But I am proud of ye, Alasdair. Why would ye think I'm not?"

He pulled her close and kissed her, as though he never wanted to let her go. Lightning sparked through her, the way it always did when he touched her, and she moaned in protest when he finally released her.

"Hold onto that while I'm gone," he said, and she wasn't sure whether he meant the kiss or the fact she was proud of him. In the end it didn't matter, since she had no intention of forgetting either. "I'll return to ye within ten days."

Chapter Twenty-Two

Four days after leaving Dunochty, Alasdair arrived at Castle Campbell, and after he and the two men who'd accompanied him dismounted, they were taken to the earl, who was on his archery range. Alasdair had no doubt about the reason why he'd been summoned.

To formally hand over Ranulph's bequest of Kilvenie Tower.

He narrowed his eyes against the glint of the sun. Good God, was that William who was with him? He was pleased to see his friend but was reluctant to discuss the reason why he'd first gone to Rum in front of him.

William, after all, was married to Freyja's sister, and even though marriages were arranged all the time—including William's own—Alasdair would far rather keep the details surrounding his own marriage to himself.

The earl spoke to William, who remained where he was, before Archibald strode across the grass and greeted him warmly, grasping his shoulder. "Welcome, and well done, Alasdair. I knew ye wouldn't let me down."

Thank God his men weren't within hearing distance. He pulled out the document Miles had given him and handed it to the earl. "Kilvenie Tower is now in Campbell hands."

The cursed guilt crawled up from the depths of his soul. Damn it. He thought he'd managed to suppress that for good.

"Excellent," the earl said as he ran a critical eye over the parchment. "I want a full report. How did ye find the men of

Kilvenie? Will there be trouble?"

The stronghold might no longer belong to Freyja, but he was determined to do all he could to keep Kilvenie managed in the way she would have herself. And the earl had just opened the perfect opportunity for him to present his suggestion.

"The men are loyal, and the stronghold is well maintained and protected. I foresee no problems if my lord sees fit to allow the current steward to continue his duties. He knows Kilvenie and the people of Rum respect him."

"Wouldn't that be an issue?"

"Miles will do whatever is best for Kilvenie, and for Lady Freyja. He won't allow any bloodshed in her name."

The earl was silent, clearly contemplating the best strategy. Alasdair had often witnessed him doing this, when considering the best path forward. At length, his half-brother turned to him.

"Yer plan has merit. We don't want unnecessary resentment on the Isles. I'm willing to keep the current steward of Kilvenie, based on yer recommendation. And I appoint ye as custodian of Kilvenie, in my name. I'll have the document prepared for ye before ye leave."

He hadn't expected that. With this additional honor, it would be far easier to ensure Freyja's wishes concerning the stronghold were upheld. "Thank ye. I'll ensure it prospers."

"I've never had cause to doubt yer loyalty. Ye've more than earned this over the last few years. Ye're now the master of three fine estates, as befits yer status."

It was only then it struck him. Three estates. Another step closer to his fiercely guarded dream of a barony.

He bowed his head in acknowledgement, and the earl once again grasped his arm. "Go speak with William. I've a meeting to attend, but I'll be back shortly."

The earl marched off in the direction of his castle and Alasdair joined William.

"I didn't know ye'd be here," William greeted him. "We should have brought our lady wives. It would've saved me an earful of reproach from Isolde before I left Creagdoun, and that's a fact."

"Freyja wasn't happy we cancelled our plans." But she hadn't reproached him. He suspected Lady Isolde hadn't genuinely reproached William, either, since his friend was grinning at him. "But she understands my loyalty to the earl."

"Aye, she'd have to."

What in hellfire did William mean by that?

"What am I missing?" he said.

William shook his head in mock despair. "Nothing, Alasdair. Keep yer hair on, man. 'Tis not intended as a stain on yer character. I'm here too, aren't I? The earl is visiting the Queen shortly and wanted an update on Creagdoun's defenses before he left. Besides, our lady wives have already made plans to see each other later in the summer. And don't forget Lady Helga and Lady Roisin are visiting us in the autumn."

Still stinging from William's barb, although he couldn't quite figure out why when he'd never made a secret of his loyalty towards his half-brother, Alasdair was goaded to respond.

"I'll speak to Freyja. She may wish for Lady Helga and Lady Roisin to spend time at Dunochty first before traveling onto Creagdoun."

He recalled Lady Helga's enigmatic remarks the first time he'd met her. When she'd spoken of ambition and how it could blind one. He still wasn't certain what she'd meant. But of one thing he was sure: When she saw Dunochty, she'd know that when it came to his own ambition, he'd ensure it was always of benefit to Freyja.

William shrugged, apparently supremely unconcerned by the possible change of plans. "If Isolde is agreeable, then so am I. I'm certain she'll understand."

And what did he mean by that? Goddamn it, why was he second guessing every word that came out of William's mouth?

"God's blood," William suddenly said and grasped his arm. "With all the communication between us through our lady wives recently I'd forgotten I've not offered my congratulations on yer marriage. So, congratulations, man. How does wedded bliss find ye?"

Thankful for the change of subject, Alasdair grinned at his friend. "It finds me well. Lady Freyja is more than I ever hoped I might find in a bride."

"Spoken like a man who is truly enthralled by his wife."

Alasdair continued grinning like a fool, until he realized William was smirking. His smile faded and doubt gnawed through him.

While he admitted to himself that his bride enthralled him, it wasn't something he needed the world to know. Or even his closest friends. A man simply didn't allow a woman that kind of power over him.

It wasn't the way the world worked.

Yet William didn't appear to care who knew how much he adored his wife, and it had nothing to do with her status as a MacDonald of Sgur.

He grunted and squinted into the distance. The sooner this line of conversation moved on, the better. Unfortunately, he couldn't think of anything to say since Freyja's mocking laugh filled his head, as though, even within the sanctity of his own damn mind, she found his disconcertment entertaining.

William, however, didn't take the hint. "What?" his friend said, sounding irksomely amused.

He didn't want to discuss it. Except a stubborn part of him did. He glowered at the other man. "A man should not be so captivated by his own wife."

William's eyes narrowed, all hint of mirth gone. A heavy silence fell between them which he had no idea how to break, and then his friend's menacing frown faded. "Ah." William folded his arms. "Ye're speaking of yerself."

Of course he was speaking of himself. "Forget I said anything."

"Easily done, since ye are talking shit."

"Marriage," Alasdair said, before he could stop himself, "isn't how I thought it would be. But then, I never expected to wed a noblewoman such as Freyja."

"I always believed marriage would be nothing but a duty to endure. Ye know how I felt about it, until I met Isolde." William inhaled a deep breath, and Alasdair gave a brief nod of agreement. William had been lukewarm at best about his arranged alliance with a daughter of Sgur.

And then he'd quite literally fallen at her feet.

"I do," he acknowledged, when it appeared William was waiting for a response.

"If ye care for Lady Freyja even half as much as I care for my Isolde, then ye're a lucky man. And don't let anyone convince ye otherwise."

He wasn't concerned about that. He knew he was damn lucky to have Freyja. But despite his noble bloodline, he hadn't been raised in that world, and she had.

Since moving to Dunochty, he'd shared her bedchamber, and she hadn't remarked on it. But did she secretly wish he'd use his own? Yet surely she would have told him, if that was how she felt. She wasn't the kind of woman to keep such things to herself.

But the disquiet gnawed, all the same. He didn't want them to ever use separate bedchambers, never mind reside in separate establishments. Yet that wasn't an uncommon arrangement among nobles. Just because their current sleeping arrangements suited him didn't mean a thing. What if the servants treated Freyja with less respect than she deserved, simply because they perceived him to be lacking because of his upbringing? What if Freyja herself thought that?

"I've no wish to lead separate lives, but Freyja is of noble blood, and what if that's something she expects?"

As though pulled by an invisible thread, he glanced over his shoulder, where the castle could be seen beyond the orchard.

"Alasdair." William's low voice pulled him back to the present. "Ye and Lady Freyja must make yer own life as ye see fit.

Don't look at the earl's situation in this matter. Lady Jean is the Queen's half-sister, and the royals do everything differently. Besides, the earl is always happier when he's away from his wife, but that's not the life I want. Do ye?"

He conceded it was not, and a weight lifted from his shoulders. He'd been so fixated on his half-brother's marital arrangements, not to mention the strained relationship between his mother and stepfather, he'd not looked further.

But William's own father, a baron no less, had always been most attentive to his late lady wife, and Alasdair couldn't recall any times when the baron and his lady had lived apart. And it was the same with Hugh's parents.

He released a long breath. There was no need to mull over nonexistent concerns. If Freyja was unhappy with any arrangements, she'd let him know. Of that he was absolutely certain.

But thinking of Hugh's parents reminded him of something.

"Have ye heard from Hugh lately? I sent him a message from Rum, to let him know of my marriage, but didn't hear back." Something occurred to him. "'Tis always possible his father forgot to pass the message onto him." Hugh's father, alas, grew frailer by the year.

William frowned. "Now ye mention it, I haven't heard from him in weeks. I can't even recall the last time I saw him."

"I spoke to him a few days before I left for Rum. He was on his way to speak to the earl." Damn, he hoped to God the earl had nothing to do with Hugh's apparent disappearance.

"I'll visit his father on my way home," William said. "'Tis strange, though. Hugh doesn't usually go for so long without word." His gaze shifted to over Alasdair's shoulder. "The earl returns."

Alasdair swung about. The earl was strolling their way, accompanied by a man in long, dark robes. When they were still some distance away, the earl raised his hand, and the other man halted while Archibald continued on his way.

"An interesting meeting," he said when he reached them. "Do

either of ye have need of a physician? I can vouch for Seoc Erskine's bloodline but have no knowledge as to his medical expertise."

Alasdair already knew the answer to that question. There was no way he'd subject Freyja to another patronizing old bastard.

"We appointed a physician some months ago," William said. "Good God, the man doesn't appear old enough to be qualified. I thought all physicians had one foot in the grave."

Alasdair frowned and took another look at the stranger. William was right. Seoc Erskine looked scarcely ten years older than the three of them.

The earl laughed. "Aye, he's fresh out of that fancy college in London. Lord only knows what new ideas he has. I'll take him with me to Edinburgh when I leave in the morning. If nothing else, he can make some good contacts."

"I'll speak with him." Freyja had spoken of the royal college with barely concealed longing. If Seoc Erskine wasn't a pompous turd, then maybe he'd invite the man back to Dunochty so Freyja could question him. He was certain she'd enjoy that.

He made his way over to Erskine, who offered him a friendly smile. Goddamn, he didn't think physicians had it in them to smile. Then again, he'd never encountered one as young as Erskine, or one who'd attended the royal college.

"Alasdair Campbell," he said by way of introduction. "I hear ye went to the royal college."

"Aye, and I'm eager to put what I've learned to good use."

There was one sure way to discover if Erskine was as forward thinking as Freyja. "Tell me, what are ye thoughts on the medicinal use of the poppy?"

"'Tis a remarkable plant. I confess I'm fascinated by its properties, but with respect, I'm surprised that ye mention it. 'Tis not in common usage, although it used to be widely available."

"Some physicians refer to it as the devil's work."

Erskine made a dismissive gesture with his hand. "Forgive me for being blunt, but that's an old-fashioned outlook. I want only the best for my patients, and I consider all remedies on their merit."

He had the feeling Freyja would get on well with Erskine. But he wouldn't offer the man a position unless she gave her approval. He'd have no man disrespect her the way Lamont had.

And now for the final test. "My lady wife is a skilled healer. What are ye thoughts on that?"

"Nothing less than admiration. Indeed, my own wife shares my love for diagnosing medical ailments."

"A happy state of affairs." And he wasn't just referring to Erskine's obvious pleasure that his wife shared his enthusiasm for his profession. It was the remarkable good luck that the physician had been at Castle Campbell today, so their paths had crossed. "If ye're willing, I should like to invite ye to Dunochty Castle to meet my lady wife. And I must warn ye, she'll not agree with anything ye say if she believes ye're wrong. Just so ye know."

"I shouldn't wish her to. My wife questions everything, and I long ago discovered that is the only way to learn. There's so much we don't yet know, but I'm confident in time we'll unlock all the mysteries of the body."

He laughed. Damn, the man reminded him of Freyja's passion when she spoke of her beloved calling. "My lady wife is the same. She speaks of an astonishing book that reveals what lies beneath the flesh. I cannot imagine such a thing."

"The Fabrica." There was a hushed note in Erskine's voice. "An astounding set of volumes, and that's God's own truth."

"Ye've seen these books?"

"Aye. At the college."

Ever since they had wed, he'd wanted to buy Freyja something that showed her how proud he was that she was his wife. But with moving to Dunochty, and the discovery of their low stocks, he hadn't found the time to search for the perfect gift.

He'd had a vague idea of a beautiful piece of jewelry. But while he was certain she'd be delighted by such a present, it wasn't who she was. Collecting priceless jewelry wasn't her passion.

Learning all she could about how the body functioned—now, that was her true passion. Freyja would be beside herself if he managed to acquire a copy of these elusive volumes that she had once, in breathless wonder, told him about.

Excitement surged through him. Until now, the idea hadn't occurred to him. And even if it had, he had no contacts in an establishment as prestigious as the Royal College of Physicians, where one might reasonably expect to hunt down such specialized books.

But now he had Seoc Erskine.

"Seoc," he said. "I need yer help."

It didn't matter how long it took or how much it cost to acquire the books. Because on the day he placed them in Freyja's hands, she'd know how much she meant to him.

Chapter Twenty-Three

True to his word, Alasdair arrived back home within ten days after he'd left. Freyja waited at the doors to the castle, ready to greet him, anticipation thudding through her. How she'd missed his smile and the sound of his voice, and the way her heart leaped in her chest whenever she caught sight of him at odd moments throughout the day.

The bed was far too large within him by her side.

Alasdair and his men rode into the courtyard, and he leaped from his horse and made his way to her. Heedless of decorum, she opened her arms and hugged him tight, and he clearly didn't give a fig for appearances either, since he lifted her from her feet and swung her around.

She laughed and smacked his arm as he carefully placed her on solid ground. "'Tis good to be home," he said.

"'Tis good to have ye home." And then she was distracted by the appearance of a wagon, and a couple standing some distance from them. The man was wearing a long, dark robe, and a thread of foreboding inched through her.

She knew of only one type of man who wore such robes. But surely Alasdair hadn't brought a physician here? Yet why wouldn't he? Dunochty and its estate was too prestigious not to have a physician, and her good mood evaporated as trepidation crawled through her like a poisoned fog.

But she knew her duty and so she fixed an enquiring smile on her face and inclined her head in the strangers' direction.

"Freyja, I've invited Seoc Erskine to meet ye. He's a physician who studied at that college in London." Excitement vibrated through every word, and her face started to ache from the effort of keeping a smile upon it. The truth was that his insensitivity hurt. He knew how little the medical profession regarded women in general and those who practiced the healing arts in particular.

Or did he? Maybe he'd forgotten Lamont's caustic remarks. A part of her hoped he had, since Lamont had been so derogatory towards her. But a tiny sliver, deep inside, grieved that Alasdair clearly considered Lamont's disregard for her of little consequence.

"Indeed," she said. She was the mistress of a grand castle, and she wouldn't let Alasdair down by betraying her true feelings.

"I've a notion ye'll be happily impressed," he said, as he led her over to Seoc Erskine. "But if ye're not, I shall send him and his wife on their way."

She shot him a sharp glance but there was no time to reply as Alasdair made the introductions, and Seoc Erskine and his wife said all the right things. To be sure, Seoc made no condescending remark, but then again, he didn't know she was a healer, yet.

"Ye've arrived just in time for dinner," she said. "I'll ensure extra places are laid for ye both."

"That's very kind, my lady," his wife, Jane, said. She looked a few years older than Freyja and had a quiet air of confidence about her, and when she crouched down to welcome Dubh, Freyja had the feeling she and Jane could easily become friends.

As they made their way into the castle, Seoc said, "My lady, forgive me for being so forward, but Alasdair tells me ye are a renowned healer. If circumstances permit, I should be honored if ye'd share yer wisdom with us."

Startled, she glanced at him, but he didn't appear to be mocking her. In fact, both he and his wife smiled at her in apparent admiration.

Well, Alasdair said she'd be happily impressed, but she was more taken aback than anything else. But if Seoc Erskine was genuinely interested in learning more about the ancient wisdom she had inherited from her foremothers, she expected something in return.

"I'd be happy to, if ye're willing to share insights ye learned from the royal college."

"Nothing would please me more." He sounded as though he meant it. If this was the type of man the royal college was producing, she was frankly staggered.

"There's nothing Seoc loves more than discussing the latest medical innovations." Jane gave her husband a fond glance as they entered the hall before looking back at Freyja. "I fear ye may have to be quite firm when ye want him to stop talking about it, my lady."

"I'm not easily offended," Seoc said. "I know I'm obsessed and thank God every day that I married a woman who shares my vision."

Freyja dragged her stunned gaze from Seoc to his wife. "Ye are also a healer?"

"I am, my lady. Alas, I couldn't enter the college, but with Seoc's tutelage I believe I could not have learned more even had I graced those hallowed halls."

There was a touch of wryness in her last words and Freyja flashed her a genuine smile. "I've always said there should be a college for women to attend."

"I couldn't agree more," Jane said. "Alas, I cannot see it ever happening, though."

"If the royal college is producing physicians such as yer husband, then I think there is hope for us yet."

"I hate to be the bearer of bad news, my lady, but I fear Seoc is one of a kind. His compatriots are generally quite rigid in their beliefs."

Ah well, she supposed that dream was too good to be true. She caught Sine's eye, who came over to her. "We have two guests, Sine. Please ensure the west chambers are made ready for them."

It wasn't until that night, when Freyja and Alasdair retired to their bedchamber, that they were finally alone to talk. She grabbed his hands and shook her head in mock disbelief.

"Alasdair Campbell, where on God's green earth did ye ever find such a pair? My head is still spinning from our conversations."

He gave her a smug grin, which she found utterly delightful.

"Does this mean ye're willing for Seoc to settle at Dunochty?"

"I am. And what's more, I'm enthralled with his wife. Ye are a very clever man, Alasdair."

"To be fair," he said, "Seoc was at Castle Campbell seeking recommendations. 'Twas only by the sheerest of good luck our paths crossed."

"How noble of ye not to remind me how I didn't wish ye to answer the earl's summons last week." She went onto her toes and gave him a teasing kiss. "I suppose 'tis only fair that I forgive the earl for disrupting our trip to see Isolde and William. Although I hope he doesn't make a habit of it."

"He wishes to meet ye when he returns from Edinburgh. After all, ye're his half-sister-by-marriage, now."

"Ooh," she said, unable to dredge up the enthusiasm Alasdair clearly expected by his comment. The Earl of Argyll, whoever he happened to be, wasn't, after all, universally admired on the Small Isles. "Lucky me."

He laughed at that and tugged her close. "Come here, wife. I'm the one who's lucky, and I'll never forget it."

She wound her arms around his neck, and her eyes drifted shut as he nibbled kisses along her throat. He often said how lucky he was that he'd found her, but she knew the truth: She was the lucky one. What were the chances that the only man she had ever wanted had come to Rum and somehow managed to gain her grandfather's deepest respect? A respect that had caused him to bind them together in a deathbed wish.

AND ALASDAIR HAD embraced it all, without a single word of reproach.

Aye, she was lucky indeed, and happier than she'd ever imagined she could be away from her beloved Sgur. Because she was with Alasdair.

The man I love.

IT HAD BEEN another long day of poring over the finances of Dunochty and ensuring the estate continued to prosper. Even when Alasdair's stepfather was still alive, the task of bookkeeping had fallen to him, although he'd not been privy to the actual disbursement of the manor's small income until two years ago, and he was thankful for the grounding it had given him.

He leaned back in the chair and rolled his shoulders as his gaze roved around the private chamber where he undertook the business of running the castle. A cabinet was along one wall, and hanging next to it was the portrait of a woman in profile. He had no idea who she was, but the likelihood she was a Campbell ancestor of his on his father's side was high.

There were several portraits scattered throughout the castle, another visible aspect of the prestige of Dunochty. But this particular one, for a reason he couldn't fathom, irked him.

She seemed to be watching him.

Damn it, what was wrong with him? He was the laird of the castle. He could move the painting somewhere else. And then an idea struck him: He'd commission Freyja's portrait, and hang it in here, where he could feast his eyes upon her likeness whenever he pleased.

He grinned at the prospect. How would she react to the notion? He had no idea, but he was determined to persuade her.

There was still some time before supper, and he decided to go for a ride. It would clear his head and stretch his cramped limbs.

As he left the castle and strolled across the forecourt on his way to the stables, Seoc joined him. The physician had only arrived two weeks ago, and yet he'd settled into the fabric of their life so well, it seemed he'd always been around.

"Do ye have time for a ride?" Alasdair asked. If anyone had told him a month ago that he'd one day consider a physician a friend, he would've laughed at them. Yet here he was. But more than that, Freyja was happy with him, and as an additional bonus she and Jane had become close over their mutual love of the healing arts.

"That would be a godsend." Seoc exhaled a long sigh. "Jane is forever telling me I need more fresh air."

Alasdair laughed. He'd never met a man of learning before who spoke so easily and with such affection about his wife. Seoc didn't appear to care if other men found his devotion unusual.

William didn't, either. And with every day that passed, Alasdair's secret fear that his father's disregard would somehow cause an insurmountable gulf between himself and Freyja faded a little more.

Even though she'd never mentioned it, he'd convinced himself that in her eyes, he was worthy of her because of his father's bloodline. She'd met his mother, but she didn't need to know the grim reality of his childhood or how hard he'd fought to gain Archibald's trust.

That was in the past. All he cared about was the future he and Freyja would share, and God willing, any bairns they might have.

He'd never believed it possible to be so content, nor filled with such pride whenever Freyja smiled at him or made one of her blunt remarks. He knew she'd been reluctant to leave Sgur, but she'd made her home at Dunochty, and now her gardens were planted and Jane had arrived, an air of happiness surrounded her.

He couldn't imagine life without her brightening every moment of his existence.

For the first time in his life, a thread of sorrow at his half-brother's life flickered through him. Archibald, the trueborn son of the late earl, who had received every honor his status demanded from the moment of his birth, and the respect of all of Argyll because of his bloodline. But one thing Archibald had never found was the kind of delight in his own marriage that Alasdair had with Freyja.

Seoc grasped his shoulder. "I almost forgot. I had a letter today from my colleague at the royal college. He has a contact and is hopeful of acquiring a copy of The Fabrica. But it will likely cost a little more than I anticipated."

"That's grand news. And I'll pay whatever the cost is." The price, however steep, was negligible when he imagined how thrilled she'd be when she unwrapped the mighty tomes.

"Alasdair." One of the men who had joined him after arriving at Oban hailed him, and Alasdair swung on his heel and went to meet him.

"What is it, man?"

"Visitors at the gate. Colban MacDonald of Tarnford Castle on the Isle of Islay and his cousin Peter MacDonald. They say they're friends of Lady Freyja."

Where had he heard the name Colban MacDonald before? He was certain Freyja had never mentioned the man to him. And then he remembered. William had spoken of him in passing, and although Alasdair didn't know what had transpired between the two men, it was obvious William thought little of him.

But they were from the Small Isles and knew Freyja. It was unthinkable that he should turn them away, despite the late hour they'd arrived. "Let them enter," he said. "I'll find Lady Freyja."

His ride would need to wait until the morning.

Chapter Twenty-Four

Freyja had the feeling she should be more enthusiastic about the visit of Colban and his cousin. They were a link to home, but the truth was Colban just made her uncomfortable. She couldn't forget the way he'd looked at her the last time she'd seen him on Eigg, when he'd asked her to accompany him to visit her grandfather.

Or the quickly masked flash of anger when she'd refused.

Well, if her sisters and Amma were right and he *had* ever harbored the wish to wed her, that was all in the past now. Maybe she was being unfair to him, and the only reason he'd come to Dunochty was to extend his best wishes upon her marriage.

Aye, she wanted to believe it. Why was it so hard to convince herself?

A few minutes ago, Alasdair had found her in her gardens, and now they were in the great hall as Colban and Peter made their way towards them. She fixed a welcoming smile on her face, since as the mistress of the castle that was expected of her, but all she could think was they'd left it so late to visit that she'd have to offer them hospitality for the night.

After the greetings and introductions to Alasdair were done, Colban once again took her hand. His presumption irked her more than it should, and she feared her smile dripped icicles.

Not that he noticed. "Lady Freyja, may I say ye look radiant. Marriage clearly agrees with ye."

Was that his idea of a compliment? She had the enticing urge to tell him it wasn't marriage that made her radiant. It was the fact Alasdair was her husband.

She suspected Colban wouldn't appreciate the differentiation. But since an answer was expected, she said, "Thank ye, Colban. Ye are looking well yerself."

"'Tis kind of ye to say so." He nodded somewhat sagely. And still didn't relinquish her hand.

"Well," she said, while her fingers itched to slap his hand. "Ye and Peter must certainly stay for supper. 'Tis all but ready to be served, and we should be happy to have ye."

"We should be honored," Colban said.

With more force than she intended, she pulled her hand free, and then to cover up her lack of etiquette, she turned and gave Alasdair a bright smile. "What a delightful surprise this is, to be sure."

The expression on Alasdair's face suggested he was bemused by her behavior, so she focused on Peter, who so far had barely said a word. "I trust ye and Colban will stay the night?"

"If it's not too much trouble, my lady." Peter inclined his head.

"Not at all." She glanced at Morag, who gave a discreet nod at her unspoken message to pass the news onto Sine before she returned her attention to Colban. "Now ye must tell me all the news from the Isles."

USUALLY FREYJA ENJOYED suppertime, when she and Alasdair would share details of their day with each other, and since Jane and Seoc often joined them, it was a lively discussion.

But tonight, she couldn't shift the uneasy suspicion that beneath his charming manners and benign smile, Colban was raging. Which was really quite absurd. It wasn't as though he'd ever asked for her hand and she'd refused him, which would at least give him cause to be offended.

For all she knew, that notion had never crossed his mind, and she was letting her sisters—and especially Roisin's—opinions affect her good sense.

She squashed her misgivings and gave him her most engaging smile. "Tell me, Colban, have ye been in the Highlands ever since we last saw each other at Sgur?"

She couldn't imagine why he'd spend so long away from his castle on Islay. It had been weeks ago that they'd last spoken.

"I haven't," he said. "I stayed with Peter for a week before returning home, when I learned of the sad news about Ranulph. Allow me to offer ye my condolences, Lady Freyja."

"Thank ye. I miss him greatly."

Colban nodded before looking at Alasdair. "'Tis a fine castle ye have here, Alasdair."

"Aye. Dunochty has been in the Earl of Argyll's family for over two hundred years."

"A noble bloodline," Peter remarked.

Freyja picked up her goblet and took a sip of wine. The conversation was all very civilized. Why, then, couldn't she shift this troubling sense of foreboding?

LATER THAT NIGHT, as the sun sank beyond the western horizon, Freyja and Alasdair strolled from the courtyard to the stables as Dubh chased shadows, and a solitary owl hooted in the distance. Alasdair tugged her close, and she leaned her head against him as his familiar scent of worn leather and wild woodlands wrapped around her like a sensual caress.

"I was led to believe ye were a friend of Colban MacDonald. That's how he got through the gate."

She sighed. She knew she hadn't managed to hide her conflicted feelings from Alasdair.

"We are old family friends. I've known him all my life." Should she tell him of her sisters' suspicions? It seemed unfair when there was no evidence to support it, especially since Alasdair might not take kindly to the notion.

"I know ye, Freyja, and there were things ye wanted to say but held back. That's not like ye."

She laughed and patted his chest. "Ye know me that well, do ye? Well, I'll tell ye this. I'm trying to curb my impulsive nature, now that I'm mistress of such a grand castle. I should be grieved if my unwary tongue ever embarrassed ye."

"There's nothing ye could say that would embarrass me." He sounded amused by the idea. "But my comment stands. Ye've known Colban all yer life and yet something feels amiss. If the man's done anything to upset ye, let me know and I'll throw him out of the castle myself."

She shook her head, inordinately delighted that Alasdair did, indeed, know her so well. "'Tis nothing, Alasdair, truly. Colban has only ever been a friend, and although I confess I sometimes found his comments irksome, I don't believe he meant any harm."

"That's generous. I believe if ye found my comments irksome, ye'd waste no time in telling me so."

"But of course. Ye're Alasdair Campbell. I care what *ye* think of me." She kept her voice light, so he might think she was jesting. But she wasn't. She cared deeply what he thought of her. And ever since she'd faced the fact, two weeks ago, that she had fallen irrevocably in love with her own husband, one question had gnawed incessantly in the back of her mind.

Does he love me?

"Huh. I'm not certain I follow yer thoughts here, but since it appears ye're looking upon me in a favorable light, I shall let it pass."

"A wise decision."

"The wisest decision I ever made was in wedding ye."

Warmth curled around her heart, and she wound her arm around him. "Then we are in perfect accord. How did Afi know we would be so right for each other?"

His arm tightened around her, but he didn't answer straight away, and she stifled a sigh. Alasdair was truly everything she'd never known she wanted in a man, and she couldn't imagine life without him. But although he was most attentive and often asked her if she had everything she required for her comfort, it didn't necessarily follow that he felt the same way about her as she did about him.

She should change the subject. They were married, and at the end of the day it made no difference to their situation if Alasdair thought they were perfect for each other or not. Why was she so hung up on that? Did she really want to force the issue and risk him telling her something she didn't want to hear?

A sane woman would leave it well alone. It was the advice she would've given if asked. At least, it was before she'd fallen for Alasdair.

'Twas no good. If she didn't press him for an answer, she'd end up stewing about it. He was certainly right that when something was on her mind, she generally had to say it out loud.

Ah well. She'd always lived by the maxim that it was better to know the unvarnished truth than a pretty lie.

"Do ye think we are right for each other, Alasdair?"

"How can ye ask me such a thing? Ye're the only woman I've ever wanted for my wife."

It was a good answer. She smiled as twilight spread across the land, but her incessant need for clarity wouldn't be appeased. "And if Afi hadn't blindsided us both with his wish for us to wed, ye're certain ye would still have asked for my hand?"

"I've told ye already. Ye spellbound me from the moment I saw ye in the stables. What is this about, Freyja? Do ye doubt how deeply I admire and respect ye?"

A strange little pain squeezed her heart. She knew he admired and respected her, and that was not a small thing. It was enough to build a strong marriage upon.

But how she longed for more. How she longed for him to say *I love ye.*

She tipped back her head and he captured her lips in a kiss that seared her to her very soul. When he pulled back, his hot breath dusted her cheeks, and he traced a calloused fingertip along her jaw.

"Do ye?" His voice was raw with passion and a shiver of pleasure raced through her.

"No," she whispered. "I don't doubt it, Alasdair."

"I'd do anything to make ye happy."

"I am happy," she assured him, and it was the truth. If his precious earl himself appeared from the shadows and offered her the chance to return to Sgur, she'd turn him down. She knew where she wanted to be, and it was by Alasdair's side.

Chapter Twenty-Five

"I CANNOT WAIT until I see Isolde again."

Alasdair, propped up in bed against a pile of pillows, watched as his wife picked up Dubh to give him a kiss before she pulled on her gown and flashed him a smile over her shoulder.

Lust coiled through him, despite their early morning bed sport, but it was more than lust and he knew it. He'd always known it; from the first time he'd kissed her when they'd stood in the cove on Rum.

Five days ago, when she'd asked him how her grandfather had known they were so right for each other, he hadn't known how to respond. Had Ranulph known it? To be sure, in the letter her grandfather had written him, he had stated he could see how Alasdair cared for her. But he couldn't dislodge the certainty that Ranulph had forced the issue because he hadn't seen any other choice for Freyja.

The notion prickled like thorns under his skin. He hoped, somehow, Ranulph could see his granddaughter was content in her new life. And then she'd asked him outright if he thought they were right for each other, and the words he desperately wanted to say to her had stuck in his throat.

Aye, she'd seemed happy enough when he'd told her she was the only woman he ever wanted for his wife. But they were just superficial words, that didn't convey even an inkling of how vital she was to his very existence.

He doubted he'd ever be able to find those words. They likely didn't even exist.

"Three weeks isn't long," he reminded her. It was enlightening how complicated arranging a trip was, now he and William were both married and had substantial estates to manage. But the date was set, and nothing would stand in its way.

"That is true," she conceded. "I'll endeavor to be patient."

He laughed and flung back the bedcovers. Her gaze drifted to his erection with unbridled interest, and he groaned. "If ye continue to look at me so, I won't be responsible for my actions."

"Do ye see me trembling in my boots at such a threat?"

"It wasn't a threat. 'Twas a promise."

"Even better."

He shook his head in mock despair. "Ye'll be the death of me, woman. Half the morning has gone already."

She sighed dramatically. "Aye. And as tempting as ye are, Alasdair Campbell, my little lad needs to relieve himself. So we shall both need to wait until this night."

With that, she flung a shawl around her shoulders, blew him a mocking kiss, and left the chamber.

He shook his head and, still grinning, strolled to his chest that stood against the wall and pulled out a clean shirt. If he had his way, they'd spend all day in bed. And nothing else would get done.

He finished adjusting his plaid and then paused, eyeing the leather pouch that hung from his belt and contained the letter from Ranulph. A foolish sense of guilt had compelled him to keep the letter close, but it was time to accept that no matter why he had first traveled to Rum, the most important thing was, however it had happened, Freyja was his wife. The letter was not a burden for him to bear. It belonged with the document Archibald had given him regarding Kilvenie Tower, in the strongbox he kept in the chamber where he oversaw the running of the estate.

He would do that later today. And to prove he was no longer bound by his misplaced guilt, he untied the pouch from his belt and placed it in the chest with his shirts before closing the lid and leaving the chamber to start the day's work.

THEY HAD JUST finished dinner, and Alasdair was leaving the hall with Freyja. She wanted to show him how well her gardens were flourishing in their new Highland home, and he was more than happy to oblige. Not just because a laird should be aware of such things, but because he enjoyed listening to her when she told him of the frankly magical properties some of her plants possessed.

Instead of going through the kitchens to the gardens, they left by the main doors so he could check on the horses first, but the sound of a rider approaching distracted him.

As the rider dismounted some distance from them, his heart sank. Christ, no. He recognized the man as one of the earl's most trusted messengers. He hoped to God Archibald wasn't sending for him.

Since there was no help for it, he greeted the man, who dipped his head in a respectful response. "I bring word from the Earl of Argyll."

Alasdair took the sealed letter and glanced at Freyja. She had a fixed smile on her face, but he wasn't fooled. She knew, as well as he did, that the chances were high the earl demanded his immediate presence.

He broke the seal and scanned the contents of the letter. As he'd suspected, the earl wanted him to leave Dunochty without delay and meet him at Edinburgh Castle, where he was still with the Queen after her safe delivery of a healthy son.

He took that in with barely a glance. But his eyes snagged on the final, intriguing line.

Old Iomhar of Glenchonnel has finally died and we must discuss a matter which I am certain ye'll find to yer advantage.

His flare of resentment against the earl vanished as fierce anticipation surged through him. Iomhar Campbell, Baron of Glenchonnel, had no heir. What matter of importance could the earl wish to discuss so urgently, if it wasn't connected to the transfer of the barony?

"I'm instructed to wait and accompany ye back to Edinburgh," the messenger said.

"Ye must be famished," Freyja said before he could respond. "Go to the kitchens, and ye'll be served a hearty dinner."

"Thank ye, milady." The man bowed before handing his horse to a stable lad and making his way to the castle.

Alasdair turned to Freyja, who folded her arms. "Edinburgh? Ye'll be gone for weeks."

"I could be back in three weeks. There's no need to cancel our journey to Creagdoun."

"Aye, but ye cannot spend three weeks in Edinburgh and then another two weeks away from Dunochty. I believe the earl needs reminding that ye're a married man now with a grand estate to manage and cannot drop everything at a moment's notice when the fancy strikes him."

He had the alarming notion that Freyja wouldn't hesitate to tell the earl that in no uncertain terms when they met.

"Freyja, ye must understand we are all of us beholden to the earl. But that's not the main reason why he has my loyalty. He's my half-brother and he was there for me when he didn't need to be."

She eyed him, clearly not understanding what he meant, and why should she? He had no idea why he'd almost told her of that time in the back streets of Oban, when Archibald had saved him from a thrashing. The last thing he wanted was to risk seeing pity in her eyes when she discovered the truth of his childhood. When she realized his father had never acknowledged him, and his bloodline had meant less than nothing until Archibald had formally recognized their kinship four years ago.

She exhaled an exasperated sigh. "Very well. I know he is yer half-brother, and I know ye are close. But I'm allowed to be irked by his high-handed demands, and I am."

"I understand, Freyja. But listen, there's—"

"Aye, I know." She rolled her eyes, and he cocked his head,

since there was no possibility she could know what he was about to tell her. "The last time ye heeded his summons, ye came home with Seoc and Jane, and I'm grudgingly grateful to the earl for that. But the fact remains, our visit to Isolde and William must once again be postponed."

Momentarily distracted by what he needed to tell her, he shook his head. "Not necessarily. I'll speak to Raso before I leave, and we'll work something out. I'll send a messenger once I arrive in Edinburgh, to let ye know how things are."

"I could always go by myself."

They'd had this conversation before, the last time he'd been summoned by the earl, and his answer hadn't changed. "No. I'll not let ye travel the countryside unprotected."

"Without ye by my side, ye mean. I'd hardly be unprotected, Alasdair."

It was what he meant, and he acknowledged she wouldn't be unprotected even if he wasn't by her side. Clyde would ensure half a dozen warriors accompanied her, but none of them could possibly protect her the way he could, and that was the end of it.

"If ye'd let me finish what I must say, Freyja, the earl wishes to discuss the barony of Glenchonnel. This could be what we've been waiting for, mo leannan. All being well, ye might soon be the Baroness of Glenchonnel."

She deserved nothing less. He just hadn't expected the opportunity would arise so soon.

Freyja, however, appeared supremely unimpressed by the possibility.

"I've no ambition to be a baroness, Alasdair, but if it's what ye want then I hope the earl delivers. I'll send word to Isolde today to let her know—" She cut herself short and a thoughtful frown creased her brow. "Wait. I could invite her and William here. Our stores are growing nicely, and ye won't need to concern yerself about rushing back, should the earl decide to keep ye at Edinburgh for longer than a day or so."

"That's a grand idea." Why hadn't he thought of it himself?

When he'd first brought Freyja to Dunochty, he'd wanted William and Isolde to visit, so he could show her sister that he was able to provide for Freyja in the manner she deserved. But as the weeks passed, the need to prove himself to her family had faded, without him even realizing it.

His wife was happy, here with him, and that was the only thing that mattered.

"Aye," Freyja said. "I'm full of grand ideas, had ye not noticed?"

He laughed and pulled her close for a lingering kiss. "I had," he growled against her lips when he finally came up for air. "'Tis one of the many reasons why I wed ye. Now I must go to the stables. Are ye still coming?"

She sighed. "No, ye go and arrange yer journey, and I'll write the letter to Isolde. It won't take me long."

Freyja watched Alasdair saunter to the stables, and she stifled a sigh. The sunlight splashed across the courtyard, causing the intriguing streaks of auburn in his hair to glint, and without quite meaning to, she roved her gaze over his broad shoulders and lingered on his mighty biceps.

Blessed Eir, she was still as obsessed with him after weeks of marriage as she'd been on the day they'd first met. Moreso, if she was being truthful. And she dearly wanted to let him know. But how did one go about saying such a thing?

She was practical to her core, and had never indulged in romantic tales the way Roisin did. If she had, maybe she'd have a clue about what to say to him. But practical or not, she didn't relish laying her heart bare when she wasn't certain Alasdair felt the same way about her.

When Isolde arrived, she'd ask her advice. After all, her sister hadn't been best pleased about her obligation to wed William, and yet within weeks Isolde and William had irrevocably fallen in love, and everyone knew it.

Alasdair had now vanished from sight and a pang arrowed through her. She shook her head in amused mockery at the notion she could miss him already, before he'd even left the castle. Sometimes, she didn't even recognize herself as the woman she'd been before he'd arrived in her life.

Still smiling at her foolishness, she returned to the castle with Dubh at her heels and made her way to their bedchamber where she kept her ink and paper. As she opened the door, a flash of white linen snagged in Alasdair's wooden chest caught her eye, and she made her way over to it. He was always shutting the lid without first checking his sleeves weren't dangling out and she found the habit ridiculously endearing, even though she pretended to scold him about it.

She lifted the lid and moved a leather pouch aside so she could refold his shirt. Dubh stood on his hind legs and peered into the chest, panting with excitement, and she laughed.

"What are ye doing, ye daft lad?"

For answer, Dubh grabbed the leather pouch in his mouth and darted across the chamber, and her indulgent smile vanished. "Ye bad lad, bring that back here this instant."

Dubh ignored her and to her horror, he not only growled deep in his throat, but he tossed his head as he ripped into the leather as though it was a tasty treat.

She dashed after him and grasped the end of the pouch, but he still didn't relinquish his prize, and she glared at him in disbelief. "What in the name of all the gods is the matter with ye, Dubh?"

With an ominous ripping sound, the leather split open and Dubh gave a gleeful little whine as he nosed the contents. Utterly mortified by his behavior, she firmly pushed him away. "I'm ashamed of ye," she told him. "Look what ye've done."

To be sure, she could mend the leather so it was once again usable, but that wasn't the point. Dubh wasn't a naughty dog. She couldn't fathom what had possessed him.

Gingerly, she opened the rip and pulled out the letter it contained. The seal was broken but there was no mistaking that it was Ranulph MacDonald's crest, and incomprehension twisted through her. She turned it over, but there was no name on the front. Had Afi written this letter to Alasdair? Or had he intended it for her? No, that couldn't be so. Alasdair wouldn't have opened it if that were the case.

With the pouch in one hand and the letter in the other, she stood up and made her way to the bed. And couldn't stop a desolate question from reverberating around her head: Why would Afi write to Alasdair, and not to her?

She sat on the edge of the bed and indecision clawed through her as she stared at the half-unfolded letter clutched in her hand. If it had been meant for her, Alasdair would have given it to her. There was no doubt in her mind. But it didn't stop the unease that gnawed through her heart at the realization that he hadn't shared its contents with her. What could Afi have possibly written to Alasdair that her husband hadn't believed worth sharing with her?

The compulsion to read it burned through her. But she wouldn't. She'd ask Alasdair about it before he left for Edinburgh, and there was doubtless a simple explanation as to why he hadn't even mentioned its existence to her.

Decision made, she expelled a long breath just as Dubh, sitting beside her, pawed at the letter and she caught sight of the first few lines written in Miles' hand. And despite her good intentions, she could not drag her gaze away.

> Alasdair,
>
> *No doubt ye are curious as to why I changed my mind and now bless yer marriage with my beloved lass, Freyja. I've watched ye with her and I see how ye care for her, perhaps more than ye realize yerself.*

The thread of guilt at reading something not meant for her eyes unraveled. This didn't make sense. To be sure, it was wonderful that Afi had seen how much Alasdair cared for her. But what did he mean that he had changed his mind about their marriage? They had never spoken of marriage until Afi had been on his deathbed. Maybe he had simply been confused when he dictated this letter to Miles. But if that was the case, Miles would have corrected him, she had no doubt.

She frowned and continued reading.

> *When ye came to Rum with the Earl of Argyll's proposition, I could not agree to it. I'd not see my sweet lass used as a pawn in men's games.*

She froze, the words dancing before her eyes as the implications spiked like lightning through her mind. No, she'd misunderstood. But reading it again, and three times, did not change its meaning.

The earl had sent Alasdair to Rum not merely to inquire after her grandfather's health. Alasdair had gone to Afi with a proposition that had involved her.

There was only one thing a man wanted with a woman he'd never met before, and that was an advantageous alliance.

Something fragile and precious cracked deep inside her breast, and a pain she'd never imagined could exist seeped from the wound like malignant tears.

The idea for her to marry Alasdair Campbell hadn't come from Afi. It had been hatched between the earl and his half-brother and was the only reason Alasdair had traveled to Rum.

He'd intended to trap her in matrimony before he'd even entered the stables where she'd been helping Ban with her puppies. From the moment they'd met, everything had been a lie.

How noble she'd thought him, when he hadn't fled after hearing Afi's deathbed wish that they should marry. She'd believed him the most honorable man alive when he'd been adamant that he wanted to wed her for herself, and not because of her grandfather's unexpected request.

She'd imagined him a man of high principles and rock-solid integrity.

How horribly, laughably, wrong she had been.

She slumped, clutching the letter in her lap as Dubh sat at her feet and pushed his snout into her hand. If only she'd left Alasdair's shirtsleeve alone. A maid would've tidied it away. And then she wouldn't have found the letter.

And instead, she'd continue to live a lie.

"Good lad," she whispered, and stroked him with one finger. He must've smelled Afi's scent on the letter, and that was why he'd gone a little mad and ripped open the leather. He whined and shuffled closer, but she could offer him no further comfort when her heart felt as torn open and exposed as the leather discarded on the floor.

What now? She couldn't pretend she hadn't read Afi's letter. She'd have to confront Alasdair, but the notion made her shrivel inside with shame. How could she ever look him in the eyes again, knowing how little he truly thought of her?

The door swung open, and Alasdair entered, a familiar smile on his face. A smile she'd grown so used to during these last few weeks yet seeing it now was like a sword plunged through her heart.

His gaze dropped to her lap, where she still clutched the letter. And his smile vanished.

Chapter Twenty-Six

*C*HRIST, NO.

Like a condemned man, Alasdair's gaze fixed on the letter Freyja held. She knew the earl had sent him to Rum to wed her.

The air grew heavy and it was hard to breathe, but maybe that was simply the guilt he carried inside eating him alive. She didn't speak, didn't accuse him of anything, but she didn't have to.

The pain in her beautiful blue eyes told him everything.

He released a harsh breath and took another step closer. Once he explained how he'd wanted her from the moment he'd met her, she'd understand. God, surely she would understand.

She straightened her shoulders, and her gaze turned glacial, halting him in his tracks.

"Freyja." His voice was hoarse. "Ye found Ranulph's letter."

What the hell was he saying? He sounded as though he accused her of something. But the truth was far worse. Because he, who had spent all his life saying the right things at the right time, didn't have the first idea what to tell her to make this horror disappear.

"I wasn't spying, Alasdair." Ice coated every word. "Yer leather pouch tore and I intended to mend it."

"I know ye weren't spying." And now he sounded affronted when all he wanted was to find the words to convince her that the letter she had just read wasn't the full truth. "Freyja, listen to me. This isn't what ye think."

She smoothed the crumpled letter on her lap with slow, deliberate strokes, and somehow that was far worse than if she'd spat venom in his face.

"So the earl, yer half-brother, didn't send ye to Rum to entrap me in marriage to stake a claim on Kilvenie Tower?"

He raked his fingers through his hair and cursed his negligence in leaving the letter where it could so easily be found. During the last few weeks, he'd convinced himself the circumstances surrounding their marriage were not so bad, but hearing her utter the bald truth out loud was so much worse than anything he'd imagined.

"It wasn't like that." Not from the moment he'd discovered who she was. But at Castle Campbell, when Archibald had given him this mission, it had been exactly like that. "Ye're the only one I've ever wanted, Freyja."

"I've no use for yer honeyed tongue, Alasdair. It means nothing to me. If ye knew me at all, ye'd know it's the unvarnished truth I want, not pretty lies."

Aye, by God, he knew that about her. He'd known it from the start, when he first found out who she was and had told her how much better it was to tell the truth rather than keep secrets and lies for fear of causing offense.

Her response had stayed with him, a prickle in the back of his mind, no matter how hard he'd tried to ignore it.

"I'd far rather face an unfortunate truth than be victim of a pretty lie."

He hadn't seen her as a victim. He still didn't. But it didn't change the fact he'd kept the truth from her. But of one thing he wasn't guilty. "I never lied to ye, Freyja."

For the first time, anger flashed in her eyes, and she surged to her feet, the letter floating to the floor, forgotten.

"Ye lied to me from the moment we met. The only reason ye sought out my company was because yer precious earl demanded it from ye."

"No. When I first met ye in the stables, I had no idea who ye were. Ye bedazzled and intrigued me from that moment, and that's God's honest truth. When I found out yer name, it seemed like fate, and that had nothing to do with the earl."

She scoffed. "Spare me yer flattery. How many years did ye and yer half-brother plan this? Were ye just waiting for my grandfather to fail before ye struck?"

Her accusation speared through him, sharper than a blade. He wanted to deny every word, yet the truth was he had no idea how long the earl had planned this. But at least he could answer for himself.

"I knew nothing of this until the earl confided in me, a week before I arrived on Rum. Freyja, ye must understand. I didn't know ye then, and I didn't know Ranulph. The earl swore me to silence, and he has my fealty. How could I have told ye his plans without betraying his confidence?"

"So ye betrayed my trust instead."

"I cannot change the past. No one can." And if he could, would he? Would she have still wed him if he'd told her the truth from the start?

He'd been so convinced that she wouldn't. But maybe he'd been wrong. Yet if she'd refused him, they wouldn't have shared these last few weeks together, and even if it damned him to hell, he knew he would've done anything to ensure he had, at least, those memories.

"I thought ye were so noble." Her voice cracked and it was like a blow to his heart. "Agreeing to Afi's outrageous request. But I didn't see the truth. It wasn't what he wanted. 'Twas your plan all along to force me into marriage."

Her accusation burned through him, even though he deserved it. The earl had wanted Kilvenie, whatever it took. And if he hadn't obtained it through a peaceful marriage alliance when Alasdair had married Freyja, he would've found another way.

And Ranulph knew that. But still he hadn't agreed to force Freyja's hand. Until death had loomed over his shoulder, and he hadn't wanted to leave Freyja unprotected.

Aye, the truth was he deserved her condemnation. But the knowledge of how she now despised him pierced him to his core.

"Is that what ye think of me?" His voice was hushed, and his gut knotted at the prospect that Freyja, his Freyja, could think so ill of him.

Something flickered over her face. Regret? Despair? He couldn't tell, and it was gone so fast perhaps he'd merely imagined it after all.

"I don't know what to think of ye." There was no mistaking the anguish that threaded through each word and lacerated his soul. "I thought ye were so keen to wed because ye cared for me. Because ye wanted our life together to start as soon as possible. What a damn fool I've been."

"Ye're not a fool." Goddam it, how could he make her see that, however shadowed his reasons had been for going to Rum, nothing about their life together was a sham? "I do care about ye. I always have. And that's why I wanted to marry ye as soon as possible."

"Are ye sure it's me ye care about?" Bitterness shivered through her words. "Or were ye more concerned about Kilvenie slipping through yer fingers?" She swept her hand around, encompassing the bedchamber. "Or maybe it was Dunochty ye feared losing? I overheard Mistress Campbell telling ye she suspected yer castle and I were connected, and we are, aren't we? I'm the reason the earl bestowed ye Dunochty."

He recalled that conversation with his mother. He'd hoped Freyja hadn't overheard and when she hadn't remarked on it later that day, he'd been thankful. But she had heard. And she'd pieced the truth together. He could say nothing. But she already knew the castle was a new acquisition, and if he didn't tell her the truth now, she would only think the worst of him.

"Ye've seen the manor. 'Tis in no fit state for a lady such as yerself." He swallowed the rest of his explanation when she made a sound of disgust. There was no help for it. She wasn't the kind of woman who wanted the hard truth interwoven with sweet-smelling honeysuckle. He sucked in a deep breath. "What I said is true. And the earl knew it. But aye, he bestowed Dunochty as a wedding gift, and that's the reason why I hadn't found the time to ensure the castle was running as it should have been before we arrived here."

"What a grand prize I was. Kilvenie Tower and Dunochty Castle in one fell swoop. Is that why ye coerced me when I was at my most vulnerable, Alasdair, as a way to ensure I couldn't change my mind and ye wouldn't lose yer fine estates?"

He reeled at her accusation, denial and horror intermingling deep inside his chest like a malevolent canker. That she could even think such a thing, let alone throw it in his face.

He hadn't forced her. He would never force her, even if his life depended on it. But her scathing words echoed in his head, regardless.

Christ, was that really what she thought?

Is that what I did?

Acid scalded his throat as guilt ripped through him, charring his heart. Archibald's orders had been clear. Before he'd arrived on Rum, Alasdair had been willing to seduce Freyja to secure her hand and ensure the earl claimed Kilvenie. But even then, before he had met her, he would never have forced her. He would never force any woman.

But now, confronted by the anger in Freyja's beautiful blue eyes, his convictions withered to dust. Even though, in the stables, he hadn't planned to seduce her, it didn't negate the fact that, when he'd first met her, seduction had been in the back of his mind.

She glared at him, as though his silence was somehow a reflection of his guilt. "Do ye have nothing to say, Alasdair?"

Quick thinking and pleasing words had been the backbone of his life for as long as he could remember. He'd learned when he was still a young lad it was the best way to distract his mother when her resentful eyes had fallen upon him. It had become a habit without him even realizing it.

But he understood it now for what it was. Not that it mattered. Freyja was not his mother, and he didn't want her to see a pale façade of the man he really was.

Yet the man she saw when she looked at him was one she believed would force her against her will. He was sickened to his soul and had no more pretty words left inside him.

"Well?" Her demand rattled through his head, and he forced himself to look her in the eyes. Her bonny eyes, that had once looked at him with such affection.

"We'll discuss this when I return from Edinburgh." He sounded as though they were discussing the weather. Thank God she couldn't see how his heart cracked inside his chest.

"Ye're still going to Edinburgh?" Incredulity pulsed through every word.

"Aye. The earl commands it." Was that a trace of bitterness in his voice? He scarcely cared. Whenever Archibald had summoned him, he'd dropped everything without a second thought to be by his side. It was the way it had always been, and always would be.

But he'd never experienced this thread of resentment before.

"Oh, of course." Derision dripped from every word. "Ye cannot possibly ignore the earl's summons. Go, then. Accept his pox-ridden barony since that's all ye care about, but I won't forget this, Alasdair Campbell. Ye can be sure of that."

"I'm not asking ye to forget about it. I'm asking ye to give me a chance to explain when I get back. Is that too much to ask?"

"There's more to explain?"

He couldn't think of anything that wouldn't damn him further in her eyes, but there had to be something that would make her see their marriage wasn't the lie she thought it was. With three weeks apart, surely he'd find the right words so she'd understand.

He had no choice but to leave, yet every instinct he possessed pounded through him to go to her and pull her into his arms. To beg her forgiveness and tell her—

God help him, why was it so hard to tell her how much he loved her?

But the prospect of spilling his heart at her feet and having her crush it with cold disdain was too great a risk.

But even worse than that was the fear she wouldn't believe him.

"Aye. We'll speak when I return." Somehow he managed to sound as though this conversation wasn't ripping him apart, and since he couldn't trust himself not to kiss her farewell if he stayed a moment longer, he gave a sharp bow of his head before swinging on his heel and marching from the chamber.

When the door closed behind him, he leaned his back against it and screwed his eyes shut. All would be well. He had to believe that.

The alternative was too bleak to even consider.

CHAPTER TWENTY-SEVEN

FREYJA STOOD BY the castle doors and watched Alasdair and his men ride across the courtyard and through the gatehouse. Her spine was so rigid she feared it might crack, but no one would ever accuse her of not performing her duties as the mistress of Dunochty in the manner that was expected of her.

No one would guess she'd just discovered the real reason why her husband had married her. For all she knew, everyone in Argyll had been aware of it, and the only reason she hadn't seen it was because she'd been blinded by Alasdair's charm.

Distress churned her stomach, but she kept a small smile on her face so the servants wouldn't gossip about the surly Lady Freyja of Dunochty Castle. She did, after all, have a tiny particle of pride left.

The courtyard emptied as the servants went back to their tasks and she was alone, save for Morag, and dear, loyal, Dubh who sat by her feet and gazed up at her with sad brown eyes.

She wasn't going to think about brown eyes. Lying brown eyes that belonged to Alasdair Campbell.

Amma had been certain her future was with Alasdair, away from Sgur. And because she'd been so enamored with him, she'd allowed herself to be swayed by her grandmother's words.

But what if Amma was wrong about the Deep Knowing? What if, by leaving her beloved Isle, she had betrayed her foremothers' legacy and as a punishment was cursed with heartache?

Yet Isolde had found happiness with William. And besides, there were no such things as curses. Damn Alasdair. It wasn't just her heart he'd destroyed. He'd splintered her good sense too.

A shudder wracked her and she turned and entered the castle as Morag made her way to the kitchens to fetch a drink. She still had to write to Isolde, but what she wanted to say to her sister weren't things she could put in a letter.

Blessed Eir, how dearly she needed to see her sisters again.

In the bedchamber, she caught sight of Afi's letter on the floor. For a few moments she merely stared at it before she could summon the energy to pick it up and her gaze drifted over the end of the letter.

> *If the veil of death were not upon me, I would not force this issue, but I cannot leave my Freyja unprotected. 'Tis for this reason I bequeath Kilvenie Tower to ye, Alasdair Campbell, upon yer marriage to my granddaughter.*
>
> *Look after my lass, Alasdair.*

Afi had signed the letter in his own hand, and she blinked rapidly, willing the tears not to fall. In the end, even her grandfather had been taken in by Alasdair's charm. So much so, that he'd even signed away her inheritance to him.

And now she was trapped in a marriage to a man who had shattered her heart and her trust, and she had only herself to blame.

He'd never professed to love her when they'd decided to wed, and at the time she hadn't expected him to. Many marriages weren't based on love. But she'd respected him and foolishly had imagined it was reciprocal.

She'd even harbored the notion that one day love would come. And so it had. For her.

Why was she torturing herself with memories of what had happened on Rum? But it seemed she couldn't stop the bittersweet images from unfurling in her mind, yet those happy moments were now forever tarnished with the darkness of deception.

Alasdair had never proposed to her. How strange she'd not realized that before. All he'd said was he needed a wife, and she, who prided herself on being so practical, had read far too much into it.

He had simply gone along with Afi's pronouncement, and, captivated by his presence all she'd thought was how honorable he was.

Slowly, she went to the window. The shutters were open, and the deeply recessed, arched window had been glazed long ago, another sign of the wealth of the Campbells. In the distance was the sea, a sight she'd always found comforting since moving to Dunochty, but today all it did was make her homesick for Sgur.

"We'll speak when I return."

Alasdair's cold parting words before he'd left the bedchamber thundered around her head in an endless refrain. How uncaring he'd sounded that her world had fallen to ashes at her feet. Or maybe he hadn't even noticed. She wasn't sure which scenario was worse.

But one thing was unmistakably clear: His loyalty to the earl was paramount, and his ambition to become a baron surpassed any fleeting concern he might harbor over the plight of his marriage. Yet why would he care how she felt about the circumstances surrounding their hasty betrothal?

He'd caught her and been rewarded for it. And, doubtless, would continue to be rewarded.

She rested her head against the window recess. She shouldn't be so hurt by the way he'd walked out. He'd always made it very plain where his loyalty lay. And if she was being honest with herself, it wasn't the fact that, like so many men, he put his fealty to his earl above any loyalty to his own wife.

It hurt because she'd foolishly believed Alasdair, like William, put his wife before any other.

Well, now she knew the folly of assuming such a thing.

A ragged sigh escaped, and she turned from the sea to gaze around the bedchamber. Alasdair had never used his own, and she'd enjoyed the closeness of waking up every morning with him beside her. She'd imagined he had forsaken his own chamber because he liked being with her, too.

But she was likely wrong about that, since she'd been wrong about everything else when it came to Alasdair Campbell.

He expected her to wait patiently for at least three weeks until he returned from Edinburgh before he deigned to discuss the farce of their marriage. Not that she was sure what was left to discuss, but regardless, he'd left in the middle of their conversation, and without a backward glance.

A flicker of anger stirred deep inside, and she welcomed it, embraced it, because anger gave her strength. She focused on it, feeding it, willing it to burn away the acrid stench of mortification that scorched her soul and scarred her heart.

Damn Alasdair and his earl to hell. She would not wait meekly in Dunochty as Alasdair expected. She'd return to Sgur, and even if it was only a few weeks' respite before he came to drag her back to his castle, at least she'd see Roisin, and her grandmother, and once again breathe in the wild, free air of Eigg.

She picked up Dubh and held him close, his warm body a comforting barricade against the rest of the world. It went against everything she believed in, but she needed to maintain an illusion in front of the servants that everything was well between Alasdair and herself and give the impression her journey to Eigg had been approved by him.

It might sicken her, but at least in this respect she was no fool. If anyone suspected she was leaving Dunochty without his permission, she'd never make it through the gatehouse.

IT WAS JUST before supper when Seoc approached her in the great hall, looking irrepressibly pleased with himself. She summoned up yet another smile as she greeted him.

"My lady," he said. "A package has arrived for Alasdair."

She glanced at the large package he carried. Since arriving at Dunochty, Alasdair had received several deliveries, but she'd always known what they were because he'd discussed them with her beforehand.

But she knew nothing of this. And a small pain squeezed her heart. How many other things did she not know about her husband?

"Would ye mind taking it to his private chambers?" she said. "It will be safe there until he returns."

"Of course." Seoc drew in a deep breath and grinned at her although she couldn't fathom why. "I'm glad it arrived before ye left for the Small Isles."

"Indeed," she agreed. Seoc was so taken with whatever this package contained, she could only deduce it was something Alasdair had purchased for the physician's use. Not that she could see why he'd do such a thing. Seoc was independently wealthy.

"I'll take it now," he added before strolling out of the hall.

Jane came up to her. "Is anything amiss, my lady?"

"No, everything is fine." She smiled at the other woman, even though her face hurt from all the smiling she'd done since Alasdair had left the castle. A part of her wished she could confide in Jane, but despite regarding her as a dear friend she was, ultimately, Seoc's wife. And Seoc was undisputedly loyal to Alasdair and would ensure she remained within the confines of Dunochty if he discovered Alasdair hadn't, in fact, given her permission to visit Eigg in his absence.

"Ye must be so looking forward to seeing yer kin again."

"I am."

"I've spoken to Seoc," Jane said as they sat down for supper. "And he's of the same mind as me. Should ye wish for another woman to accompany ye on yer journey, I'm happy to come with ye."

Taken aback by the offer, Freyja took the other woman's hand. Any other time she'd be tempted to take her up on her offer, but how could she speak freely with Roisin and Amma, if Jane was around? "That's very kind, Jane. But there's no need."

"Well, if ye change yer mind in the morning, the offer stands."

DAWN HAD BARELY risen when Freyja left her bed the following morning. She'd tossed and turned all night, and despised herself for missing Alasdair, but there was no point deluding herself. She'd missed the way he held her at night, how his steady breathing after he fell asleep soothed her, and how she loved snuggling against his familiar body in the early hours of the morn.

Doubtless she'd get over it.

Of one thing she was certain: When she returned to Dunochty, she'd insist he utilized his own damn bedchamber.

The thought didn't bring her any comfort.

Yesterday, she'd sent a messenger to the port, and her passage was booked for this afternoon. Alas, it was far too early to leave Dunochty, and so after she'd washed and dressed, she went downstairs to find Sine.

To be sure, she'd spent a good hour with her, and the steward, Raso, yesterday afternoon, ensuring that everything in the castle would run smoothly until Alasdair's return. He may have broken her heart, but that didn't mean she wanted him to accuse her of neglecting his beloved castle.

After speaking with Sine, and ensuring she understood her explicit instructions when it came to tending her precious medicinal gardens, she found Clyde waiting for her in the hall.

"The wagon is loaded," he announced.

"Thank ye, Clyde." She gave him a bright smile, but his glower merely darkened. She had the feeling he hadn't been taken in by her story, but thankfully neither had he questioned her about it.

She was only taking one chest with her, containing her gowns and personal items, and a small casket with a selection of essential tinctures and powders, as well as her medical satchel. Clyde had arranged for four of Alasdair's men to accompany them to the port, but only she, Clyde and Morag were sailing to Eigg.

"The men will be ready to leave in an hour," he said, and she nodded. That would give them plenty of time to arrive before the ship sailed.

She looked at Dubh. "Come on, then. One last walk before we leave."

With Morag by her side, she left the castle, but before they'd even crossed the forecourt, half a dozen riders clattered through the open gates.

She shielded her eyes from the glare of the sun as the first rider dismounted and made his way to her.

"Colban?" Good Lord, what was he doing here? Her glance traveled over his companions, but she only recognized his cousin, Peter.

"Lady Freyja." Colban came to her and kissed her hand. "Bad tidings, I fear. 'Tis Lady Helga. I came as soon as I heard, to escort ye back to Sgur Castle."

Fear gripped her heart. "What's happened? Were ye there?"

"No. 'Twas sheer luck my uncle heard just before he sailed from Eigg to Oban. Doubtless a messenger has been sent on the next boat, but I knew ye'd want to be told as soon as possible. Peter gathered his men, and we will take ye back to Sgur without delay."

She gripped her hands together to stop them from trembling. Amma had always been such an immovable presence in her life, it was hard to remember that, in fact, she was not a young woman, and the ravages of age could strike her at any time.

No, blessed Eir, please don't let Amma die. She couldn't bear it, so soon after losing Afi, and discovering how little Alasdair thought of her.

No good would come from her falling apart. She dragged in a sharp breath to try and clear her mind. "I must send word to Lady Isolde." At least they could travel to Eigg together.

"No need, my lady. A messenger is already on his way to Creagdoun. My ship is ready at the port, and we'll wait for Lady Isolde there."

She grasped Morag's hand. "Find Clyde and let him know we will be leaving instantly."

"Aye, milady." Morag hurried off as she tried to untangle her thoughts. "Colban, where is yer uncle? I must speak with him, to find out what he knows about my grandmother."

"He's on his way to Creagdoun."

She supposed that made sense, since Isolde was the elder sister and should receive the news of their grandmother's health firsthand. But it was a terrible thing, not knowing what ailed Amma.

Clyde marched over, leading a horse pulling the wagon, accompanied by the four men who were escorting her to the port. She glanced back at Colban and caught shock on his face before he quickly masked it. Not that she blamed him, and she felt compelled to explain.

"I had planned to visit Eigg while Alasdair is with the earl." In the back of her mind, a discordant note stirred. There was no reason why Colban would know Alasdair wasn't in the castle. So why hadn't he requested to see Alasdair when he arrived? No matter what she thought about it, 'twas normal practice to ask a man's permission before escorting his wife to visit her sick relative.

But the notion was fleeting, for what did it matter? Colban had known her grandmother all his life and his concern for her health had likely caused him to forget standard protocol.

Colban eyed her, almost as though he didn't quite believe her. But the sensation vanished in an instant. God help her, her mind was playing tricks on her.

"'Tis fortunate ye are already packed for the journey," he said, and she had the oddest feeling he didn't think it fortunate at all. "But there's no need for the laird's men to accompany us. As ye see, we have Peter's men."

Before she could respond, Clyde stepped forward. "Lady Freyja's safety is my concern, and the men will accompany her."

His tone brooked no argument and Colban gave a tight smile before inclining his head in assent.

Jane hastened over to her. It was obvious from the concern on her face that she'd learned of the news. "My lady, I'm so sorry. How fortunate it is ye are ready to leave without delay. Do not worry about Alasdair. Seoc will send a messenger after him, so he'll know what's happening within a few days."

"Thank ye, Jane." It would be at least two days before a message reached Alasdair, but considering his haste to reach the earl, it was more likely he wouldn't receive it until after he arrived in Edinburgh. Not that it made any difference. There was nothing he could do, and he certainly wouldn't forsake the meeting with the earl simply because Lady Helga was ill.

What's wrong with her? Had she succumbed to sickness? Or broken a bone in a fall? Why on earth didn't Colban have more information?

But it was no good driving herself mad with questions that couldn't be answered until she saw Amma herself. She just needed to collect her satchel, and they would be ready to leave.

As they rode through the gates, a forlorn wish whispered through her mind, no matter how hard she tried to quell it.

If only Alasdair were coming with me.

Chapter Twenty-Eight

Alasdair rode through the gatehouse of Dunochty, the image of Freyja standing by the doors of the castle etched in his mind. Anyone observing her would think nothing was wrong. She had smiled and said the right things as he'd kissed her hand in farewell, but he'd seen the ice in her eyes.

The hurt.

And the wretched certainty settled in his chest that no matter what he did, she would never forgive him.

They rode in silence, the two men he'd brought with him as disinclined to converse as he was himself, and the earl's messenger was never one for idle talk. But his cursed thoughts wouldn't quiet, and no matter how he tried to distract his mind, Freyja's contemptuous accusation haunted him with every tortured breath he took.

"What a grand prize I was. Kilvenie Tower and Dunochty Castle in one fell swoop."

He couldn't deny the truth of it, not even to himself. She had been a grand prize. He'd known it from the moment the earl had shared his strategy. Freyja MacDonald was a noblewoman with an ancient bloodline she could trace back to a fierce Pict queen, and he'd never been good enough for her.

As she'd accused him, Dunochty Castle had been a fine reward for carrying out his half-brother's plans. But just as importantly, it had been another step closer to his dream of a barony.

He'd ignored any reservations he'd harbored over keeping the full truth from her. The Campbells, after all, were renowned for making advantageous alliances, and their brides invariably brought great estates and impressive residences with them.

But then he'd got to know Freyja, and even the promise of the castle had paled beside his burning need for her to willingly agree to be his bride.

"*Is that why ye coerced me when I was at my most vulnerable, Alasdair, as a way to ensure I couldn't change my mind and ye wouldn't lose yer fine estates?*"

An iron band compressed his chest as he once again heard the contempt in her voice. As he once again recalled their frenzied lovemaking, when he had made her his and he'd believed nothing could tear them apart.

Archibald had more than implied that if nothing else worked to win Lady Freyja, then seduction was a viable solution. Yet that wasn't the reason Alasdair had taken her into his arms that day in the stables. The earl's strategy hadn't even crossed his mind. All he had wanted was to comfort her on the loss of Ranulph. But God knew, she'd been vulnerable. And afterwards, she had been left with no choice but to wed him, in case he'd given her a bairn.

The afternoon was warm and the sky blue, but a chill crawled over his arms and a blanket of dark fog wrapped itself around him. Had Freyja's every smile and laugh since they wed been false? While he had blindly imagined they had something special between them, had she secretly resented him for taking away her choices?

THEY STOPPED FOR the night at an inn, and after the four of them had eaten a hearty stew, he escaped from the men's ale-induced banter and retired to his room. He placed his oil lamp on the table and sat on the edge of the bed, his elbows on his thighs and fingers interlocked between his knees.

Whenever he'd traveled to see the earl before, there had always been a sense of anticipation and, aye, excitement. Archibald inhabited a world that could have been his, had his father acknowledged him. But now, thanks to his half-brother's support during the last four years, he'd been welcomed and accepted into that world and nobody cared about his past.

But tonight, all he wanted to do was return to Freyja. To wrap his arms around her and tell her—no, to hell with it—*beg* her to give him another chance.

When he returned from Edinburgh, that was exactly what he'd do. Christ, he'd do anything to win back her trust. If only he knew how.

The glow from the oil lamp flickered on the whitewashed walls, and in his mind's eye he was transported back to Rum, just after he'd watched Freyja race along the beach, heedless of anything but the pure joy of her freedom.

A freedom she could never have at Dunochty. Or Oban. Or anywhere in the Highlands, if it came to that. She'd told him how thankful she was that she didn't need to heed the restrictions imposed beyond the Small Isles, and he hadn't thought much about it since.

"Eigg is where my heart lies, and Rum is very dear to me, too."

Guilt speared through him. Not once since they'd moved to Dunochty had she breathed a word on how she felt about leaving her home and everyone she loved behind. Yet on the two occasions they'd made arrangements to visit her sister at Creagdoun, he'd had to cancel.

He should have allowed her to visit her sister, even if he wasn't there. They both knew she'd be well protected in his absence, and it was just his damn pride getting in the way. Well, it was too late for that regret now. He'd tell her when he returned from Edinburgh.

But disquiet still lingered, gnawing into the edges of his mind, and he couldn't dislodge the suspicion he was missing something vital. Something that would show her, without any doubt, just how dear she was to him.

The Small Isles. If he told her she could visit her isle whenever she wished, whether he accompanied her or not, would that be enough to show her he wanted only her happiness? But still something did not feel right, and he gripped his fingers together as an inkling of an idea too outrageous to consider hovered just beyond his grasp.

And then it fell into place, and he exhaled a ragged breath. She loved the Isle of Rum almost as much as she loved the Isle of Eigg. And until he'd entered her life, Ranulph had planned to bequeath Kilvenie Tower to her. Her own home, where she would be mistress and answer to no one, somewhere she could run along the beach if she pleased, and no one would condemn her for it.

The earl had appointed him custodian of Kilvenie Tower. He would transfer the custodianship into Freyja's name. It wasn't the same as her owning it outright, but it was all he could do to return what he could of her birthright.

The earl would not be happy. But then, the earl did not need to know everything. Alasdair found his writing case, went over to the table, and picked up his quill.

IT HAD BEEN a torturous night, filled with broken dreams and haunting echoes of the last conversation he'd had with Freyja. As the first pale streaks of dawn illuminated the room through the gaps in the shutters, he remained in bed, staring at the ceiling, unable to summon even a flicker of urgency to make haste to Edinburgh.

There was little doubt in his mind that Archibald planned to bestow upon him the barony of Glenchonnel. But no anticipation fired his blood. No fierce pride filled his chest at the prospect that his dream would soon be granted.

There was only a bleak certainty that the wondrous delight he had discovered with Freyja had irrevocably shattered.

Lately, he'd told himself he needed the barony because it was no less than she deserved. But Freyja didn't care about becoming a baroness. It was all about his own ambition and burning need to prove himself good enough in the face of his peers.

But what goddamn use was that if he wasn't good enough for Freyja?

"Ambition is not a bad thing."

He'd said that to Lady Helga, the first time he'd met her, when he'd been sure she was judging him for who he was.

"I agree. But sometimes it can blind us to what is truly important."

He hadn't understood what she meant. What could be more important than acquiring power and prestige, of gaining the respect of those who had once derided him? It was the only way he'd never be vulnerable again. His ambition had fueled every breath he took, every action he'd taken, since he was nine years old. His loyalty to the earl was absolute.

But Freyja held his heart. There was no point in possessing a barony, or a dozen castles, if she wasn't by his side because she wanted to be there. How could he survive, knowing she was with him only because she couldn't leave, if she believed he put Archibald before her, that if it ever came to a choice, he'd choose his half-brother over the woman who had transformed his life in ways he'd never even imagined could be possible?

And finally, he understood what Lady Helga had always known: Ambition was not a bad thing. But it wasn't the most important thing. And while his thirst for power had set him on the path to winning Freyja, if the choice before him was losing her and gaining a barony, or once again earning her respect and affection and turning his back on his half-brother, there was, in the end, no choice to be made.

Freyja was the one he'd choose. Every time.

She alone was his vulnerability.

Once he'd been so certain he needed to hide from the world

how much his bride enthralled him. He'd believed it wrong that a woman could have that kind of power over a man. It wasn't the way the world worked.

How sure he'd been of that. How wrong he had been. It was the way his world worked, and God help him, he'd have it no other way. But she didn't know that. And she never would, unless he showed her.

HE FOUND THE earl's messenger downstairs, having breakfast with his men, and the man made his way over to him.

"Is all well?" he said.

"I must return to Dunochty."

The man stared at him as though he'd lost his mind. Maybe he had. And there was no guarantee Freyja would listen to him when he arrived home so unexpectedly, but that was a chance he had to take. All he knew for sure was if he didn't see her for another three weeks, the likelihood of her forgiving him was remote.

"But the earl is expecting ye."

"Aye. But there's a matter I must speak to my wife about." He handed the man a succinct letter he'd composed before leaving his room. Archibald deserved that, at least. "Give the earl this, with my sincerest apologies."

The messenger took the letter with obvious reluctance. "This is unprecedented." He sounded vaguely unnerved.

"The earl is a fair man. He won't blame ye for my non-appearance."

With that, he turned on his heel, summoned his men, and departed.

IT WAS MIDMORNING when Dunochty came into view, and instead of the usual surge of pride that consumed him at the sight, only apprehension gripped his gut. Would the gift of Kilvenie Tower, a stronghold that should, by rights, be Freyja's anyway, be enough to soften her anger against him? At least enough for her to listen to what he needed to say?

Christ, the things he needed to say. He hoped this time, unlike yesterday, he would be able to find the right words, so she'd know how much she meant to him.

As soon as he reached the courtyard he leaped from his horse and hailed a passing maid. "Where is Lady Freyja?"

The girl stared at him, wide-eyed, as though she had no idea what he was talking about. Luckily, Seoc emerged from the castle, and Alasdair repeated his question.

"Lady Freyja?" Seoc frowned. "But she left for the Isle of Eigg this morning, Alasdair."

Blankly, he stared at Seoc as his words thundered around his brain. Freyja had gone to Eigg?

She had left him?

"What?" His voice was hoarse, and he only just stopped himself from grabbing the other man's shoulders. He knew, as laird, he shouldn't allow his feeling to show so readily, but God help him, he couldn't hide the cold sense of finality that slithered through his veins and squeezed his heart like the deadliest of poison.

"My lady planned to visit Eigg. She booked passage for this afternoon." It was obvious Seoc had believed Alasdair knew all about that plan, and now realized he'd been in error. If his world wasn't falling about his feet, he would've felt sympathy for the other man. "But then Colban MacDonald and his men arrived with word that Lady Helga was ill, and my lady left earlier with him."

Lady Helga was ill? That would be reason enough for Freyja to depart Dunochty, but that wasn't the case. She'd already made arrangements to leave before she had received the message from

Colban.

Whatever her reasons had been, and unfortunately he could guess them, she was now facing the prospect of her beloved grandmother's ill health. It wasn't ideal, but since there was no other option, he'd join her in Eigg.

"How long ago did she leave?"

"A good two hours. But the wagon will slow them down."

Aye. A wagon would slow them down considerably. If he left now with a fresh horse, the chances were good he could catch them at the port before they sailed.

He hailed a stable lad and while a horse was readied for himself, he prayed to God, and to Freyja's formidable foremothers, that he hadn't left it too late to try and make amends.

Chapter Twenty-Nine

They had been traveling at a leisurely pace for a good hour, and frustration twisted through Freyja. To be sure, they had a wagon which slowed them down, but they could still go a little faster. Still, she should be thankful she was on her way at all. If Colban hadn't arrived when he did, they would've only just been leaving Dunochty now.

She rode behind the wagon so she could keep an eye on Dubh, who was most miserable at being confined to his basket. It was clear from Colban's attitude that he'd expected her to ride up front beside him, and where his men were. But at least this way Dubh could see her from where his basket was wedged between her chest and casket. And her darling lad's peace of mind was far more important to her than appeasing Colban's pride, even if she was grateful to him.

Clyde and Morag rode either side of her, and Alasdair's men surrounded them, taking turns to drive the wagon. There couldn't be a safer way to travel, and yet Alasdair's words haunted her mind.

"I'll not let ye travel the countryside unprotected."

They had both known what he really meant was he wouldn't allow her to travel without him by her side. Yet here she was, and not even traveling to Creagdoun, but all the way to Eigg.

And yet still a stubborn, stupid part of her wished Alasdair was, indeed, by her side.

She shook her head, trying to force him from her mind but he remained, like a ghostly shadow darkening her every thought. Did he ever think of her when they were apart? Until yesterday, she'd harbored the fanciful notion he did.

It was time to stop the romantic nonsense. Her marriage was nothing more than another political alliance, like so many noble marriages were. There was nothing special about the connection between Alasdair and herself, and if she'd kept her wits about her, instead of letting his pretty words seduce every last grain of good sense she'd ever possessed, she'd have known it.

She forcibly relaxed her grip on the reins, adjusted her satchel, and breathed in deep. Enough. She couldn't brood on the state of her marriage when Amma needed her. And no longer could she unburden herself when she arrived at Sgur. Roisin would need her strength, and Amma needed her healing skills.

With a resigned sigh she focused ahead where Colban and Peter were deep in conversation, and for some reason an uneasy shiver crawled along her arms. Did Colban always spend so much time in the Highlands?

Maybe he did. It wasn't her concern how he spent his time. But instead of letting the matter rest, the odd prospect of his uncle having been on Eigg at the exact moment when Amma had fallen ill prickled through her mind.

She couldn't remember a single time when Colban's uncle had visited Sgur Castle. Why had he been there?

And why hadn't Colban answered her when she'd asked what was wrong with her grandmother? Surely, his uncle would have told him. Yet Colban had glided over her question, and with everything happening so fast, she hadn't pressed him.

Something didn't feel quite right, but she couldn't fathom what. She was certain that when Colban had arrived at Dunochty, five men had accompanied him, including his cousin Peter. But now there were only four men. Maybe she was just suspicious because she was tired, and her trust had taken a beating.

She gave Clyde a sideways glance. His grim expression didn't ease her troubled thoughts. Then again, he was close to Lady Helga and was doubtless worried in his own stoic way.

The sooner they reached Sgur, the sooner they could put their minds to rest.

ANOTHER HOUR PASSED, and as they approached a village Colban rode to her side. "Lady Freyja, we'll stop here for a while so ye might refresh yerself."

"I have no need to refresh myself, Colban." Somehow, she managed to keep the irritation from her voice. Why would he think she needed a rest after merely two hours in the saddle? Now if he'd suggested Dubh needed a break to stretch his legs and relieve himself, that would be a different matter.

"'Tis no trouble," he said, as though she'd expressed it was. "The men will understand. I'll secure a private room for yer use in the tavern."

With that, he rode off, and she exhaled a frustrated breath. Alasdair wouldn't have presumed to know whether she needed to rest or not, and neither would he have dismissed her reply as though her opinion was of no consequence.

Curse the man, why did she remember his good qualities when their entire marriage was based on a masquerade? Maybe now she knew the truth Alasdair wouldn't be so accommodating. She willed herself to believe it and was disgusted when she couldn't. Whatever else he had done, she simply couldn't accept his willingness to listen to what she said had all been a pretense.

By her side, Clyde grunted, and she caught his eye. It was clear he shared her exasperation with Colban.

They rode into the village and found the tavern, and since there was no help for it, she dismounted before Colban could insist on helping her. They secured the horses, released Dubh from his basket, and Alasdair's men remained with the wagon as she, Clyde and Morag made their way to the old stone building with its freshly turfed roof.

She glanced over her shoulder at Colban's men.

Five of them, now. Was she losing her mind?

Colban disappeared inside and Freyja focused on Dubh as he had a good sniff of the wild grasses and piles of manure that were scattered about, since if she didn't, she had the feeling Colban's men would notice her rising vexation.

"Lady Freyja." Colban emerged from the tavern and gave an imperial wave, beckoning her over. Clyde stiffened with affront by her side, and she swiftly grasped his arm before he said or did something they might all regret.

"'Tis all right," she said under her breath as she released him and tapped her thigh for Dubh to come to heel.

"'Tis not all right," Clyde growled as they went over to where Colban waited by the tavern door. "He shows a lack of respect, and I don't trust him."

She didn't have time to respond, as they'd reached Colban, but Clyde's confession unsettled her. The two men had known each other for years. How long had Clyde distrusted Colban?

"This way," Colban said, sweeping his arm towards the open tavern door, where a man and woman stood, presumably the tavernkeeper and his wife. She smiled at them in thanks, since none of her turbulent thoughts were their fault, and followed them to the back of the tavern where the woman showed her into a small room.

"I shall leave ye to rest for a short time, my lady," Colban announced as though he was doing her a great favor, before he retraced his steps, the tavernkeeper and his wife following in his wake.

Clyde cast a suspicious glance around the room. Shelves took up most of the space, laden with crockery, and in the middle of the floor were two stools, one of which bore a pitcher of ale and a tankard. It was clear the tavernkeeper kept no private rooms for passing patrons and had hastily made accommodations for her.

"I'll be right outside." Clyde left the room and shut the door behind him and Freyja rubbed her aching forehead. It wouldn't take a moment to find a soothing remedy in her satchel, but she had the irrational conviction that if she did, Colban would return, see what she was doing, and conclude he'd been right to force her to rest.

With that absurdness faced, what on earth was she meant to do until Colban deigned to return? She was starting to wish she'd declined his offer to accompany him to Eigg on his ship and instead had stuck to her original plan of sailing that afternoon.

She went to the window, but it was small and cracked and she couldn't see much besides the stone wall of the neighboring farrier.

"Shall I pour the ale, milady?" Morag gave the pitcher a doubtful glance.

"No thank ye, Morag. I'm tempted to see if there's another way out of here, so Dubh can enjoy himself before we resume our journey."

It was likely unfair to bring Dubh into her argument for leaving the room Colban had assigned her, when the real reason was she was simply irked at being unnecessarily confined when she didn't know how desperate Amma's condition was. If Colban and his men wanted to stop for an ale, why hadn't he just said so, instead of pretending she needed to rest because she was a woman?

"There may be another way outside through the pantries." Morag glanced at a door in the far wall. "Should I look, milady?"

"We'll look together." Freyja opened the door, and sure enough, it led into a pantry filled with cooling pies and tarts. With a stern word to Dubh to behave himself, she and Morag crossed the rammed earth floor, and she opened another door that led outside.

It was only a small yard, but the important thing was it wasn't a room where she'd been consigned like a piece of baggage. Alasdair would never have treated her so.

For the love of God, she had to stop comparing everything unfavorably with how Alasdair would handle it. At least she could be sure Colban wasn't trying to trick her into marriage by underhanded means.

The notion didn't lift her mood, and she stifled a sigh as she kept an eye on Dubh. There was a narrow alleyway between the tavern and the farrier that led to the road where they'd left the horses and wagon. She strolled to the corner of the building where the alleyway was, and stopped dead, heart pounding.

Colban and one of his men stood not a mare's length from her.

Stealthily, she backstepped, even though her head berated her. Why did she care if he saw her? The truth was, she didn't, but she'd rather avoid a confrontation with him. The way she felt about the machinations of men right now, she'd likely give him some home truths that could never be forgiven.

"We're ahead of schedule." Colban's voice was low, and although she'd intended to retreat further, something in his tone made her pause. "I'd allowed an hour for Lady Freyja to pack her belongings, but I could scarcely delay when she was ready to leave."

Why would he want to delay? He had his own ship. It wasn't as though he had to wait on another captain's timeline, the way she'd had to when she'd booked passage for this afternoon.

Something didn't sit right with her and when she caught Morag's questioning gaze she raised her hand in warning. Morag stilled and Dubh ceased his exploration, his eyes fixed on her.

"We weren't expecting the extra men," Colban's companion said, and alarm scraped through her. Any last remnant she'd harbored that she was in the wrong by eavesdropping vanished. "We were prepared for Clyde. But four more will cause problems, Colban."

"Ride ahead and give the men fair warning. They'll know what to do."

"'Tis not straightforward." The other man sounded sullen.

"Do as I tell ye." Colban's voice was hard. "The reward will be great for ye and yer men. But there are to be no mistakes, ye hear?"

"We'll need more men from the ship to join mine in the ambush. Can ye vouch for yer own men, Colban?"

"With my life."

Freyja gripped the strap of her satchel, the leather biting into the palm of her hand, as her stomach churned in distress. It had been no coincidence that Colban had arrived so soon after Alasdair had left to answer the earl's summons. He'd waited for the right moment before coming to Dunochty with his tale that her grandmother was ailing.

Is she ailing?

She didn't know the truth of that, but of one thing she was certain: Colban planned on murdering Clyde and the men who accompanied her, and there could be only one reason for it. He wanted Kilvenie and sought to gain control of Rum through her. Clearly, his spies hadn't informed him that since her marriage she had lost her inheritance to her husband and his earl.

She had to tell Clyde. He would know what to do. But before she could silently retrace her steps to the pantry, Colban's accomplice spoke.

"The messenger dispatched from Dunochty for Alasdair Campbell was intercepted. He'll have no idea what's happened until it's too late."

The puzzle of Colban's missing man, who had suddenly reappeared, fell into place. He'd stayed behind, to deal with the messenger Seoc had sent, and Freyja's paralysis cracked. The poor man, simply doing his duty. Colban would not get away with any of this outrage.

"Good," Colban sounded satisfied. "Once I have Lady Freyja safely secured, yer men can lay in wait for when Alasdair Campbell leaves Edinburgh Castle. With him gone, nothing will stand in my way to claim what is rightfully mine."

Iced terror gripped her heart. They meant to murder Alasdair in cold blood. In an ambush, most likely, which he'd never see coming, and how could he defend himself against unseen forces?

She swung about and hastened back to the pantry with Dubh at her heels and Morag close behind. Heart thundering and hands shaking, she closed and locked the door behind them before hurrying back to the storage room.

For a moment she stood there, immobile, as terrifying images pounded through her mind, and her thoughts tumbled, incoherent.

Focus.

She breathed in deep, before slowly releasing her breath through her mouth. Panicking would get her nowhere. She had to think clearly, the way she did when a medical emergency presented itself.

Alasdair didn't know he was in any danger. He had to be warned. If she sent one of their men to Edinburgh now, he could pass on a message to Alasdair before he left the castle to return home. Surely the earl would scout the area and find the would-be assassins.

'Twas a sound plan. Colban's cowardly scheme relied on the element of surprise, and once that was gone, his men would be found. The earl thought highly of Alasdair, and he'd ensure justice was served.

Alasdair would be safe. He wouldn't die an ignoble death because of her. Relief washed through her, causing her knees to wobble, and she had the overwhelming urge to sink onto the stool and bury her face in her hands.

And then her grandmother's voice whispered in the back of her mind.

Keep perspective in all matters to be a fair judge of truth.

She shook her head. There wasn't time to think of Amma now. Yet her wise words would not be silent, and she could no longer ignore how she had been guilty of disregarding her grandmother's most solemn tenet.

The truth couldn't be denied. She'd been so hurt when she'd

read Afi's letter and discovered her marriage was nothing more than another political alliance she had, indeed, lost all perspective.

Alasdair hadn't told her the whole truth about why he'd visited Rum. But he'd never spun a web of lies around her the way Colban had, nor plotted to kill anyone who stood in the way of his objective.

His loyalty was with his earl, just as most men's loyalty remained with their lord. It didn't mean he thought any less of her. If he'd truly wanted to trick her into marriage, he would've seduced her into compliance. It was a stratagem as old as time itself, to force a woman to wed by impregnation. Alasdair had no way of knowing she could protect herself against conceiving a bairn.

But he hadn't forced or coerced her. She'd wanted him that time in the stables, and he had been the one trying to show caution.

Grief and regret twisted through her as she recalled the accusations she'd thrown in his face before he'd left for Edinburgh. Aye, she was mad at him and would always harbor the secret wish he could love her the way Willliam loved Isolde. But the anguish and horror that had flashed across his face when she'd flung those words at him would haunt her forever.

He deserved her condemnation. But he hadn't deserved that.

Please let me see him again to tell him I didn't mean it. And she didn't know whether she implored Eir, the ancient Norse goddess of healing, or God Himself.

Only then did the realization hit her that her plan wouldn't help Clyde or the three men who remained with her, if they were attacked by a large contingent of mercenaries. And should her faithful Clyde fall, it was easy to guess the fate Colban had in store for her.

She had to save Alasdair, but she also had to save her people and herself.

Her gaze fell upon the jug of ale on the stool. Colban's men were doubtless enjoying themselves in the tavern, where ale flowed freely. But no matter how many tankards they had consumed, if offered wine she was certain they'd accept.

She pulled her satchel from her shoulder and carefully sorted through her precious stocks. Aye, she had what she needed to ensure Colban and his men fell insensible. All she needed was the means to deliver it.

"Fetch Clyde," she said to Morag, who did as she was bid. Clyde listened in stony silence as she quickly told him what she'd overheard. "Do ye think ye can ensure his men drink the drugged wine, Clyde?"

"Aye." That was all he said, but the word was filled with simmering rage.

She nodded, before kneeling on the floor and preparing her potion.

"Make it strong," he said.

She glanced up at him. "Don't worry. A goblet of wine with this infusion would knock out a horse." And give her time to return to Dunochty to alert the rest of Alasdair's men.

When it was done, she handed Clyde the phial. "Make sure it's mixed thoroughly in the jug of wine," she instructed him. Certainly, it would be better if she could dose each goblet individually, but since that wasn't possible, this was the best she could do.

He gave a single nod, took the phial, and left the room.

Now all they could do was wait until the potion took effect.

Chapter Thirty

Clyde entered the room. "It's done. And I've dispatched one of our men to Edinburgh."

Freyja released a relieved breath. "Good. Come, Morag, there's no need for us to remain in here."

They followed Clyde through the tavern to the small forecourt, where Colban's men stood around, enjoying their wine. They nodded genially in her direction and raised their goblets, and she inclined her head and even managed a gracious smile.

It appeared the man she'd seen Colban with had left as soon as they'd spoken, since Clyde had only handed out five goblets of drugged wine.

But where was Colban now?

As she stroked the neck of her mare, a couple of the men staggered before slumping to the ground, still clutching their goblets, as the wine splashed over them. Their compatriots jeered and Freyja surreptitiously tried to see where Colban was lurking.

It was possible he'd passed out already, but unless she saw him herself, they couldn't be sure. Anxiety twisted through her as another man slowly slid down the wall of the tavern, and then Colban strode through the door into the courtyard.

He surveyed the sight of his men, and Freyja's heart lurched in her chest. He wasn't affected by her potion.

He hadn't drunk the wine.

Colban grabbed his cousin, Peter, who stood swaying as he gazed with bemusement at his fallen countrymen. Without a word, Clyde marched over and pulled Peter from Colban's grasp. As Peter collapsed without his cousin's support, Clyde smashed Colban to the ground with one mighty punch.

Colban didn't move.

"Tie them all up," Clyde ordered his men before turning to her. "I'll inform the tavernkeeper these traitors are wanted by the Earl of Argyll. They won't dare release them for fear of the earl's retribution."

"Shouldn't we take them back to the castle?" Centuries ago, the Great Keep had been used for prisoners, and although those days had long passed, it was still the most secure part of the castle, and surely would suffice until such a time the earl decided what to do with them.

"My priority is yer safety. I'll have one man remain here to ensure my orders are followed. Once ye're back at Dunochty, I'll dispatch a contingent to bring them back."

"And send a messenger to Sgur, to discover if anything Colban said was true." Although she doubted her grandmother was ill. It had simply been a ruse, to ensure she accompanied him.

As Clyde went to speak to the tavernkeeper, Freyja quickly scooped up Dubh and put him in his basket on the wagon. Within moments, Clyde, Morag, and the two remaining men were heading back to Dunochty.

The pace was painfully slow because of the wagon, and she couldn't help frequently glancing over her shoulder to see if they were being followed.

They weren't, of course. The threat of the earl's displeasure would be enough to prevent anyone from freeing them. But she wouldn't rest easy until they were safely within the castle, and Colban and his men had been rounded up and imprisoned in the keep.

And when Alasdair was safely returned from Edinburgh.

Her stomach churned. What if Colban's mercenary got to Alasdair, despite everything?

Stop. She wouldn't dwell on such an unlikely outcome. He

would be fine. He had to be. Because she needed to tell him that even though she was hurt by his deception in Rum, she understood it. And didn't condemn him for it.

In the end, it was better that she had her eyes open, instead of living in an imaginary bubble of her own making. Just because theirs was a political alliance didn't mean they were doomed to unhappiness. Her marriage might not be the great love she craved, but the truth was she'd rather keep what they'd found together than leave him and have nothing at all.

Clyde rode ahead of the wagon, and two of the men flanked her and Morag, when Clyde suddenly raised his arm in warning. A rider was galloping towards them and even though it was nonsense, apprehension gripped her at the possibility it was bad news about Alasdair.

She narrowed her eyes against the glare of the sun. God help her, she was seeing things now. Because she'd swear on her life the rider was Alasdair. No other man possessed such entrancing hair that glinted with hints of auburn, nor looked so magnificent astride his horse. But Alasdair was on his way to Edinburgh, and it didn't matter how desperately she wished he was here, wishing never made anything come true.

The rider pulled up alongside Clyde and there was no mistake.

He was Alasdair.

She spurred her mare on as the wagon halted and came to his side. There were a thousand turbulent thoughts colliding in her head but the only words that emerged were an incredulous, "Ye're here."

He gazed at her with those brown eyes that had captivated her from the day they'd met. She gripped the reins tighter in the vain hope that might steady her nerves. "Aye." He sounded faintly unnerved. "I was told ye were on yer way to Eigg."

"We were." She shook her head, the events of the last few hours losing their terrifying significance in the face of seeing Alasdair, here in front of her, when he was supposed to be traveling to the other side of the country. "But why are ye here, Alasdair?"

"I had to see ye."

She couldn't fathom his mood. He glared with an intensity that made her heart lurch and yet there was a thread of uncertainty in his voice. Had he received bad news about his half-brother?

"What of the earl?'

"The earl can wait."

Had she heard right? "He can wait?" she repeated. "Do ye mean to tell me he didn't send word for ye not to travel to Edinburgh?"

"I made the decision this morning, Freyja. I couldn't leave things the way they were between us. I couldn't wait another three weeks before seeing ye."

She understood his words. But she could scarcely believe what he was saying. He'd turned his back on his earl, because he needed to speak with her. "Ye came back to Dunochty to see me, instead of obeying the earl's command?"

"I did."

"But what of yer barony?" She knew it was his dearest wish. And she was certain the earl wouldn't grant such an honor to a man who refused his word. Even if they were half-brothers.

"Freyja—"

"I don't mean to intrude." Clyde's frown could've blocked out the sun if such a thing were possible, and she sucked in a ragged breath, swallowing her hasty words, but if only he had kept his peace for just a few moments longer. What had Alasdair been about to say to her? "We need to secure Lady Freyja at the castle, Alasdair. Colban MacDonald has betrayed his name, his family, and his clan."

"What?" Alasdair sounded bemused and she pulled her scattered thoughts together. Of course, Clyde was right. It was disgraceful she had forgotten their situation for even a moment. But the most important thing was that Alasdair was here, he was safe, and the earl could pick up the men sent to assassinate him without her worrying that her husband was in danger.

Quickly, she gave him a brief account of what had occurred this morning, and his face grew dark with anger.

"He didn't hurt ye?"

"No. I've told ye everything. We must make haste back to the castle and send men to bring them to justice."

"We've a man watching them to ensure they don't escape?" He directed his question to Clyde.

"We do."

"They're tied securely, Alasdair," she was compelled to remind him.

He turned his gaze to her, and for a fleeting moment she fancied she saw raw agony gleam in those dark depths. Then he gave a sharp nod, and the moment vanished.

"Return to Dunochty," he said to her. "I'll go on to the tavern and wait for reinforcements."

"No, ye must return to Dunochty with us." How could he think otherwise? "Ye cannot go back alone, Alasdair."

"A man will do many things if promised a reward, and Colban will promise anything for the chance to escape. I cannot risk yer safety, Freyja. I need to make sure no villager or passing traveler is tempted to listen to his lies. One man alone could be easily overcome."

"But—"

"Freyja." He leaned over his horse and took her hand, his gaze never leaving hers. "I wasn't here when ye needed me. I must do this, at least, and I need to know ye're safe."

But I need to know ye're safe too.

She looked down at his hand covering her own so he wouldn't see how deeply she disagreed with him. But before she could wrap her fingers around his, he pulled back, as though he'd just realized what he was doing.

"I'll see ye back at Dunochty," he said, and then he urged his horse on, and she watched him disappear into the distance.

She expelled an exasperated breath as she glared at Clyde.

"There was no need for him to go back, was there?"

"It's true that two men are better than one should some villagers take it into their head to accept a bribe to free Colban."

"Then we should have loaded the men onto the wagon and brought them back with us, as I first suggested."

Clyde grunted.

"I'm going after him."

"No, ye are not."

"Morag, bring me my writing case." She dismounted, ignoring Clyde's infuriated glower, and when Morag found her things she quickly wrote a note to Seoc, explaining the situation and that men needed to be sent to arrest Colban and his cohorts. After she sealed it, she handed it to the man driving the wagon.

She comforted Dubh, who gave her fingers a doleful lick, and then she turned back to Clyde. "I should be glad of yer company, Clyde."

"Ye're as willful as yer mother," he growled, but it wasn't said unkindly, and he motioned one of their men over before glaring at her once again. "Promise me ye won't put yerself in any danger."

She smiled and accepted his disgruntled help in mounting her mare. "I promise."

Chapter Thirty-One

As Alasdair left Freyja, it was an effort not to glance over his shoulder at her. But if he did, he might not leave her at all.

And he had to make sure Colban and his men didn't escape. If they did, Freyja would never be safe and any chance of freedom, even on her beloved Isles, would be lost to her forever.

He'd never let that happen. He should have been here, to protect her. Instead, he'd put the earl first, but thank God he'd come to his senses in time.

And yet when he found her, she'd already broken free from Colban's grasp because of her knowledge and skill with her medicinal plants.

Fierce pride surged through him, mingled with despair. Would he ever find a way to tell her how proud he was of her? How deeply he wished he had sailed to Rum all those weeks ago without the earl's orders ringing in his ears?

But one thing was certain: He had no intention of letting justice run its course when it came to Colban MacDonald. The man had planned to abduct Freyja, and once she was widowed, it was easy to guess what he'd had in mind.

He'd ensure Colban was dealt with permanently.

With grim determination, he skirted the woodlands on his right, and as he rounded the bend in the road, he sucked in a sharp breath as Colban MacDonald came riding towards him.

His fears had been justified. The bastard had managed to

bribe someone to release him and overpower the man Clyde had left behind.

They both pulled up, horses snorting, and Alasdair cast a calculating glance over the two men that accompanied the other man. They, like Colban, didn't appear to be affected by Freyja's sleeping potion. Goddamn it, his chances against three were slender at best, but whatever happened, Colban wouldn't be walking away from here.

It was clear his unexpected arrival had unsettled Colban, but he quickly recovered. "Good day, Alasdair."

Did the man possess not the slightest shred of honor? But then, Colban couldn't be sure he'd met Freyja on the way and knew of his actions, and congeniality was a tactic to take one's enemy by surprise.

Too bad for Colban he wasn't falling for it.

"A good day for justice," he said, and drew his sword.

Colban, the moldering louse, actually laughed. "Are ye serious, man? We shall dispatch ye in an instant, and I'll have Lady Freyja for my wife, the way it was always intended."

"Lady Freyja was never yer intended bride."

Colban's sneer turned ugly. "Aye, she was. I've always wanted her. And what's more, the MacDonalds of the Isles will not yield any more power to the cursed Campbells. It's imperative Kilvenie Tower remains under MacDonald control."

Raw fury pumped through him at Colban's reasons for wanting to wed Freyja. Would he have felt any better had the other man professed undying love for her, instead? Likely not, but at least that was an honorable motive.

Abducting her for her inheritance turned his guts. *How am I so different?* He'd married her because his earl had commanded him to do so. And for the same reason.

His rage melded with self-disgust, but it only served to strengthen his resolve to end this danger against Freyja once and for all. If he needed to sacrifice his life to do so, he wouldn't be going to hell alone this day.

But instead of coming to face him, Colban pulled back and the other two men rode forward. Damn the lily-livered maggot. He bared his teeth and gripped his sword tighter; then all three men stilled, their gazes riveted over his shoulder.

He wouldn't fall for such a pitiful ruse.

The sound of horses from behind him alerted him that the men weren't trying to distract him, but he kept his gaze on them, nevertheless. From the corner of his eye, he saw Clyde and one of his men flank him, and there wasn't time to wonder why the devil Clyde had decided to leave Freyja and follow him, as Colban's men attacked.

Alasdair urged his horse forward, ignoring the two men and focusing on Colban. The last remnants of his sneer had vanished, and he fumbled for his sword, swinging it wildly at Alasdair.

The clash of steel against steel splintered the air and familiar exhilaration pumped through Alasdair's blood. He'd best this bastard, and Freyja would be safe.

FREYJA CLUTCHED THE reins, her gaze riveted on Alasdair as he fought Colban, and white-hot terror seared her heart. When Clyde had knocked him out, she should've poured another of her potions down his throat, to ensure he wouldn't wake for hours, but it hadn't even occurred to her.

Was her error going to cost Alasdair his life?

But if two of his men had already recovered, it appeared her knowledge had failed her when she'd needed it most, so would it even have mattered if she'd drugged him?

Blessed Eir, merciful God, please let Alasdair live.

Clyde dispatched one of the other men and, momentarily distracted, she watched him tumble to the ground. She didn't recognize him. He wasn't one of the men who had accompanied Colban this morning. She glanced at the other man, but she'd never seen him before, either.

Alasdair and Colban's swords clashed ferociously as Alasdair inexorably drove the other man backwards. If only she was as proficient with a sword as Isolde. But she'd never understood the appeal, even though she admired her sister's skill.

A tortured yell filled the air as Clyde's man reared back, his arm hanging uselessly by his side. Before Colban's man could finish his attack, Clyde plunged his sword through the man's throat, and he fell to the ground with a hideous gurgle.

Clyde grabbed his man's reins and led the horse away from the carnage. He clutched his arm as blood seeped through his shirt sleeve, and Clyde returned to the battle to capture the two riderless horses.

Finally, something she could do to be useful. Hastily, she dismounted and opened her satchel to find what she needed to ease his discomfort and close the wound. As she pulled out a bottle of astringent she glanced up and a gasp caught in her throat as Alasdair thrust his sword through Colban's chest.

For a blood-streaked moment, memories of when she and Colban had played together as children flashed through her mind. He had always possessed an abundance of arrogance, and she had never imagined a life with him, but she'd never wished him ill, either.

But that was before he had set his sights on murdering her husband, and relief washed through her that the danger was over. Alasdair was safe. She had the alarming urge to sink to her knees, but there was work to be done.

Thank ye, blessed Eir. Thank ye, merciful God.

"My lady," croaked the injured man, and she glanced at him to see his eyes wide with shock, just as someone grabbed her braid and wrenched her head back, and the sharp sting of a dagger pressed against her neck.

Incomprehension pounded through her but before her stunned thoughts could form further, a hot breath grazed her ear.

"Not so fast, Lady Freyja," snarled a voice, and incomprehension mutated into confusion. What in the name of God was Lamont, Afi's former physician, doing here?

Chapter Thirty-Two

A LASDAIR PULLED HIS sword free and watched the life drain from Colban MacDonald's eyes. With their leader dead, it was doubtful the men he'd gathered would pose any danger, and besides they would be long gone from the tavern by now, since clearly Freyja's sleeping draught hadn't kept them unconscious for as long as she'd anticipated.

But he fully intended to see Colban's cousin, Peter, brought to justice.

Freyja would never be threatened again, and he released a jagged sigh of relief that in this, at least, he had not failed her.

They'd pile the bodies onto the horses and return to Dunochty where he'd send the earl another message. But more important than that, he would speak to Freyja.

The way she'd greeted him on the road earlier had given him a flicker of hope that all was not lost between them. He hoped to God he hadn't imagined the concern in her eyes for his safety when he'd told her he was riding to the tavern. He couldn't wait to get back to her. He might even catch up with her on the road before she reached the castle.

He swung about, anticipation and hope that his future might not be as bleak as he'd feared only this morning pounding through him, and then froze at the sight of Freyja in the clutches of a mad-eyed Lamont.

Christ, no. His heart thundered in his ears, momentarily drowning out every other sound, and for a terrifying moment the world blurred. *Why is she here?*

She was supposed to be safe from harm, on her way to Dunochty. But the question didn't matter. She was here. And she'd been captured by Lamont.

"We meet again, Alasdair Campbell." Contempt dripped from every word, and without taking his eyes off the physician, Alasdair dismounted, placed his sword on the ground, and raised his hands. His dagger remained hidden, and if he could just get close enough without rousing the other man's suspicions, he'd take him out like a mad dog.

"Lamont. Release Lady Freyja. Whatever it is ye want, we can talk about it like civilized men." He took another step closer until he was standing next to Clyde, who had also dismounted.

"Civilized? Campbells don't know the meaning of the word. As for ye, ye're not fit to lick my boots." The poisonous gleam in the physician's eyes chilled him to the bone. He well remembered their confrontation in the stables, just after Ranulph had died, when he'd warned Lamont to never speak so disrespectfully about Freyja again. When he'd told the other man he wasn't fit to wipe her boots.

It seemed Lamont hadn't forgotten, either. Christ, was this some kind of twisted retribution because he'd defended Freyja against the physician's slander?

"I know all about ye," Lamont continued, "and ye're nothing but a bastard to yer core. Even yer own father couldn't bring himself to acknowledge ye."

He'd had far worse insults thrown at his head, and while he'd never wanted Freyja to know the truth about his past, it no longer mattered. Nothing mattered except getting her away from Lamont before he injured her.

Or worse.

No. He wouldn't think about that.

"Were ye working for Colban, Lamont?" Freyja said as her gaze caught his, and when Lamont's attention wavered from him, he understood what she was doing. As one, he and Clyde stealthily moved forward another step as the physician glared at Freyja's head where he grasped her hair.

"Working for that pup? Don't insult my intelligence. I've known his father since we were lads, and I stayed with him after ye killed Ranulph with yer primitive concoctions. Colban was still so infatuated with ye even after ye wed Campbell, it was clear he intended to have ye one way or another. Not that his father realized. I've been biding my time with Colban these last few weeks, and it's fortunate my men and I found him where ye'd tied him up. At least the MacDonalds of Tarnford Castle know a woman's proper place, and it isn't meddling in affairs she should leave to her betters."

Alasdair kept his mouth shut but only because it was clear Lamont was mad, and the slightest word might push him over the edge. If he pushed that blade into Freyja's neck, nothing would be able to save her.

"I didn't kill my grandfather, and ye know it."

He and Clyde inched forward since Lamont was fully focused on Freyja, but even though he knew what she was doing, he wished she wouldn't provoke the physician.

Lamont bared his teeth. Alasdair had the surreal sensation the other man had forgotten he and Clyde even existed.

"I know what I know."

Lamont didn't raise his voice, but an eerie shudder skittered along his spine at the man's tone. Freyja was barely a horse length from him now. All he needed was another moment and he'd reach her.

"Ye and yer wretched foremothers, polluting the Small Isles with yer evil ideas for generations. I know what ye are, Lady Freyja of Sgur Castle." He released her hair and drew back his hand that held the dagger. *"Thou shalt not suffer a witch to live."*

It all happened so fast. As he lunged forward, Freyja twisted around, dipping low, before springing up and smashing the underside of Lamont's jaw with the palm of her hand. The physician reeled and Clyde pulled Freyja to safety as Alasdair pulled out his dagger.

He ducked to avoid Lamont's frenzied attack, before spying an opening and plunging his blade deep into the other man's heart.

BY THE TIME Alasdair and Clyde had gathered the bodies and secured them to the horses to take back to Dunochty, Freyja had tended to their wounded man whose arm was now in a sling.

He raked his fingers through his hair as he watched her close her satchel, but all he could see in his mind's eye was how Lamont had wrenched her head back, and the gleam of his dagger as he'd held it against her neck. He doubted he'd ever forget the cold terror that had gripped him at the image.

Freyja glanced up at him and their gazes meshed. Now the aftermath of the skirmish had been cleared up, he had no excuse not to talk to her, but even now the words wouldn't come.

He dragged in a deep breath. There was one thing that required no words, and he pulled out the letter he'd written her in the early hours of this morning. Was it really only this morning? It felt like a lifetime ago.

"Freyja," he said, but he got no further as she pressed her hand against his chest, and he damn well forgot how to breathe.

"Alasdair, 'tis not true." Urgency thrummed through each word, and he nodded, even though he had no idea what she was talking about. "My foremothers weren't witches. I'm—I'm not a witch. There are no such things as witches."

Bemused, he gazed at her. "I know that."

She released a ragged sigh. "I was certain ye did. Ye're not driven by wild superstitions like some. But Lamont—"

"Never think of Lamont again. He'd lost his mind, Freyja. Ye must know that."

She didn't look convinced. "He's always believed these

things. But I'd never harm anyone with my knowledge, Alasdair. That is not a healer's way."

Before he could stop himself, he took her hands. "Ye're truly the most talented healer I've ever encountered." He recalled the medical books he'd wanted to give her. If they had arrived before she'd read Ranulph's letter, would that have been enough for her to understand how deeply he admired her? "Lamont's evil will never touch ye again, and neither will Colban or his kin."

She gazed at him, her blue eyes shimmering with unshed tears, and he wanted to kill both of those bastards all over again for causing his brave wife a moment's fear. Yet as those images unfolded once again in his mind, a realization struck. It would have been far harder to rescue Freyja without harm, had she not managed to shove Lamont back.

"How did ye know how to escape his clutches, Freyja? 'Twas an impressive move, I must confess."

"Oh." She gave a small smile. "Isolde showed me. 'Tis not simply the sword she is proficient with."

"Thank God," he said with feeling. Silence fell between them, and with Clyde standing grimly behind Freyja, and their injured man slumped over his horse, he could scarcely tell her how much he wanted to make amends for the past. Instead, he released her hands and handed her the letter.

She frowned at it in evident confusion before breaking the seal and reading the contents, while he stood like a dumbstruck fool, waiting for her reaction.

Her confusion transfigured into shock, and she looked up at him. He offered her a smile that hurt every muscle in his face.

"Ye're granting me custodianship of Kilvenie?" Her voice was hushed as though she didn't believe the evidence of her own eyes. "Ye haven't spoken to the earl of this, have ye?"

"Aye, I'm granting ye custodianship. And no, the earl knows nothing of this."

She looked back at the letter and swallowed. "I didn't expect this. I am not certain what to say."

"Well," he said before he could think better of it, "that's a first."

She gave a small laugh and his heart lightened at the sound. "Freyja—"

"We should return to Dunochty." Clyde cast a dark glance between him and Freyja, and even though it seemed Clyde was always interrupting them at the worst possible moments, Alasdair couldn't disagree with his sentiments.

They needed to return to the castle so this mess could be dealt with.

Chapter Thirty-Three

WHEN THEY ARRIVED at Dunochty, Alasdair gave orders for the dead men to be taken to the keep, where they'd stay until he heard back from the earl. And Colban's men who, he surmised, were still insensible from Freyja's potion at the tavern needed to be rounded up. He just hoped the man Clyde had left there hadn't been killed.

His immediate concern was informing the earl of what had transpired. But even that urgency faded when he compared it to how very close he'd been to losing Freyja forever.

After he instructed his men, he couldn't help but watch her, as a visibly upset Jane held her hands while they stood on the forecourt before the castle doors. Before he'd wed Freyja, it had troubled him that she would feel like an outsider when he brought her to Dunochty. The way he'd always felt like an outsider, even as a child living in his stepfather's manor.

He watched her hug Jane, obviously reassuring the other woman she was unharmed, and a strange sense of calm wrapped around his wounded heart. Freyja was not an outsider. She'd made the castle her home, and she'd been accepted for who she was.

And at Dunochty, with Freyja, he'd found the first true home he'd ever known.

But it wasn't the castle that made him feel he had come home. He knew, now, it didn't matter where he lived. If Freyja wasn't also there, then a castle would be nothing more than cold blocks of stone.

He'd returned her birthright to her, and he wouldn't stop her if she chose the Small Isles over the Highlands.

Over him.

Inside, he would die a little, but if that's what it took to make her happy, to ensure that, in some way, their marriage could survive, then separate households were a small price to pay.

But before she made that decision, she needed to know what she meant to him.

From almost the first moment he'd met her, she'd told him she preferred the unfortunate truth to pretty lies. And despite his misgivings throughout their marriage, he'd been quietly adamant that he'd never lied to her.

And finally, the words that had eluded him for so long blazed through his mind.

When he reached her side, Jane pulled back, and he gave Dubh a pat in greeting just as Seoc emerged from the castle.

"Thank God ye are all safe," Seoc said.

Freyja glanced at him before returning her attention to Seoc. "Doubtless bards will compose epic poems about it, and in years to come no one will believe a word of it."

He knew it was her way of making light of the situation, but the threat of having almost lost her was too raw. "They can mock it all they like. At least it didn't end in tragedy."

She shivered. "I'm ashamed my kinsmen behaved so dishonorably. The MacDonalds of Tarnford will not escape justice."

He knew she was referring to Lady Helga's brand of justice, and he suspected Colban's father's plea of ignorance as to his son's plans would not be well received.

But that was all secondary.

"Ye're not to blame for Colban MacDonald's actions, Freyja."

An awkward silence fell between them, and he had the urge to take her hand and spirit her away somewhere remote, where they could be alone and not interrupted, but since that was nothing but an impractical fantasy, he wasn't certain she'd appreciate him dragging her into the castle while Jane and Seoc stood before them.

Seoc cleared his throat. It was clear he wished to be anywhere but there and was preparing an excuse to disappear. "Here, Alasdair, this arrived yesterday."

The physician thrust a large package at him, and its size and weight meant it could only be the books he'd ordered for Freyja. He grunted his thanks, and with a nod, Seoc took Jane's arm and they walked across the courtyard to the stables.

Freyja cast the package a curious glance, but didn't comment on it. For which he was thankful, since he didn't want to get sidetracked.

Together they entered the castle, and it seemed Freyja was of the same mind as him, as she led the way up the stairs to their chambers. As they entered the bedchamber, she gave him a bright smile. But it didn't reach her eyes, and a pang of despair squeezed his heart at the notion she might never truly smile at him again.

"With all the excitement today, I'm not certain I thanked ye for coming to our rescue. But it's much appreciated, I assure ye."

If things weren't so strained between them, he'd be certain she was mocking him. But despite her polite smile she looked deadly serious, and somehow that was far worse.

"I'm not sure who rescued who. If ye hadn't decided to follow me after I told ye to return to the castle, I doubt I'd be standing here now."

The remnants of her smile vanished. "I didn't even think about the possibility of Lamont having joined Colban's cause. But of course he would, if he believed Colban would lead him to me."

Once again, he saw the blade glint against her neck. It was a nightmare he'd never forget. "There's no reason why ye'd think such a thing. Freyja, I'm proud of how ye put his men to sleep so ye could escape his clutches."

This time, her small smile didn't look forced. "Alasdair, if ye think it will help, I'll write to the earl myself explaining the situation. I'm certain once he understands why ye didn't answer his summons to go to Edinburgh was because I was abducted, he won't withhold yer barony."

They both knew he hadn't returned to Dunochty because Freyja was in danger. He'd known nothing of it until he'd reached the castle. He also knew how easy it would be to twist the truth when explaining things to his half-brother. Everything had happened so fast, no one would question his version of events.

But it wasn't the truth, and both he and Freyja knew it. She, who valued the truth over pretty lies, was willing to close her eyes to something she held so dear—for him.

He tried to swallow, but there was a constriction in his throat. If she did this for him, he would never forgive himself for being the reason she had compromised her integrity. Nothing was worth that.

He shook his head. "'Tis kind of ye to offer, but I'll take my chances. The barony is not that important to me."

She looked taken aback. "But I know how dearly ye crave it, Alasdair. I should be grieved if I'm the reason why ye don't achieve yer ambition."

"Don't be grieved. I have other ambitions now."

She didn't appear to realize he was desperately trying to tell her something completely unconnected to the damn barony.

"I didn't understand, before. I thought ye had lived a life of privilege as the late earl's son, and the barony was simply something ye felt due to ye because of yer status. But that's not the reason, is it?"

Damn Lamont and his scathing words. But Freyja had heard him and there was nothing for it but to tell her the truth. "There was no reason why Archibald should acknowledge me as his half-brother, when he became earl. I was nothing but an unclaimed bastard. But he did, and aye, I'm grateful for it. But priorities change, Freyja."

"That's why ye said no one spits in the face of a baron. I thought it an odd thing to say at the time, but I understand it now, Alasdair. Truly, I do."

Christ, had he said that to her? Heat crawled through him as he recalled he had, indeed. What the hell had possessed him?

He grunted, unable to hold her gaze and went over to the table to put the heavy package down. And saw the letter from Ranulph, where Freyja had left it. Was it really only yesterday that she had confronted him with it?

Freyja came to his side, and he tried not to breathe in her irresistible scent of roses and rain, but he did, regardless. It took every particle of willpower he possessed not to swing her around, pull her close, and beg her to stay.

He would not beg. He had to give her the choice. But when she didn't speak, when she merely gazed at the letter on the table, he knew he owed her an explanation as to why he'd concealed Ranulph's final words from her.

"I should have shared yer grandfather's letter with ye, Freyja. I know it was written to me, but I'm certain he didn't expect me to keep it from ye."

She didn't look at him as she gently traced her finger over the letter, and then she sighed. "If I'd read Afi's letter the day we had wed, I wouldn't have had all the memories we've made together since that day. I won't deny I was hurt that yer only reason for going to Rum was to win my hand. But I've had time to think about it all, and I believe our marriage is worth saving, if ye're of a like mind."

She was giving him the second chance he'd so desperately wished for. More than that, it seemed she cherished the memories they shared just as he did.

How easy it would be to agree with her and let the past fade into insubstantial shadows.

But it wasn't enough. He didn't want a political alliance, or a wife who believed he had wed her purely because his earl had commanded it.

"'Tis better than keeping secrets and lies for fear of causing offense."

He'd told her that once. Now it was time to make good on that pledge.

He'd once believed the words he needed to say to her, that showed her how dearly he loved her and needed her by his side, didn't exist. And maybe they didn't. But the words that had eluded him for so long now lurked in the corners of his mind and they weren't ones that declared his devotion. Once spoken aloud, he risked losing everything. Yet there would be no peace, and no chance of redemption, until he confessed.

"Freyja, I've always consoled myself that I've never lied to ye. And I haven't in so many words, but it's not the truth. When I first met ye, I told ye I was the earl's half-brother, but I kept a secret from ye because he swore me to silence. But it doesn't change the fact I lied to ye by omission. And for that, I'll never forgive myself. I know how highly ye prize the truth, and God knows I'd do anything to make it right, but I can't change the past."

She didn't reply but her bottom lip trembled. He swallowed, tormented by what he had to say next, but there was no fleeing from it.

"In the stables, after Ranulph died." His voice was hoarse but somehow he pushed on. "Ye were right. I took advantage. I took away yer choice, Freyja, and for that I'm sorrier than ye'll ever know."

"No." The denial burst from her, and she pressed her hand against his heart. "Don't ever think that Alasdair, for it's not true. I knew exactly what we were doing, and I wanted it more than anything. I only said ye took advantage of me because I was hurt and angry, but I didn't mean it, even as I said it."

Relief spilled through him and a tiny flicker of hope stirred. But it still didn't change one thing. "Ye still had no choice but to wed me, though."

A blush heated her cheeks, but she didn't look away. "I'm a skilled healer, and I know many things that some men believe should not be known. I knew I wouldn't conceive yer bairn that day, Alasdair."

He wasn't entirely sure how she could know such a thing for

certain, and in truth he didn't want to delve further into such things, but it was enough that she hadn't been compromised into marrying him because of what he'd—what they'd—done.

"I'm thankful to hear it." He sucked in a great breath. There was only one thing left to tell her, and after everything he'd confessed already, it surely wouldn't be too hard. "Freyja, ye've had my heart since the day I met ye. I don't need a barony, or a fine castle, or even my bond with the earl. 'Tis ye I need, and without ye, all else is meaningless."

"Alasdair Campbell," she whispered, as she gently traced her fingers along his jaw. "Ye have a honeyed tongue, indeed."

"No." He captured her hand and pressed a kiss upon her fingers. "It's the truth. I'll never coat my words in honey with ye, Freyja. There's no need, and never has been. I love ye, and always will, whatever the future may bring."

"Ye love me, do ye?" She shook her head, and a single tear escaped even though she smiled at him. "Well, I'm happy to hear it. A one-sided love would be a great burden to bear and that's a fact."

"A one-sided love?" Did she mean what he hoped she did?

"Thankfully not, as it transpires. I love ye too, Alasdair. Why do ye think I followed ye today, instead of retreating to Dunochty? Why do ye think I'm so content here in the Highlands, when I was always so certain I could never leave Sgur Castle?"

Fierce joy, that he had never imagined could exist surged through him. His wife, his beloved Freyja, loved him. Whatever else happened, all was right in his world.

"There's no need now to postpone our visit to William and Lady Isolde," he said. "But before we go to Creagdoun, we shall travel to Eigg to see yer sister and ensure Lady Helga is well. I've been remiss. We should have visited sooner. I know, in yer heart, ye miss yer isle terribly."

A strange expression settled over her face. "I do," she said. "But, Alasdair, there's something I didn't tell ye about our Pict queen ancestor."

"Yer warrior queen foremother." He grinned at her and wrapped his arms around her, even though he didn't know why she'd brought up her ancestor right now. "What else did she do? I can scarcely imagine."

She shook her head as her fingers tangled in his hair. "I shouldn't tell ye, for 'tis a secret handed down from mother to daughter, but I want ye to know." She took a deep breath before she whispered, "*The bloodline of the Isle must prevail beyond quietus.*"

A shiver chased along his arms, although he wasn't sure why. "What does it mean?"

"I thought it meant if the daughters of Sgur abandon our Isle, our bloodline will die. It's what all three of us were taught, and that tenet is a part of us. I have wondered if only one of us needs to remain on Eigg to fulfil the legacy. But now I'm not convinced that's what the Deep Knowing truly means. Maybe ye were right, after all, when ye said our Pict queen will never be forgotten as long as her story is told. Maybe it's her memory that must prevail beyond the Small Isles."

"I don't know," he confessed. "All I want is for ye to be happy, Freyja."

"I am happy," she whispered. "I'm happy to be here, in the arms of the man I love."

With a groan, he walked her backwards, towards the bed. But as they passed by the table he paused, his gaze falling on the package.

Later.

Unfortunately, she followed his glance. "Is that for Seoc? He was uncommonly excited when it arrived."

With a sigh, he released her and picked it up. "No. 'Tis for ye."

Her eyes widened as he handed it to her. "Good Lord, did ye buy me a slab of marble?"

"What use would a slab of marble be to ye?"

She smiled before placing it back on the table and untying the string that bound it. She pulled off the packaging, and then went as still as marble herself.

Time seemed to still as she gazed at the volumes, and then, reverently, she traced a finger over the cover of the first massive tome before opening the book.

Awe transfigured her face as she gasped softly and turned a page or two, clearly enthralled by the wonders it beheld. And as he watched her, a half-forgotten conversation rippled through his mind.

Her light must never be dimmed.

He'd always thought Ranulph was reminding him to keep his word and not trick Freyja into marriage. But that wasn't what he'd meant at all. He'd been referring to her healing skills. Telling Alasdair to respect her knowledge. But he'd never needed Ranulph's reminder for that.

"Is it all ye hoped it would be?" His voice was hushed.

She tore her gaze from her book. It was a trick of the sunlight through the window, but regardless, all he saw was her bathed in an ethereal glow.

"Aye," she breathed. "'Tis so much more. I never believed I'd get the chance to see these books, let alone own them. I don't know how to thank ye, Alasdair. 'Tis the most thoughtful gift in the world."

He almost quipped *better than a diamond necklace?* But he swallowed the words for they weren't necessary. He knew her answer.

He always had.

"I'm glad." His voice was gruff. "I know how dearly ye wanted to read it. Now ye'll be as good, if not better, than all those physicians in that fancy London college."

"But to think ye recalled our conversation. We scarcely even knew each other back then." She drew in a tremulous breath before coming to him and cradling his face. "Only a man with a truly caring heart would've thought of purchasing his wife such an unconventional gift."

He wrapped his arms around her and swung her off her feet,

the sound of her laughter washing the last remnants of guilt from his soul. "That's because no other man is as fortunate as I, to be wed to such an unconventional woman as ye."

They tumbled onto the bed, facing each other, and he tenderly brushed back an errant curl from her cheek. His words echoed in his mind, and a strange realization struck.

He'd never formally asked her to be his wife. Events had simply unfolded, after Ranulph's deathbed declaration.

Doubtless it was a foolish move, and Freyja would laugh at him. But it didn't matter. It needed to be done.

He pushed himself from the bed, pulling her upright so she sat on the edge, and then sank to his knees before her.

"Lady Freyja of Sgur Castle, if we had our time over again, would ye do me the honor of consenting to be my bride?"

She didn't even hesitate. She took his hands and pressed them to her lips, before she gave her answer. "Alasdair Campbell, laird of my heart, I'd marry ye a thousand times over, and that's the truth."

Laird of my heart. He kissed her, his clever, incomparable wife, and the last shadows of his past withered until they vanished forever beneath the sun-filled future that beckoned with Freyja by his side.

The End

Author's Note

The Royal College of Physicians in London was founded by Henry VIII in 1518.

While the medicinal and recreational properties of the poppy have been known for thousands of years, during the Holy Inquisition it was linked to the "work of the devil" and subsequently almost entirely purged from most of Europe. It was "rediscovered" in the mid-16th century by a German-Swiss physician, Paracelsus.

The books mentioned by Freyja and acquired for her by Alasdair are De Humani Corporis Fabrica (The Fabric of the Human Body) by Andreas Vesalius, published in 1543. The volumes are considered to be one of the most significant publications in the history of medicine and anatomy.

Acknowledgements

Once again, a big thank you to Sally Rigby and Amanda Ashby who have talked me down from the ledge more times than I care to remember! May our tiaras forever sparkle.

Thank you to Kathryn Le Veque and the wonderful team at Dragonblade. Audrey Salo, my amazing editor, who sees the things I can't, and Kim Killion for another stunning cover!

And a big thank you to my readers for choosing to spend your time in the worlds I create.

About the Author

Christina grew up in England and spent her childhood visiting ruined castles and Roman remains and daydreaming about Medieval princesses and gallant knights. She now lives in sunny Western Australia with her high school sweetheart and their two cats who are convinced the universe revolves around their needs. They are not wrong.

Christina's Website:
christinaphillips.com

Christina's Newsletter:
christinaphillips.com/pages/newsletter

Christina's Facebook:
facebook.com/christinaphillips.author

Bluesky:
bsky.app/profile/christinaphillips.bsky.social

www.ingramcontent.com/pod-product-compliance
Ingram Content Group UK Ltd.
Pitfield, Milton Keynes, MK11 3LW, UK
UKHW020420260825
7566UKWH00007B/594